Save Them All

A novel

This is a work of fiction. Names, characters, places, and incidents either are the products of the author's imagination or are used fictitiously. Any resemblance to actual persons, living or dead, businesses, companies, events, or locales is entirely coincidental.

Second Edition, April 2018

Printed in the U.S.A.

ISBN-13: 9781980923220

To Katha, Karen, Mitzi, Laurie, and Rita: thanks for helping cultivate the brain that came up with this crazy stuff.

There is no true love save in suffering,
and in this world we have to choose either love,
which is suffering,
or happiness.
Man is the more man - that is, the more divine –
the greater his capacity for suffering,
or rather,
for anguish.

Miguel de Unamuno

ONE

"This world isn't for me anymore," Evon Brisk said out loud to himself as he sat on the hood of his new car. Never mind that it was stolen, purloined from some dumb fuck who thought keeping the keys tucked away in the visor would be a safer bet against car theft than keeping them in his pocket.

Oak Harbor was a little chilly on this rainy April night, but the radiating heat from the engine made Evon feel good. He felt good that the weather couldn't dampen his mood, that the decision he settled on this night was for the best, and that he had done all there really was to do in this life.

At least everything he had the power to do.

There was a time when Evon had all that a man could ever want. He had the all-American looks with his 6'2" fit frame, a full head of thick, well-groomed hair, and piercing brown eyes. He was comfortably rich, too, having developed a line of technological goods for use in the Silicon Valley. Every company worth their weight had come to rely on those goods in these times ruled by electronic advances that made for an easier life.

He also had what he felt was the sexiest woman alive as his trophy wife, and the most beautiful daughter in the world.

But bad decisions with where he invested his money and bad advice from his stockbroker had left him with half of his previous fortune. That was his two cents. The remaining half of his fortune his sexy-yet-greedy bitch of an ex had gotten her hands on and if Evon hadn't spent their marriage playing his cards right, there was no doubt she would've gotten much more.

Evon was smart, though, and he had prepared himself for times like this. He never thought he'd lose his money to bad business transactions, but he knew that marrying a stripper would eventually come back to bite him.

He remembered it clearly. He'd met Chastity on one of his regular trips to his favorite club, Exile, and from the first time she stepped on stage fully nude—aside from her 6-inch, see-through heels—for a show that made him pitch a tent in his pants, he kind of knew she was the one.

At least on that night.

Evon liked to fuck because that's the way it worked. He was young and rich and that's what guys like that do. He tried to make sure it was a new person on every occasion because he wanted to experience new things, new bodies, new… techniques, and he couldn't learn anything new by sticking with the same old person every night.

So, after a few drinks and the obligatory private lap dance in the V.V.I.P. section of Exile, Evon used his gift of gab to let Chastity know what he *really* wanted to do with her body.

He still remembered the smell back then.

It was thick with the mixed aromatics of perfumes and sweat from the dancers and the nervous desperation of rich men who had their wives and girlfriends in the backs of their minds. It wasn't a scent Evon was giving off, for his conscience was free and clear.

Chastity didn't give off the aroma he initially thought she would, either. Hers instead was a fruity, yet seductive fragrance that he breathed in fully as she climbed on top to straddle him.

He felt himself slip inside her and experienced the newness she had to offer. There was no need for a rubber because that ruined the amazing feeling of the inside of a woman.

Even Catholic men knew that.

She rocked back and forth, rhythmically, and he hadn't forgotten that she was a dancer, first and foremost. Her arms were wrapped around his head, pulling him close to the crevice between her breasts.

They were both eerily quiet, only letting a few moans and gasps escape from their lips. He dug his fingers into her back, gently at first, then gradually more forceful as he approached the climax.

When it came time for that orgasmic release, Evon made no attempt to pull out of her enveloping warmth and came inside of her.

Just like that.

He didn't much care if she got to feel as good as he did, that's not what he was there for.

The feeling was indeed amazing and he thought at the time it was a poor decision on his part to not put on any protection to ward off any surprises, but there was a plan B available in times like these, and it only cost him a Ulysses S. Grant every time. Evon didn't take that route on this occasion, however. Something different came over him.

Something… new.

Funny as it may sound, he heard wedding bells after filling her up, or maybe it was the sound of his keys and loose change jingling in his pocket as he pulled his jeans back up. Evon liked to think it was the former and gave Chastity his name and phone number on a Ben Frank. She slowly took it out of his hand with a smile and kissed him on the cheek, leaving a faint, purple impression of her lips.

"What kind of name is Chastity for a stripper?" Evon whispered to her.

She held up the one-hundred-dollar bill to the dim light in the room and said, "What kind of name is *ee-vahn*?"

He shook his head with a grin.

"It's pronounced exactly how you'd say *Evan.* Blame my mom. Let's practice so you get it right. Say it with me: *Ev—"*

"I get it! I get it."

And with that, Chastity chuckled to herself and started to walk out of the room, dusting herself off to get ready to perform for the crowd full of horny, fat, old men that had accumulated.

Watching her ass jiggle as she exited, Evon said, "Is that your real name?"

Chastity looked back at him with a smile.

"Yeah," she said as she waved goodbye.

People sometimes liked to think that life moves at a molasses-like crawl, that time has only one speed, though we'd like for it to move faster through difficult times and slow down for the more enjoyable ones.

Life for Evon definitely had one swift pace in mind when it fashioned a shotgun marriage three months later and then produced a baby girl six months after that. They decided to name her Sunny, being that she was delivered on the first day of Spring.

Chastity looked stunning to him when their lives had first intersected, and continued to be an awesome looking woman, even after childbirth. She was blessed with long, brunette hair with blonde highlights, perfectly sized tits that were great for grabbing, a nice flat stomach, and man, could she bring the house down in bed. Much better than the first time they had sex.

She was a dumb bitch, though, and Evon knew that.

And to keep the dumb bitch from realizing how stupid she really was, he made sure to tell her how smart and beautiful she was every single day that they were together, no matter what.

He liked to think of it as a necessary conditioning.

That was the only way to make sure that when the inevitable divorce proceedings went down, she didn't take him to the cleaners and end up with money she had no business with. Money that he had earned through hard work and ingenuity.

The conditioning worked to some degree, which is why Evon was left with roughly a fourth of the money he started with and weekend visits.

That was all 15 years ago since the night he walked into Exile.

Fifteen years.

That's all it took to make his fortune—*poof*—virtually disappear. That's all it took for him to impregnate a stripper in the back room of a seedy nudie joint. That's all it took for him to create something as beautiful as a human life and then be relegated to spending less than 48 hours a week with that creation.

And now… he was left with this.

Sitting on the wet hood of a beat up, red '93 Mustang that he stole because it was unremarkable. Who was going to notice he stole this? Hell, at this point in his life, Evon *looked* like a guy that would drive a shitty car like this. Maybe he even did a favor to the male this surely belonged to.

Unremarkable.

Just like his life had become in the five years since he signed the final divorce papers and agreed to what his lawyers had worked out for him as far as visiting Sunny was concerned.

Unremarkable.

That's what wandering around town blowing the rest of your money on Stella Artois, pizza, and hotel rooms was. And when that was all gone he completed his precipitous fall from grace by taking refuge with the other bums and vagabonds of the city who undoubtedly had made the same bad decisions in life he had. That wasn't very hard to do in Oak Harbor, Washington, though.

This had once been a prosperous little enclave in the Pacific Northwest that catered to building planes for the Air Force and vessels for the Navy during the heyday of the nation's excursions into world affairs. Now, the town tried to switch things up by opening a facility to build the Growler line of fighter planes. But ever since the U.S. became a little more peaceful and secretive, deciding that drones and hacking were more effective at defeating its many enemies, there were still some economic consequences to be had for the town.

So there Evon found himself on a nightly basis—living, eating, and relieving himself wherever the wind had blown him, along with everyone else who had screwed up the opportunities life had afforded them.

That's how Evon liked to look at it anyway.

It would be too much of a blow to his ego to acknowledge he was the only person in this town who fucked everything up beyond all repair.

Misery *loves* company.

In reality, he thought, it was much easier to fail than to maintain a success such as the type that he came across. That line of thinking provided *some* solace.

With a sigh, Evon hopped off the hood of the car and walked slowly to the glistening rusted-silver rails of the bridge. The loose gravel crunched underneath the weight of his tired feet.

He looked down at the railings, the ones that were supposed to prevent accidents, taking stock of the damage they'd sustained over the years. They were marked by a multitude of dents and scratches of paint, telltale signs of careless drivers who owed their lives to these pieces of metal.

He involuntarily shivered, the chill and the wetness of this evening making his body feel a little uncomfortable considering he was becoming soaked, but he ignored the fleeting uneasiness and focused on the atmosphere. Looking around, he couldn't help but notice and truly appreciate the distinct beauty of the millions of raindrops that quietly fell from the sky, of seeing them hit the still water below. Though he was high up, he could make out subtle ripples disturbing the surface.

He looked on as the droplets of water cascaded down the leaves and branches of the trees that covered the cliff's face right beneath the bridge. They gave off an unmistakable fresh scent filling the air to be appreciated one more time.

"This world isn't for me anymore," Evon said again.

Not so much as to repeat it so that someone, *anyone,* venturing on the road would hear and try to talk him away from the edge, because he didn't want that.

Evon *wanted* to go and he needed just a little more hyping up to take that final plunge.

April was a great month to do it, too, from what he'd once read online, and the hundreds of thousands of poor souls who made this the number one month for these kinds of things would agree if someone asked them. One would think people offed themselves in droves during the frigid and lonely winter months, but that wasn't the case. Lives came and went, flashed in front of people's eyes just as the seasons changed from a frosty darkness to the inviting warmth of the spring.

This spot couldn't be more perfect either, right off Deception Pass Bridge near a slightly forested area. The bridge had earned its namesake because it had spanned a body of water that deceived an early group of explorers into thinking it was a calm and serene place to sail a fleet of ships, when in fact it was anything but.

Now, it would prove to be a fitting name because anyone who got to a point where jumping off this bridge seemed like a more palatable thing to do than to go on living a miserable existence was deceived into believing there was life in vigilance. But in reality, there wasn't anything left to *live* for when you hit rock bottom, and in his case, there was nothing left to do but to literally *hit* rock bottom.

He posited that if he calculated his fall just right, he'd hit the water, give or take some impacts from the rocks jutting up, and end up as food for the fishes. He cringed at the thought of having to feel the pain of any impact, but he knew it would be expeditious before unconsciousness soothed him.

If his body didn't make it to sea, it would at least be obscured by the surrounding greenery, and eventually the creatures of the wild who inhabited these parts would feast upon his corpse, leaving nothing left to be identified by if he was found.

So, this was it. He was preparing to join the natural cycle.

Forty-three years old and taking your own life on your birthday took balls, he thought. Maybe there was something symbolic about ending your life 43 years to the day but he couldn't quite put his finger on it.

Fuck it.

Evon turned around so that his back faced the water, raised his arms out wide, just like an eagle, tilted his head back, closed his eyes, and felt his senses take over one last time.

There were no tears shed from his eyes.

No, what was streaming down his face were the tears the heavens had provided for him on his last night on this plane of existence.

He inhaled deeply, felt the crisp surrounding air fill his lungs, tasted the sweetness of it on his tongue. It was invigorating, though much too late.

"From the earth I came and to the earth I shall return," he whispered quietly to himself.

Then Evon Brisk cast himself from the edge of the bridge and waited for that new experience to come over him.

TWO

"Dude, can you hold on?"

"Shut up and keep walking!"

"Seriously, would you slow the hell down? Then maybe I could keep up!"

"Look, do you want to get home and out of this rain or what?"

"Yeah, I do. But if you had listened to me before we left then we'd be more prepared for this weather and not in such a rush to get home. I told you I looked at Weather Bug and it said we'd have to deal with this stuff a few hours after we took off!"

Joey shook his head, disgusted. "Man, don't give me that shit. The app said 40% chance. I erred on the 60% side, so what? Besides, we'll be home in like 30 minutes anyway."

"Well, ok. Still, you know my mom is going to want to know why we didn't wear a coat or bring an umbrella or something. I'll just blame you again, Joey."

"Fine with me! The old broad knows every kid in the neighborhood doesn't call me Joey Danger for nothin'!"

Mitch just shook his head and kept walking.

He was pretty soaked and the cold wasn't going to be too forgiving to him if he didn't get home soon. But he was getting sluggish and his feet were killing him after walking on the trail with Joey for the past few hours. Not to mention the steady rain was making the dirt trail transform into a mud trail, making it an extra tough walk.

But when the coolest, smartest kid in the neighborhood tells you he wants you to be his assistant on Discovery Day, damn it, you became his assistant!

As the only thirteen-year-old in the neighborhood, Joey Danger, as he liked to be called, would regularly recruit some of the younger kids to be his assistant on what he called Discovery Day. This was his special event for the first Saturday of every month in which Joey and his handpicked assistant would trek the trails of the wooded areas near Deception Pass searching for treasure.

Joey always told the neighborhood kids that they could find some pretty cool stuff out on the trails that people left there all the time, and he liked to go once a month to give the treasure trove a chance to fill up.

The only part that sucked was that he always insisted he and his assistant walk there and back instead of taking their bikes or scooters.

He said he once watched a cartoon about it building character and that bringing bikes would only hamper their journey.

Whatever.

Mitch was only twelve and figured being without a *teen* in his age meant that he should leave the tough decisions to those who had crossed that threshold into teenager territory. He also figured that the extra year in age gave a physical advantage to Joey because he didn't seem to be bothered by the cold, rain, and mud. He just kept walking, seemingly without the slightest discomfort despite how long they'd been out.

Joey turned around so he could face Mitch and while walking backward said, "Well, since you're walking so slow, might as well take this time to talk about our awesome discoveries, my esteemed assistant."

"Esteemed? What does that mean?"

"It means I think you're a little less stupid and weird than the rest of your little 12-year-old buddies, for today at least. Now, shut up and tell me what you got in the backpack."

Mitch wanted to tell Joey to go to hell and take his fancy vocabulary with him, but he just sighed, took off his backpack, unzipped it, and looked down into it.

"Well, for today's haul we've got a baseball, half a pack of gum, a bracelet, a book of CDs, some matches, a video game magazine, and some pretty cool looking rocks."

Mitch looked back up at Joey with a proud smile to see what he thought of all the cool treasure they had found. He didn't think it was every time that Joey and whoever else he brought along found stuff like this.

Joey stopped walking for a moment and just stared.

"Wh- what's the problem?" said Mitch, worried that he'd done something wrong.

"You've got to be one of the worst assistants I've ever taken out for Discovery Day, that's what the problem is! What the hell is all that shit? Some damn gum? A girl's bracelet? Matches? *Really*? And no one even uses CDs these days! Man, dump all that shit out!"

"Chill out, Joey! I think some of this stuff could be pretty awesome to check out once we get home. I'm keeping it. Plus, it's my backpack that you told me to bring and I'm the one that did all the discovering while you played on your stupid phone."

Joey formed a word with his lips, ready to argue, but decided against it. He *did* let his assistant do most of the heavy lifting. It was how you built guts and grit in these little kids. There was going to be a time where he might not want to take part in these adventures. According to the movies he saw, he'd have to worry about girls and older kid stuff soon. It was up to the little pipsqueaks of the neighborhood to keep his tradition going.

He started walking again and said, "Alright, look, I'm taking the CDs and you can keep all the rest of that crap. Let's just hur–"

Before Joey could finish his demands, he'd fallen hard onto the muddy trail and was laying on his side.

"*Shit*! Damn tree branch!" Joey yelled.

"Are you alright, man?"

"Does it look like I'm alright? Look at my clothes, dumb ass! This is a new outfit I got for this occasion! And I think I scraped my elbow. Here, take a look at it and tell me what you think."

Mitch leaned a little closer to get a better look at the injury. The fall definitely scraped the skin enough to make a small amount of blood start to trickle.

"Well, um, I don't know. I guess it kind of looks like you need a Band-Aid or something."

"Hey, I'm not asking if you think I need medical care or something, doc. I'm asking if you think this looks like a battle scar after a long day of treasure hunting. I have a reputation to keep in the neighborhood you know."

"That's right, you *are* Joey Danger."

"Damn straight! And don't you forget it! Now, help me up, dude."

Mitch reached out his hand to Joey to help him up, then Joey bent over to brush off his pants.

"Damn it, this mud isn't coming off. Screw it, I'll just make sure I'm changed before my mom gets home from work. Ain't trying to hear her mouth today. Anyway, these damn park services people need to get out here and clear these trees off the trail path. A guy can only collect so many bumps and bruises, right, Mitch? But what do you know? You're just an assistant."

Mitch had already tuned Joey out, though, and was too busy staring at what had tripped him up.

He pointed at the ground, fixated, and stammered, "That wasn't a tree branch, Joey. Take a look."

Both of the boys stared at the foot that stuck out onto the trail from inside the brush.

"Holy *shit*! That's a fucking leg, dude!" Joey said.

"M- maybe it's just a doll. Or a dummy or something," said Mitch.

"Well, don't just stand there! Go over and check it out! See if you're right!"

"W- why do I have to be the one to do it?"

Joey got real close to Mitch, grabbed a fistful of his dampened shirt, and stared into his eyes as if he was prepared to burn a hole through him.

"Because you're the one who found it. Now, get your ass over there and see what that is or I'll make sure I tell all of your little friends how much of a little punk you were on Discovery Day."

To Mitch, that was a threat he dared not test the validity of and he didn't want that kind of notoriety following him around every time he stepped outside to play, so he made the decision to go check out the leg that had been thrust out, seemingly to test his resolve on a day like this.

He took a deep breath and slowly walked over to the protruding leg. He thought he could feel Joey glaring at him, staring darts into his back. Mitch took one glance over at him and confirmed that he was indeed shooting lasers at him, standing there with his arms crossed.

Joey uncrossed one arm and held it out, raising up his eyebrows in unison with his hand in a gesture that suggested Mitch needed to hurry up or be prepared to face the consequences of his inaction.

Mitch gathered himself once more and bent down next to the leg, trying to get a better look to see if it was human. He also tried to listen closely to the area of the brush where the leg stuck out for any indication that he and Joey should get the hell out of there.

"Look, if you just stand there staring at that leg, you're not going to find out if it's real or not. Climb in the bushes and *see!*" Joey said.

Mitch nodded and wiped away the rain that was collecting on his eyelashes and blurring his vision, then slowly crept into the bushes near where the leg was poking out. With the disturbance he was causing, he thought any animal that was hiding would've come out by now. He was relieved to find out he wouldn't have to contend with any hostile beasts.

That's when he discovered that the leg he was investigating was indeed connected to a body, a man's body.

"What do you see in there?" Joey shouted out to him.

"Um, well, there's a white guy in here lying face down. His clothes are messed up a little bit. He's, um, kind of bloody it looks like."

"Is he dead?"

"I don't know, but he looks really beat up and like, his arms are bent all weird."

Mitch watched Joey slowly nod his head and start to look around at their surroundings. He thought about the situation they'd found themselves in. This was precisely the kind of moment he imagined advanced thinking skills such as Joey's were needed to put together the pieces of the puzzle.

"Sounds like to me that he was out here doing who knows what and got robbed by who knows who, tried to fight back, they kicked his ass, threw him in the bushes. Look at all these footprints in the mud. We didn't make those," Joey said.

Mitch looked down to take stock of the footprints Joey was talking about. He was right. The prints belonged to someone with feet much bigger than theirs. Plus, they were fairly fresh.

"You say you can't tell if he's dead though, Mitch?" Joey said.

"Yeah, I don't know. How can you tell?"

"Shit, let me think. Oh, I know! I saw it in this movie once! Reach down and touch his neck. If you feel a pulse, then he's still alive."

"What's a pulse?" Mitch asked.

"Seriously, dude? A pulse is like a heartbeat, only softer. Now would you hurry the hell up? I don't wanna waste too much time out here."

Mitch wasn't going to argue with that. He didn't want to spend any more time out on the trail than Joey did. Even though his chest was pounding, he wasn't the teenager in this operation, just the esteemed assistant, but that had to count for something.

He reached down and touched the man's neck with two fingers to feel for this pulse he was supposed to be looking for.

And then he felt it, faintly pulsating underneath the tips of his fingers.

Sure enough, by what Joey said, this man was still alive.

"Dude! I feel it! This guy's alive!"

"Good," Joey said, "Now you won't get in any trouble just in case that guy was dead."

"Why would I get in any trouble? I didn't do anything to him."

"Yeah, you and *I* know that but would the cops have known that? Your fingerprints are on him now! Why do you think I made *you* do it? I wasn't about to get myself caught up in this shit."

"Gee, thanks a lot, Joey."

"No problem. Now, what do you suppose we do with this discovery? Check his pockets? See if there's some cash or credit cards in there?"

"You wanna *take* things from him?"

Mitch looked down at the mysterious man. He'd clearly already been through enough trouble. Mitch didn't want to add to his problems if he woke up to find out his body was broken and all his money was gone.

"Don't you think we should call the police or 911 or something?" Mitch offered.

"Well, yeah, but why don't we get ourselves some reward money for finding this guy alive!"

"No way, man. I'm not touching him again. You want that stuff, you do it yourself. Besides, we're soaked, it's getting colder and darker out here, and we're almost home. Can't we just leave?"

"Ok, ok. Chill the hell out. You're right. Let's get home and *then* we'll call 911 when we get there. That way we're far away from this area by the time they come."

Mitch was happy with that answer. It was creepy to him being in this wooded area and finding someone's body. He didn't like the idea of being around as it got darker to intensify his uneasiness.

The two boys started walking toward the area where they first entered several hours ago.

Joey patted Mitch on the back and said, "I don't know about you, my esteemed assistant, but I think Discovery Day was a success."

THREE

In the book of Proverbs, if someone flipped over to chapter 16 and then scrolled down to verse 27, they'd find an interesting set of the words God sent down to Solomon with the intention that he'd spread them to future generations.

It says, "Idle hands are the devil's workshop; idle lips are his mouthpiece."

Now, granted, this was a translation one can only find in The Living Bible; a version Evon had gotten his hands on because the Bibles made available to him were written in a way that was too hard to fully understand.

Understanding was exactly what he needed in these trying times, and he only wanted to hear from one voice while he fleshed out his thoughts: God.

He vaguely understood *how* he was here but the answer that had eluded him was *why*.

The word of God is such a valuable resource that is right there in plain sight for people to take advantage of and yet, so few of them actually do it; Evon wasn't going to be one of those people anymore. Initially, he didn't really understand why he was drawn to Proverbs upon opening up this Bible—a Bible he had asked for while he laid lame in bed. It was like his hands just took him there magically.

No, not magically. Divinely.

But one internet search on the tablet borrowed from a nurse gave him the simple answer.

The book of Proverbs, for the layman, is a book about wisdom. Hidden between Psalms and Ecclesiastes are 31 chapters that help a man understand, become wise, and "explore the depths of meaning in these nuggets of truth."

Proverbs 1:1.

That first chapter, that first verse of the book he was initially drawn to, was the basis for which he would make all future decisions with his new lease on life.

To hear the various nurses and doctors he encountered tell it during his six-month stay at the University of Washington Medical Center, Evon had been found wet and unconscious with a multitude of potentially life-threatening injuries. He was transported from Oak Harbor to Seattle to begin immediate treatment on what read like a laundry list of body parts you don't want to willingly injure: partial fractures of the thoracic and lumbar spine, broken neck, shattered jaw, broken teeth, several fractured ribs, dislocations and compound fractures in both arms, multiple wrist fractures, broken fingers, and one nearly shattered leg.

Then there was the punctured lung and the busted skull that knocked him into a coma, which turned out to be a good thing because having to alertly deal with the amount of pain caused by all of those injuries would've been too much to bear while waiting for the various pain-killing medicines to take effect.

Evon was truly blessed, because the odds of people coming out of comas weren't favorable. Neither were the odds of someone not becoming permanently paralyzed from injuries such as his. He felt that he shouldn't even be here because even amongst all of his failures in life, he couldn't even successfully end it with a fall from a 180-foot-high bridge.

Yet, there could be no doubt that he was made to fail for a reason, that the fall was part of a grand equation.

There were periods of time in his 43 years on this earth that he felt humans made their own decisions, paved their own futures in life, were solely responsible for what follows when they open their eyes in the morning. It didn't make sense to him that there was some divine puppet master pulling all the strings for the more than seven billion inhabitants of this green and blue sphere. He couldn't wrap his head around the notion that an unseen force governed human life from inception to their predetermined termination.

But now?

What other answer could there be?

Evon didn't think he survived his attempt to avoid reaching 44 because he merely failed to calculate his fall correctly or because of some other human factor.

Being in a near vegetative state for all these months made it abundantly clear that the sands in his hourglass still trickled through the neck of the glass bulbs.

Someone was looking out for him.

As for who was watching over him while he recovered in his sterile-smelling, winter-shaded room? That would be Nurse Morris, a full-figured woman in every sense of the word, who had long, perfectly coiffed, red hair. There was an ever-so-slight hint of gray at her roots, which meant that as much as she tried to maintain a positive attitude in a place as depressing as a hospital, the physical manifestation of stress wouldn't be denied a chance to show off.

Being that Evon couldn't talk for some time while he was recovering from the multiple surgeries to fix his jaw and make his mouth look a little less like a jack-o-lantern, Nurse Morris would come into his room smiling, with a sort of bounce to her, and help him drink or eat whatever liquified food he could. She would always announce herself by cheerfully saying, "Time for sustenance, Mr. *Ee-vahn*!"

Evon would always force a painful smile when she said this because of her peculiar word choice and because she was pronouncing his name completely wrong, but he couldn't correct her since he couldn't verbalize much more than grunts and moans. Nurse Morris took it as a sign that he was happy to not only get something of substance in his stomach, but also to see her, which was partly true because she would always get really close to him, and Evon loved to smell her flowery perfume as she helped him sit up. He would even sneak a few glances at her alluring breasts that peeked out of her plunging scrubs top, which he wasn't sure if she revealed on purpose just for him or if that was her personal style of dress. One would think that in a setting such as this, nurses would choose to dress more conservatively, but Evon was confident that Nurse Morris was a hit with all of the male patients and doctors in the building.

He felt a little ashamed that he took notice of her chest and in another life he would've loved to experience this woman, just once, and then never speak to her again. But he was baptized, washed anew by the April rains falling over Oak Harbor and couldn't be bothered to entertain such thoughts longer than he already had.

For the brief moments when feelings like that arose, Evon reminded himself that he was more than satisfied with just her healing hands.

Healing.

He had read quite a few passages in his new favorite book during his recovery, but one of his favorites had come from the little-known Nahum, which ironically meant "comforter" in Hebrew.

Chapter 3, verse 19 read: "There is no healing for your wound—it is far too deep to cure. All who hear your fate will clap their hands for joy, for where can one be found who has not suffered from your cruelty?"

To some, this might seem like an ominous, hopeless verse for someone in Evon's position, but he didn't look at it that way. If anything, it made him positively introspective.

It was true, and the acknowledgment of such stung him.

Where *could* one be found who hadn't been a pawn on the board in his game of life?

He'd had sex with enough women to fill every day on the calendar in a leap year. He had cheated and bamboozled hundreds, if not thousands, of employees and business partners on the way to making his fortune. Evon had even stolen some of the meager belongings of the vagabonds he often took refuge with during his time on the streets of Oak Harbor.

If all the people from his past didn't collectively stand to deliver a rousing round of applause while watching him fall into that pit of despair and homelessness, surely knowing he had been reduced to a crippled lump of a man for half a year would provide a reason to do so.

Evon often wondered if anyone from days gone by would hear of the news that earned him a hospital stay and become sympathetic enough to at least come pay a visit.

He didn't have to wonder much about at least two people who sojourned to his hospital room.

Securing an exclusive spot right on the stand next to his bed was a diminutive white card that was folded in half. On the front was a crudely drawn, yellow smiley face and an odd looking, multi-colored flower. Inside was a message that simply read: "*Git wel daddy.*"

Even when his mind was at its cloudiest and the days ahead seemed dark, Sunny found a way to shine through.

Evon couldn't help but smile at his 15-year-old daughter's card, misspelling and all. Those were the kinds of things that happened when your only offspring was mentally retarded.

In this politically correct world, though, many chose to re-coin the term as being *intellectually disabled*, but Evon couldn't get away from that old-school term because the alternative made it sound like her affliction wasn't all that bad. The sanitization of a malady so terrible didn't sit well with him; it was avoidance and a fear to confront something for what it really was. Sunny wasn't intellectually disabled to him.

No.

She was mentally retarded, which meant she was slow.

Weak.

Simple.

Defective.

All synonyms that meant Sunny wasn't so bright.

Regardless, he loved that girl with all his heart despite his occasional feelings of guilt that he might be the cause of her scourge. He helped create that beautiful life form and was very grateful that Chastity had enough goodness left in her to let their daughter visit him in the hospital. Evon only wished they had done so when he was awake and aware and not in a medically induced stupor.

He asked Nurse Morris if she was present when his visitors came and she had told him yes, and that she witnessed Sunny placing kisses on his cheek. She was initially going to stop her from doing so, fearing that she'd disturb the wiring he was hooked up to but thought better of it when she saw the tender exchange.

That brought some comfort to Evon and that's when, on one of his last days in the hospital since his rehabilitation had reached an acceptable point, he started to understand why God had saved him.

Wisdom.

Healing.

Comfort.

God had presented a mission to Evon. He was to use his second chance to do the things he failed to do in the first 43 years of his life. He was to use his newfound, Bible-wrought wisdom, to bring healing and comfort to those he knew that were suffering and to those he knew who were struggling with a profound sadness. This world we lived in had become a place where being a good Samaritan and helping others out of the kindness of one's heart was almost frowned upon. People were becoming so selfish that in order to provide aid to someone in need, it was a prerequisite to ensure that something material was to be attained in the end.

Was not a "thank you" enough? Or a simple embrace? Or a promise to pay it forward?

Evon didn't want any extrinsic reward though, whether that be material or a verbal acknowledgement. What he was going to offer to those who had the fortune of getting close to him in his new, spiritual state would provide a much higher reward, not only for him but also for those God wanted him to show mercy to.

What he was going to offer them was their release from any ties to this physical world because it was clear that was what God wanted him to do.

Evon, having failed to take his own life, would succeed in spades to take the lives of those suffering. Not take their lives in the sense that he would become personally invested and as such, provide comfort so that they could move forward. No, he knew it was up to him to help them breathe their last breath in this painful world and reach the serene home of their Creator.

He leapt off Deception Pass Bridge with his arms spread as if he were an eagle, only to be spared to become an angel of death.

Tears welled up in his eyes because he felt an overwhelming joy that he of all people had been chosen to end the pain, the agony, and the torment of the many people in his life who didn't want to be here anymore. No one he would encounter will admit it to him and they will not have mustered up the courage to end their own lives before he reaches them, but that was ok.

When Evon came to offer that sweet relief, there is no doubt that they will embrace him and show unmitigated gratitude at the opportunity he was going to provide.

The thought of changing lives for the better broke whatever invisible dam that was holding the tears from being released in his eyes and Evon wept uncontrollably.

This is what he had been saved for, so he himself could save those he loved from the torturous life this future hell-on-earth was quickly bringing upon them.

He picked up his Bible and frantically flipped the pages, searching for something, *anything,* that would affirm that he was truly on the right path, and after a few minutes, Evon came across his sign in Acts: "But anyone who asks for mercy from the Lord shall have it and shall be saved."

He knew of many people who this verse applied to, and Evon now knew he was the human embodiment of the mercy they had asked for.

The Lord wanted him to save them, and he would save them *all.*

He would not let his hands nor his lips remain idle.

It would not be an easy task but he had heard a saying that God saved his toughest tasks for His strongest soldiers, and Evon knew exactly who he needed to help first.

Nurse Morris was due to come in at any moment to deliver her trademark line, even though at this point in his recovery, Evon was capable of feeding himself.

He was sitting on the edge of his bed with his head down but perked up to gaze directly into her eyes when she came in.

She took one look at him and could tell something was wrong.

Her usual smile had slowly faded and she said quietly, "Oh no. Streaks on the cheeks means someone's been crying. What's wrong with Mr. *Ee-vahn* today?"

"Nurse Morris? What's your first name?"

"That would be Tiffani."

"Well, Tiffani, I need to tell you that you've been saying my name all wrong since you've known me. It's pronounced like you would say *Evan*. But since I like you, I've let that slide," Evon said with a slight grin.

She smiled back and said, "Well, thank you for letting me butcher your name, Evon. Now, are you going to tell me why you've been crying? And don't you lie to me."

"You're right, I have done a lot of crying, Nurse Morris, but nothing is wrong. Actually, everything is right, now. I need a favor too, though, and I have some questions for you that I need answers to. I was found in Deception Pass Park by paramedics, right?"

"As far as I know, yes, that's right."

"But someone had to have found me first to alert the paramedics as to where my body could be attended to, right?"

"You're two for two, sir!"

"Well, I need that person's name, Tiffani. Is there any way you could find out who that was?"

"I don't see why not. I have some friends in high places that could give me that information. You sit tight!

Oh, what am I saying, you're not going too far right now. I'll only be a few minutes!"

"You know where you can find me!"

Nurse Morris patted him on the back and headed out of the room, and Evon took this chance to gingerly saunter to the bathroom.

He didn't need to relieve himself; instead, he walked over to the mirror, placed his hands on the cold, porcelain sink, and stood there to look at his reflection.

What stared back at him was a different man, one he didn't recognize. Not just physically either. Sure, Evon's dashing good looks would never return, replaced now by what could only be described as a monstrosity, but he didn't care about those things anymore anyway. The jagged incision scars that lined his neck and lower jaw didn't bother him. Nor did his now misshapen nose or his snaggletooth grin. He was missing pretty much all his top and lower front teeth, and with no money to cosmetically fix what would be a vain feature at this point, it would remain that way. Looking attractive was of no concern to Evon after his recent revelation.

He had changed on the inside and that was all that counted.

Wanting to fulfill carnal desires, acquire wealth, and any other material accolades were in the distant past. The wealth he wanted, the desires he longed to fulfill, were rewards that could only be obtained on a higher plane. But he wasn't selfish and he couldn't wait to share.

"Knock, knock!" Nurse Morris said. "Anything you got hanging out, go ahead and put it away and come on out with your hands up, mister! I've got some great news for you!"

Evon took one last glance at his image in the mirror and walked out of the bathroom, ready to receive what he'd been waiting for.

Nurse Morris stood there, looking positively giddy to share the good news with him.

"Sit down, buddy. You ready for this? Turns out the first people to find you were a couple of kids that were getting a little exercise when they came across you being lazy and napping on the ground. Shame on you."

"You're quite the comedian, Nurse Morris. So, it was a group of kids that found me you say? Boys? Girls?"

"Well, the transcript from the 911 call indicates it was a group of boys but only one gave their name. A 12-year-old by the name of Mitchell Jeffers."

"Mitchell Jeffers… Is there a way for me to contact him?"

"Ah, I thought you'd ask. I'm really not supposed to be doing this. Since he's a minor, *usually* you'd have to contact the parents first. But…"

Tiffani then proceeded to pull out a folded-up piece of paper from her back pocket and handed it to Evon. He unfolded it and looked down at it, scanning it over slowly.

"I'm assuming you want to send a 'thank you' card?" Nurse Morris said. "Or give the young man a call to show how thankful you are that there's still good little boys in the world?"

Evon, still reading over the information on the paper, said, "Yes. Poor kid was probably traumatized a little bit finding my body in that condition. I imagine he's hurting a little bit mentally from such an experience, wouldn't you say so? Maybe I can help with that."

FOUR

In this life, one can choose to either make themselves very visible for all the world to see, or they can make themselves invisible and slither along like a wraith creeping through the night. No one really makes that choice for them. That is their choice to make and theirs alone. There are some consequences that come with that choice, though. They will either have to deal with the people, the sounds, the responsibilities, the happiness, and the eventual sadness that a visible life brings, or… deal with the people, the sounds, the responsibilities, the happiness, and the eventual sadness that an invisible life brings.

Deon really thought that being invisible, virtually non-existent to society at large would help him escape, but he found that there was no difference between the two types of lives. Being homeless and meandering around with the other homeless people in Oak Harbor brought with it the same thing that not being homeless would have.

Here in the Dreg City section of Oak Harbor—where the big wigs of the town would like to keep all of the dregs of society and prevent them from making themselves visible to the rest of the normal citizens—you could experience all that life had to offer.

Normal, well-off people think that the homeless are damaged to the point where they're not even real humans that experience the same things that they do, that there's no parallels between the two versions of reality. Deon, and his cohorts, too, had to find their way amongst a group of people where certain jobs, duties, and rules were set up to make the area they lived in run efficiently. They had to deal with the cacophony of broken glass, clanging metal, slamming doors, laughter, wails, arguments, and people talking to themselves. There was a thriving economy where money, and sometimes drugs, alcohol, and sex were traded for services, and without these services Dreg City might devolve into chaos.

Chaos that could spill out into the rest of Oak Harbor.

But even with the semblance of order that they had created, there was still crime, violence, and other problems that were solved with a unique brand of justice where all of Dreg City were the judge, jury, and sometimes the executioner.

Even though the thought of an official executioner sounded harsh, people here never killed anyone; maybe just some verbal lashings or every once in a while, the meting out of a good ass-kicking or two.

However, they certainly excommunicated those who had committed the most severe violations of their version of the legal code and that in itself was akin to a slow burning version of death to those in the homeless community because it was hard to survive in the main portion of town.

Sure, there was the Opportunity Center and other similar places in Oak Harbor that aimed to help the bums people had ostracized and virtually kicked out of their normal society but what they provided either was too much or wasn't enough for some folks. The people who worked at the Opportunity Center always wanted to *change* someone, when some of the homeless just wanted something to eat and temporary shelter so they could get back to the only way of living that made them comfortable.

That was what made them happy, and happiness could be found in Dreg City, too, like when somebody kicked an addiction that had a fierce grip on them, or when someone finally got a job with some real income. Conversely, profound sadness had no problem rearing its ugly head either, like witnessing someone fall back into the same addiction they had worked so hard to overcome, or tending to the emotional and sometimes physical wounds of someone who had been abused, or consoling someone who had lost everything due to a catastrophic event with no family to turn to for help. Weren't these the same things that the visible, normal people experienced?

If you dug deep, there really was no difference that clearly separated the two groups of people, save the amount of material possessions they had accumulated. If only they truly understood that they were one fire, one accident that permanently tore the fabric of their family apart, one little experiment with drugs that turned into a debilitating addiction away from finding themselves in Deon's position.

Deon, whose full name was Gideon but was given a shortened version after spending some time in Dreg City, had experienced all those things.

Born in Seattle to a white mother and a black father, he and his mother were fortunate enough to escape relatively unharmed from a car accident while returning home from dinner and a Disney movie one night.

It was funny how, try as one might to avoid those tragic moments, they just seemed to find you. You can be as safe as you've always been or even more so depending on a certain set of conditions, but when fate wants to introduce a new wrinkle into your life that you have to iron out, there isn't much you can do.

The wrinkle on that fateful night was a drunk driver, and drunk drivers are a bitch.

Deon still remembered the moment like it was yesterday.

He was sitting in the middle section of their minivan; the very rear was empty save for some household junk that never made it inside the actual house.

His father was driving; his mother was in the passenger seat. They came to a stop at a red light and were preparing to make a right turn. His father was hesitant to peel out because his view of any approaching traffic was obscured by a tall set of bushes adjacent to the driver side. When he felt the coast was clear enough, he slowly crept out to his right, only to be slammed into by a red SUV that sped much faster through the intersection than they were supposed to. Deon knew it was red because he saw his mother forming a scream while beginning to point in its direction, and he turned his head to see the flash of it before he blacked out. When he came to, it was smoky inside their car but not from any fire. It was the lingering powder that coats airbags when they deploy. His mother had managed to make it out of the car and was yanking on his seatbelt, trying to get him loose. She'd suffered a bruising shot to the face from the impact of the airbag, and Deon was sore from head to toe.

His dad wasn't very fortunate though, for he suffered damn near crippling injuries to his back that cost him his high-paying construction job. Having lost that gig, he moved the family to Oak Harbor where the cost of living was more in line with what he was reduced to, secretarial work at a bank, and it didn't sit well with him that he went from work fit for a man to being essentially emasculated. He went from setting an example for his idea of what a boy is supposed to grow up to become to showing what could happen when estrogen is involuntarily forced through your veins.

Day in and day out, Deon's mother tried to assure her husband that he was still very much a man, a man that she loved and admired even more strongly for still having that desire to provide for his family in the face of his new physical limitations. She stressed to him that a lesser man would've happily crawled into a pit of despair, never to leave the comfort of self-pity, leaving his family to fend for themselves. She hoped her words would provide comfort to his bruised ego but those frequent reassurances did little to assuage his feelings of guilt, shame, and anger, despite the truth he knew was behind her words.

Add to that the pain he was going to deal with for the rest of his life, and it wasn't long before he became addicted to pain pills—an addiction that grew into the need for even stronger drugs. Oh, he definitely got a hold of those stronger drugs, too, which wasn't very hard because the police were very hands off when it came to drug enforcement in cozy Oak Harbor.

That meant only emotional pain and suffering for the families who had to sit idly by and watch as drugs ravaged the bodies, minds, and souls of those who fell victim to the false promises and half-truths of the substances they ingested.

Take me! I'll make the pain go away. I'll make you feel good.

Oh, taking me puts your loved one in pain? They don't feel good?

Well, never mind them, how do I make you *feel?*

They made Deon's father feel great. They made him feel relaxed, so relaxed that he could fall asleep without being gripped by pain.

They made him forget about the lit cigarette in his hand as he lay next to his wife.

They made the home, the safe haven for Deon, turn into a blazing fire that he could only stand outside and watch as emergency responders held his flailing, willowy body back from running into the home, and he watched the firemen try desperately to put out the flames and keep them from damaging the surrounding homes. Luckily, or unluckily depending on how you wanted to look at his current situation, he had been at a friend's house for a sleepover and only returned home because he forgot some clothes. He returned just in time to see the firemen make a feeble attempt to go inside the inferno and save his parents, to see everything he had ever known being reduced to ashes, and, with tears streaming down his face, to literally see his whole life go up in flames.

Life after that was quite a wild ride. No family members wanted him, so his childhood became filled with trips to foster parents who could never fill the void left by his real parents. Then he'd run away from those faux sanctuaries only to be picked up by police who seemed to care about his wellbeing, but hadn't cared about his father's when he was out buying drugs right under their noses. Those little excursions landed Deon either in juvenile detention facilities or in foster care with other messed up kids who had the audacity to call him their brother, and he repeated that cycle several more times until at eighteen the powers that be could no longer control him. It was then that he set out on his own, *truly* on his own, and he didn't care who pretended to have a desire to lend a helping hand.

All he knew at that time is that he spent nine years with parents who, though flawed, loved him and provided guidance. The nine years without them, Deon was like a leaf in the wind, going wherever the breeze took him. The only true guiding force was that of time, always pushing him forward because that was how it worked; it was only in your memories that you could move backwards. Thus, he forged ahead.

From the age of eighteen to his current age of thirty, he found his way to Dreg City and was one of its senior members. Despite his veteran status, there was to be no pomp and circumstance associated with the annual experience he was accumulating.

In those 12 years, he was only rewarded by *living*. He got a chance to see, hear, and read damn near every possible scenario a person could.

From horror stories to happy tales, from fighting off assaults of every conceivable nature to warm embraces with those he had become somewhat close to, Deon had experienced more than the average 30-year-old. And even though he avoided making any deep connections with anyone for fear that they'd become like sand through his fingers, he had managed to form a bond with a scrawny little 18-year-old kid who reminded Deon of himself.

He was a short kid for his age. Dusty brown hair, stubble on his chin, satellite-like ears. Flip was his name, or at least that was what people called him around here. When you came to Dreg City, you left everything about your past behind, including your name. Your name was a reminder of a failed past life and you needed to be christened with a new beginning.

If you wanted to fit in here, and more importantly, be allowed to *stay* here, then you had to go through a certain rite of passage. So, Philip with the speech impediment when he told everyone his name, became Flip, the closest sounding word that had any resemblance to what was coming out of his mouth.

"Whatcha up to over there, Gideon?" Flip asked with a unique hitch in his voice.

Deon got annoyed by anyone other than Flip calling him by his full name and even if someone else did, he had been in a trance, eyes transfixed, but yet not engaged with anything in particular.

"I'm not really sure, Flip. Kind of just staring out over the scenery, observing, taking things in."

Flip stood over him while he sat on the ground with his back against a deteriorating wall, staring at nothing, yet everything.

Eyes were windows to the soul, Deon believed, but they also allowed you to get a sense of the soul that resided in another person, a thing, a place.

Deon looked up and followed Flip's gaze to a soiled napkin amongst the leaves that the crisp November wind pushed toward Deon's outstretched feet. It briefly stopped its advance before a brief gust thrusted it against his leg.

They both looked away and off into the surroundings and Deon wondered if Flip could see the same things he did, although he knew he couldn't. He imagined that all Flip really saw was a group of three men and a woman standing over a trashcan fire, a woman who had on threadbare garments, considering the weather, playing with a stray cat, and a few other men huddled over a milk crate, laughing and enjoying some drinks.

Two people could be *looking at* the same thing with their eyes and *seeing* totally different images in their minds, just as someone could *hear* but not truly *listen.* Deon figured that's what the case was this time. He had talked to Flip a lot in two years, since he came here as a sixteen-year-old runaway, and it always seemed like Flip was wise beyond his years, that he saw and understood things that others around here couldn't and likely never would, that he could *feel* a little bit differently than those around him. That's why he tagged along so much and Deon didn't mind.

"Flip, you ever wonder why you're here?"

"Fuck no, bro. I *know* why I'm here. My parents always on my ass, going to school really sucked with all the kids that always messed with me. I never really felt I belonged anywhere and no one understood me. So, I just said forget it. I'm gonna run away and live my life the way I want for a while. No strings, no obligations, no worries. I don't plan on being here forever though. This sleeping outside all the damn time kind of sucks. How in the hell you've been doing it all this time, I'll never know."

"Thanks for all of that, but you've told me that stuff before. It's insightful, really. What I meant was, have you ever wondered why you're *here*? Alive. On this earth. In Washington. In Oak Harbor. In this exact spot with me in particular, at this exact time, telling me why you ran away from home."

Flip raised his eyes from Deon, who was still staring off into the distance. He was asking questions no one had ever cared to ask before or that he had even taken the time to think about before. He thought about more pressing things, like the here and now. What was he going to eat that day? Where was he going to sleep? How was he going to fix that nagging pain in his leg? All that existential stuff hadn't occurred to him. However, he had no choice but to think about it now that Deon had posed the question. He wasn't quite sure of his answer though. Were these the kinds of things a 30-year-old thought of? Granted, Deon wasn't that old and he certainly didn't look like he'd been through 30 years of living, but Flip knew he had been through *something* that made him think about his place in the world. What he didn't know was what that was exactly. Deon never told him what landed him in the home of the dregs, and he didn't feel like it was his business to ask. The temptation to ask swelled up in him because of the human nature to be curious, but he always resisted. When that time came that Deon wanted to share some of his history with him, he'd be there to listen. Until then, the circumstances of his life were his to know about and his alone.

"Naw, man. Never really thought about it. But by the way you're zoning out right now, I'm assuming you have?"

Another bout of wind jostled the napkin loose from Deon's leg.

"Yeah, Flip. Every single day, man. Every single day."

FIVE

"Henni Road, Imperial Lane, Ponderosa Drive. Ah, here we have it. Noble Place," Evon said out loud. "8326 Noble Place, and Lord, what a noble place indeed!"

After spending a few more weeks in the hospital for the doctors to make sure he was in a suitable enough condition to leave on his own, Evon had reached the home of young Mitchell Jeffers. He had designs of making sure the young man's mental ordeal was properly addressed.

The journey here to complete this mission was quite an interesting one, too.

He was stuck in Seattle with no way to get home, and the staff at the University of Washington Medical Center weren't going to just release him out into the world by himself. He was still gimpy and dealing with a great deal of pain and would need a friend or family member to help him get to follow-up visits at a local facility when it was time for those. Luckily for him, he had someone in Oak Harbor that he was close to and knew had his back. Whether or not he felt actually going to those follow-up visits was worth it was another matter.

Regardless, there was someone in Oak Harbor he could depend on based on their history. It was just too bad it wasn't Chastity. He had tried to call the last number he remembered for her in hopes of chatting and telling her thanks for bringing Sunny to come visit, but either she had changed her number or had refused to pick up. No worries though. His friend in Oak Harbor said she would be more than happy to support him after being released but he needed to make sure he got there first.

He had some money, but that needed to be saved for later, for he had plans for its use in order to complete his mission from the Father above. He came to the realization that he would need some sort of transportation to get back home; borrowing a car like he did in April wasn't in the cards this time. Since he knew that wasn't an option, he figured the Lord would provide a way, and He did. Jesus took the wheel in the form of a nice young man that Evon flagged down as he was sitting outside the entrance of UWMC, pondering his next steps.

There was a sense of irony Evon felt as he stepped inside the good Samaritan's red, late model Mustang.

God truly did work in mysterious ways.

Evon told him that he needed to get back home to Oak Harbor. The young man said he could take him as far as the Mukilteo Ferry Terminal and then Evon would have to take the ferry to get to Whidbey Island. During the drive, they exchanged small talk to make sure there wasn't any awkward silence. It turned out the driver was a university student who was an east coast transplant. He told Evon that he came from a family of Middle Eastern immigrants who were well-respected in their former home. He didn't want to follow the family tradition of getting into medicine because he wanted to forge a new future for himself but was eventually persuaded by not wanting to be a disgrace to his entire family. Then of course, there was the earning potential that aided his decision.

Evon told him about what landed him in the hospital, and the young Middle Eastern driver spewed off some medical facts pertaining to his injuries, all of which were things Evon knew because of what the doctors explained to him. He was a little bit disappointed that the student omitted some facts, and even worse, had gotten a few completely mixed up. It was clear that he either needed to study harder or get out of the profession entirely, before being a disgrace to his family became the least of his worries.

Before dropping Evon off, the student provided him with the funds to fetch a ride and told him to keep the change. Evon was almost certain that his physical appearance had something to do with the young man's generosity; he just looked like someone who could use all the help he could get.

The ferry ride over was a serene one. It gave Evon a chance to enjoy the sights and sounds of God's earth while contemplating what he needed to do. There were a few couples and families on the ferry with him, pointing with their fingers and cameras at everything outside of the boat.

Smiles on their faces.

Excitement in their voices.

The same displays of pleasure that he would be experiencing very soon, he thought.

After arriving on the island, he got on the Island Transit bus from the drop off point in Clinton all the way to Oak Harbor, roughly a two-hour ride, and from there he began his trek to meet up with Mitchell.

Evon pulled out the folded-up piece of paper with Mitchell's address on it that Nurse Morris had given him and decided to walk all the way there with nothing but the donated clothes from the hospital and his backpack full of supplies. Considering what part of town he was in and the physical condition he found himself in, walking there would be like self-flagellation, showing the man upstairs just how far he would go and what agony he'd put himself through to prove that he loved Him and was grateful that he was selected for the task of delivering His mercy.

It took some time, but when he finally stood outside staring at the light blue, two-story home, he knew the journey was worth it. He turned his head in the direction of a dog barking somewhere in the otherwise quiet neighborhood. It was getting dark out; the chill in the air was nipping at everything that was left exposed.

The coat he had on provided some warmth but not much. He didn't mind though. The feeling of the cold hitting his skin was a reminder that he was *alive.*

He looked up at the clear night sky and honed in on the almost full moon. Something dark flew by in his line of sight, perfectly silhouetted for a fleeting moment. A bat? A bird? Maybe a raven perhaps. He turned his attention back to Mitchell's home. The kid must've been financially well off because he had a large porch, yard, and the lawn was perfectly manicured, even with it being autumn; a time where everything outside tends to die off.

Fatigue, as well as doubt, started to creep in, though. God was testing Evon, he just knew it. He slung off his backpack and dug inside for his Living Bible, another gift from the hospital. It was green with a faux leather binding that was beat up and scratched, as he imagined many hands and lost souls had likely handled it hundreds of times over the years. However, just like what was an important quality to find in a human, it was the inside that counted to him.

Evon walked to the lone tree that was in the front yard and sat down so he could get off his feet; the tree had started to succumb to fall and was void of any leaves that would block the moonlight he needed to be able to read.

After what felt like hours, he finally centered on a verse that seemed like an appropriate answer to his questioning if he should approach Mitchell on this night. Psalms 127:2: "It is senseless for you to work so hard from early morning until late at night… for God wants his loved ones to get their proper rest."

It was settled then. He would not question the Word, and the cold—though initially inviting—was getting to be too unbearable to deal with anyway.

He stood and put his backpack on. He needed temporary shelter but didn't want to bother the other resting families in the neighborhood. Even though people were supposed to be kind to the meek, at this time of night he knew that he wouldn't exactly be welcomed with open arms by anyone. Besides, there was the risk that he would be turned away and then his strange presence in the neighborhood would cause someone to alert the authorities. They would come and probably escort him away from the area after questioning him, thwarting his mission.

That's when he spotted the garage in the Jeffers' backyard.

As he walked and approached the door, he paused for a moment to see if it was unlocked. It was. He would step inside to rest his body for a while but when he awoke, it would be time to soldier on for the Lord.

***

Evon shot up from his slumber after being startled by the barking dog somewhere off in the distance. From the sound of it, it was the same canine he'd heard earlier. Either the mutt had been barking incessantly for all these hours or it was reminding an irresponsible owner to feed and water it.

Evon had lost track of time and was afraid he'd slept much longer than he planned. He wasn't quite sure when he'd arrived at the Jeffers' residence, as he had no watch or phone to keep track of the time, but what he did know was that the moon he'd looked up to hours before had been replaced by the sun and it shone just as brightly. It had cast some of its rays inside the dark and pungent garage and one look around at all the freshly used lawn equipment was all it took to know why the smell was so strong.

He arose from his aching knees just enough to see out of the garage door window to notice there were no parked cars. This didn't bother him when he first showed up last night because he thought that maybe a parent of Mitchell's worked late, but now he began to worry that he was indeed in the wrong place. He slumped back down with his back against the garage door and took out the address written on the paper, then took one quick look out of the window to make sure no one was watching him. When he felt satisfied that he was in the clear, he gathered his belongings and exited the garage.

The warmth that embraced him was a more welcome feeling compared to what he felt last night. His feet felt sufficiently rested, too. But sleeping on the hard garage floor did no favors to his back and joints. He reached behind with one hand and lightly massaged his back, but it provided little relief.

Evon casually walked to the front of the house with the address in his hand. He didn't notice it when he'd first arrived, because it was dark, but he saw that there were home security cameras attached to the side and pointed towards the garage. He looked up at one and waved. Continuing on to the front of the house, he saw in black, plastic numbering the address reading *8326*. He turned around to look at the green street sign. Noble Place. He was definitely at the right location, there was no doubt about that.

The neighborhood was still as quiet as it had been the night before. He felt like he was the only person awake and moving amongst all the people that occupied these homes. That's when he heard it: the dog barking again. He was too busy pondering if he'd arrived at the wrong location to notice if the dog had stopped barking, or perhaps it never stopped. Yet, there was the loud yapping again.

Evon decided then it was as good a time as any to get to work and he carefully approached the porch. He climbed the steps slowly, not yet sure what he would do when someone answered the door, but getting the script ready in his head for when they did. He saw that there were more cameras attached to the front and offered a wave to them. When he reached for the metallic handle on the screen door, he noticed a piece of paper that seemed to be taped on the inside door. It was too difficult to read with the screen door shut, but as he proceeded to open it, he realized it was a note: *In Seattle for vacation!*

Please leave any packages on the back porch. Happy Thanksgiving! -The Jeffers.

All Evon could do was smile and drop his head. He released the handle and let the door close on its own before deciding to sit on the porch to think for a bit.

He guessed it was getting pretty close to Thanksgiving and this wealthy, yet foolish, family had decided to not only vacation a little early, but had announced to anyone wishing to do them harm that the home was unoccupied and they were free to make off with as much property as they could handle. Evon wasn't there to take any material property, though, and apparently, the Lord hadn't meant for him to take any property in human form, either.

There was only one answer for this current conundrum: this had been nothing more than a test to see if Evon was really fit for this spiritual journey. He hoped that he had passed with flying colors. If he would walk across town only to find out that God showed His playful side by sending Mitchell Jeffers to the same city Evon had just left, what more could he do but laugh and take pride that his creator had a weird sense of humor?

Enough time had been spent here, he thought.

"Thank you anyway, young Mitchell Jeffers. Clearly you were put on this earth to perform duties that can never be repaid," Evon said to himself.

He thought momentarily about leaving a note himself, saying that he'd stopped by, but it would be pointless.

He stepped off the porch into the grass, letting it crunch beneath his feet. There were still no neighbors anywhere to be seen, and the dog, wherever it was, was no longer barking.

All the walking and nervous energy he'd expended did a number on his stomach. Where was Nurse Morris with sustenance when he needed it? Evon knew where he could get food, though, and he could meet back up with his longtime friend.

"Well," he said, "on to see my fellow dregs."

SIX

Evon made it to the center of the town and needed a headquarters for the next step in his process. He didn't have a lot of funds to work with but he needed a private place to be and decided he would get a hotel room for a couple of days. That made his decision to settle on The Dutch Inn that was close to Dreg City an easy one.

This was a place that was popular among Oak Harbor's transients. It was in a prime location and was a cost-effective way, with what little money someone had, to take care of your Johns and indulge in the drug or drink of your choice in peace. It also provided temporary shelter from the elements that could get harsh sometimes in the Pacific Northwest.

It was a desolate, single story brick and concrete building with more than 20 rooms. It wasn't exactly inviting to a stranger who might've been looking for a cozy place to stay for a night, though.

The outside had a sign on a post that read in bright green letters: "THE Dutch Inn," though Evon had no clue why the first word was in all-caps. Attached to that was what looked like a laminated red poster that read: "*$33.99 a night. ANY nihgt!*"

Whoever ran this establishment loved the use of capital letters but not so much checking the spelling of what would be displayed to prospective patrons. It must've been part of some plan to give the place some much-needed character.

He walked inside to be met by an older looking, rotund man who looked to be the human embodiment of a mid-life crisis.

Do I just shave off what's left of my hair? Or do I keep the horseshoe look with a shiny strip right down the middle? Should I keep wearing this flannel button-up over my t-shirt to make me look professional? Or do I take it off and say forget it?

Evon walked up to the counter and the man behind slapped it with both hands, asking with a booming voice, "What can I do for you today?"

"I need a room," Evon said.

"Not a problem, my man. That'll just be $34 bucks a night. That's the price without tax, of course."

Evon turned around to look outside and said, "The, uh, sign outside says $33.99, though."

The two men went silent for a moment, staring at each other. It could be that the man was taking stock of Evon's unusual appearance or that he had come to the realization that Evon wouldn't be shorted, even if it was just a penny.

"Ok then, $33.99," the man said smarmily. "How many occupants you got?"

Evon looked down at the man's chubby fingers. They were black and oily to the hilt, with chipped nails and had obviously seen better days. There wasn't a ring visible, either, which didn't surprise him.

"One. Just me. Does each room have a refrigerator?"

"Yes, they do. A mini one. You cool with that?"

"Yeah, I'm cool with that."

"Ok. Total comes up to $51.95. That includes tax and a one-time convenience charge, in case you're wondering."

This slightly annoyed Evon but he nodded in the affirmative.

"Oh, and we only take cash. If that's a problem, there's an ATM over there," he said, pointing to a gray and green machine in a corner.

Evon waved him off and handed the man three $20 bills.

"I'd like a room with a little bit of privacy. Maybe somewhere toward the back?"

The man chuckled and shook his head.

"One of those guys, huh? Alright, room 14, in the back. That'll give you all the privacy you need. You need a bodyguard too? Or a look-out? That'll cost you a little bit extra," the man said, laughing at his own joke.

Seeing that his humor wasn't landing, he dropped his impromptu stand-up act and handed Evon his change and the key. It wasn't a plastic card like the current industry standard but instead a regular metal key with a series of numbers and letters on it.

"Check-out is at 11 in the morning. If you want more days, come up to the counter no less than an hour earlier and pay more cash. Can't get no simpler than that."

"Thank you," Evon said.

He started to walk out of the door and head to his room when the man behind the counter shouted, "Hey, do you have a car?"

Evon turned back around and said, "Excuse me?"

"Do… you… have… a… car?"

"No, I don't have a car. Why?"

"I do mechanic work out back," he said, thrusting a thumb backwards. "Just tryin' to make an extra buck. You know anybody needs work, send 'em my way."

Evon realized that explained the muck all over the man's hands.

"I'll keep that in mind, um…"

"Hank."

"Hank. I'll keep that in mind, Hank."

Evon didn't offer his name in return and walked outside, heading toward his room.

Before entering, he stopped to look around and take inventory of the surroundings. There seemed to be maybe 50 feet between his room door and a limp, rusted chain-link fence. On the other side was Hank's auto repair business, if one could even call it that. Yes, there were several cars parked in that lot that seemed to be in varying states of repair, but he couldn't tell how much work was actually being done to them. Given the appearance of Hank's fingers, either he was working diligently to get these cars in running shape to get back on the road or he was tinkering around to make it *look* like he was a good mechanic to attract the confidence and dollars of prospective customers.

He knocked on his red hotel door; it was satisfyingly solid.

Evon unlocked it and stepped inside. He was immediately hit with the scent of stale cigarette smoke and cleaning agents that served only to add a layer to the funk, not completely get rid of it.

The room was small but that was to be expected for the price. The floor was made up of stained laminate hardwood that feebly mimicked the real thing. He figured that Hank was tired of trying to constantly clean the carpets after unkempt guests and replacing it with flooring that was easier to maintain was the only option.

Pushed up against the window there was a meager particle-board desk. He slid his hand across the surface.

Bumps from water damage.

A light coating of dust.

Oddly, there was no chair in the room to sit at the desk with, not that Evon planned to do much sitting and writing.

The bed looked to be queen-sized, with a red and green floral design on the comforter. He couldn't be completely sure but he thought the comforter hadn't seen a fresh wash in months. Hotels could probably get away with that and stains could be hidden throughout the dark colors of the design, but upon closer inspection, it had all the tell-tale signs of a place like this: conspicuous stains, both bodily and otherwise, and burn holes from cigarettes. He pulled the comforter back to inspect the sheets; at least they were white and clean.

He sat down on the edge of the bed. It was springy, with a loud creak. He could only imagine how much and how vigorously it had been used over the years.

Directly in front on a beige counter protruding from the wall was a 19-inch black cathode ray tube television—the big, boxy glass ones that no one would be proud to admit they have these days. A stainless steel mini fridge sat adjacent to the TV; surprisingly, it was immaculately clean, almost brand new it seemed.

After finishing his cursory inspection of the room, he reached inside of his backpack to retrieve some items that needed to be put inside the fridge.

When Evon was recovering in UWMC, he thought about the mission God had saved him for. Sure, he would deliver souls to Him, but *how*? This was new territory for him and he didn't want to displease.

The tablet he was allowed to use provided him with a means to research ways he could be successful.

The only problem was he only learned how and what to do, but he still needed to collect the tools for the job.

There was no doubt that, despite the fall from Deception Pass Bridge, Evon's supreme intellect that had lifted him to the highest of highs in his career was very much intact. He was smarter than almost everyone he knew at one point and the fall didn't impact that.

Back when he was still recovering at the hospital is when he decided to act, at night of course, a time when security and activity in a hospital slowed to a crawl.

The nurses left a wheelchair in his room so he could get around with the least amount of stress inflicted on his healing body. During the day, they encouraged him to get in that wheelchair to move around and start gathering strength in his arms. During the night, he used it to strengthen his ability to save the ones he cared about.

He first asked a nurse for a flashlight, saying that he was afraid of the dark when he got up to use the bathroom. This was a ruse, of course, because he wasn't really frightened by the lack of light. Though she was initially puzzled, she obliged and after that, night after night, he rolled from room to room, quietly searching every cabinet and every drawer for the things that he needed.

Most of the time he was never caught in the action, but when he was, he just started crying and telling the person that caught him that he was confused and had gotten lost; then they'd always return him to his room with a smile. This didn't come without some consequences, though. Nurses always reported back to the doctor in charge that Evon seemed like he would benefit from a longer stay and more observation, delaying his release. Despite those obstacles, he managed to get everything he needed and even enlisted some unlikely help for the more important items.

Returning to his thoughts to his present situation, Evon searched for the remote so that he could watch a little TV. It had been a while since he sat and vegged out. Having flipped through some channels and not finding any programming that tickled his fancy, he relieved himself and then freshened up in the shower. He piled up his dirty linens on the floor in a corner and changed into his only fresh change of clothes, which came from a donated collection the hospital had for patients in his economic condition.

Once he was satisfied that he looked presentable, he put on his backpack and walked out of the door feeling good. The angel of death was ready to take flight.

SEVEN

Receipt duty.

Deon didn't like when his rotation was up, but this was something that needed to be done to contribute to his fellow vagabonds. In the past, he had to go it alone, but lately he at least had Flip with him to keep him company.

Receipt duty was a clever way that the denizens of Dreg City could nourish themselves on any given occasion. What it entailed was simple: when people went to the grocery store and bought all the Pepsis, Twinkies, Snickers, and potato chips their unhealthy stomachs could handle, they bagged up their items, put all their money away, and usually threw their receipts on the ground.

A teenaged girl in the homeless camp named Jenny observed this convenient phenomenon and decided to take advantage of it. She would gather receipts that were left being whipped up in the wind in the parking lots, confirm that cash was used to pay, check the dates on them to make sure they matched the current day, take them inside, and gather up all the items on the receipt, as if she'd shopped for them before. Then she headed to the customer service area and asked for a full refund of all the items, stating that she had decided she no longer wanted anything due to problems with her finances.

The moment was an ironic one, sure, but the people behind the counter didn't question it. There was an impending plastic bag ban for the city that was already sweeping the state, but for the time being, to disarm their suspicions on why the items were no longer bagged, she simply said she threw them away because there were holes in them or that she was making it easier for the clerk to get to all the items. The girl got her money to spend on whatever else she wanted, and she ran back to tell all her homeless family of the successful scheme. Everyone used that script going forward and it worked every time.

To keep the people that worked at the various grocery stores from catching on and trying to stop their cunning enterprise, the matriarch of Dreg City, Ruthie Bonner, dictated that they should hit every store once a week and send a different person each time, rotating to a different store on each occasion. She said it would be like the five-man weave in basketball, only in this instance it would be a team of twenty plus nonathletic and dispossessed men and women whose only goal was to swindle the dollars they needed to survive out of the opposing team.

On this day, Deon and Flip stood outside the entrance of the local Wal-Mart, watching their unassuming accomplices.

It was crisp outside, getting close to evening. It was a perfect time and place to pull off receipt duty because not only was Thanksgiving just around the corner, but this was a store that people would spend much more than they originally planned.

Pre-made lists didn't stand a chance at a place like this, and Wal-Mart was smart, depriving the shopping public of small, easy to carry baskets and instead forcing them to use the big, rolling carts, daring people to resist the urge to fill it up with the new flavor of Oreos.

"Right there, dude!" said Flip, pointing to something Deon couldn't immediately see.

"Huh? Right where? What are you talking about?" Deon said.

"*There!* Look at that cart she's pushing! It's so full, she's got her kids putting their hands on it to hold the shit in!"

Sure enough, Deon spotted it. A thin, blonde woman with an executive pixie cut was trying to handle the overflowing cart long enough to make it to whatever car she had and she employed the help of her four kids to do it. There were two on each side of the cart, boys and girls each, little ones, laughing and seemingly enjoying the task their mother had put them on: protect the cereal and milk at all costs!

"I bet you she's got a minivan, Gideon," Flip said.

"Nope," Deon said. "Look at her hair. She's still trying to hang onto her youth; she hasn't let age decide it's time to give up on cool cars yet. And take a look at what she's wearing. Her yoga pants are painted on and she's got pink and black Puma's on. Definitely not a minivan woman. She's probably driving some kind of rich-lady SUV. She can still pack in all those damn kids and look good doing it."

Flip stared at Deon incredulously, then back at the woman.

"Well, let's just see. Loser has to do all the talking to the refund clerk this time."

"Deal."

They both watched the woman and her kids walk the cart through the busy parking lot, bending their necks to get a better view through all the people walking in their lines of sight. She and her kids stopped right behind a merlot-red Dodge Grand Caravan and seemed to be ready to put their groceries away.

"Ha! Fucking told you, dude! Get those lips ready to do some talking!" said Flip.

The mother of four began to look around, perplexed. Then one of her daughters mouthed something imperceptible and pointed behind them. They turned their cart around and started to walk across the lot. The woman pulled a set of keys out of the purse that hung loosely on her shoulder and pressed a fob that opened the gate to a black BMW SUV.

A smile spread across Deon's face.

"Get the fuck outta here!" Flip said dejectedly.

"What can I say," started Deon, "this thirty-year-old knows his shit."

"Whatever, man. That works out for us anyway. I bet you that broad spent a fortune in there! And four kids, too? You thinking what I'm thinking?

"Yeah, that receipt."

"Exactly."

"Did you see her drop anything when you spotted her?"

Flip looked around and scanned the parking lot. There were all sorts of pieces of paper being tussled by the wind. Napkins, sandwich wrappers, receipts alike.

"Naw, I didn't see her drop anything. She probably still has it with her or threw it away. That'd be our luck."

Deon's eyes were still trained on the mother and her kids. The little ones were joyfully taking turns lifting the bags out of the cart with all the might their diminutive arms could muster and loading them into the trunk. Their mother had her eyes focused on the phone in her hands. One of her boys was lifting the last bag out of the cart. He was struggling with the last heavy load and it clipped the side of the cart right before he could clear it. That's when Deon saw a small piece of paper fly out of the bag.

"Flip! That's the receipt!" Deon said, pointing in the family's direction.

"I got it," said Flip.

He started to run out into the lot in that direction when he heard a car horn blare loudly. He jumped back in shock.

"Hey, watch it asshole!" a bespectacled, old Asian man screamed as he stuck his head out the driver-side window.

Flip flashed him a middle finger and yelled out, "Fuck you!"

The Asian man gave him a salute back and glared at Flip before he sped out of the lot.

Flip continued through the lot, moving at a jog. He briefly lost sight of the receipt but spotted it again, slowly turning in the wind. He continued on past the little boy whose mother had helped him get their last bag of groceries in the back of their BMW. The receipt stopped moving for a moment and Flip stomped on it with his right foot, making a loud slapping sound on the pavement.

"Got you, you little fucker!" Flip said, within earshot of the family.

The mother turned to look at him, scowling, and ushered her kids into their car.

Flip bent down to pick it up and then jogged back toward the entrance, where Deon was standing with his hands shoved into the pockets of his black jeans. He stopped quickly to look out for any remaining angry Asian men, then continued on.

He held out the receipt to Deon and said, "Got it."

Deon took the receipt from his hand, scanning it for the total spent.

$294.17.

"Flip, we've got a lot of shopping to do."

***

"Good thing we just got the most expensive stuff on the receipt, even though we didn't get the full refund. There was no way we were getting everything she bought!" said Flip. "And did you catch the way she was looking at us when we came up with the cart?"

"Yeah, because you just had to make a big deal about returning those Tampons and the silky red panties," said Deon.

Deon and Flip were walking out of the Wal-Mart parking lot, heading home to share their newfound wealth. The lot had emptied out substantially by the time they had finished.

"Hey," Flip said, "I had to let her know that my girlfriend didn't appreciate me bringing home Fruit of the Loom underwear and prefers pads. Besides, some theatrics don't hurt. It keeps 'em from getting suspicious when you make them uncomfortable instead."

It was darkening outside, chillier too, a good time for snow, although in these parts abundant rain was the more likely weather. Fortunately for them, they wouldn't have to battle any elements to make it back to the camp.

As they exited the parking lot, walking on the sidewalk against traffic, cars drove by, headlights making trails through the evening as people made their way home. Deon thought about the BMW mom and her kids. Her and people like her commuted through the streets at night, at times oblivious to what was going on outside the safety of their metal, plastic, and glass havens.

Sure, they were able to *visually* see what their windshields allowed them to, but they might never have to see themselves walking, virtually alone, back to an outdoor transient community after fleecing a multi-billion-dollar company for pennies just to live for a few days.

Deon hoped, for their sake, they would never have to experience it.

Flip broke his train of thought. "What do you think Ruthie will say?"

"About what?"

"About all this cash we're bringing back, man. This is a lot more than we usually bring back. She'll probably think we stole it from someone."

"Flip, I think that's kind of what we did."

Flip laughed. "Ha, I guess you're right, huh?"

"I don't think she'll say anything but 'thank you,' to be honest. This will give someone else a break from being on rotation. Plus, we'll have more money to buy shit for her little Thanksgiving feast she likes to put on."

"Damn, you do have a point there," Flip said.

Being the self-proclaimed matriarch of Dreg City, Ruthie tried to live up to the role in any way she could. A former prostitute and heroin addict, she had been fairly clean since Deon had known her, which had been a few years. Her former profession and choice of recreation made her astute when it came to the business of handling money, which was why she liked the proceeds to be handed over to her so she could be a human bank account of sorts. No one objected because she was honest, always going out of her way to buy things her homeless family needed, *truly* needed; she strongly refused buying any drugs for anyone, for any reason.

Flip and Deon were just yards away from the tents and crude shelters that made up Dreg City. There was a discernible buzz of activity in the air, much more so than usual. Upon inspection, they didn't notice anything different in the people. Everyone was doing what they usually did, but still, there was *something.*

They spotted Ruthie sitting with her back to one of the tents, talking to someone. As they got closer, Deon noticed that there didn't seem to be anyone else around.

"You on some kind of trip? Talking to yourself again?"

"Wise-ass," Ruthie replied.

Flip said, "We hit a jackpot tonight, Ruthie! About $200!"

That's when a man familiar to Deon stood up out of the tent Ruthie was talking by and said, "Ah, receipt duty. I sure don't miss those days."

It was him.

EIGHT

"Two-hundred dollars though, that's a nice haul," Evon said.

He stared at Gideon and Flip as they stared at him. He figured they were somewhat in shock that he of all people was back at the camp.

"What's wrong?" Evon said, "You two look like you just saw a ghost or something."

He extended his hand out to Deon, who let it hang in the air briefly before extending his own. They shook hands and Flip replied, "You might as well be! Where the fuck you been? Decided to take a little vacation?"

"Evon here," Ruthie started as she stood up, "decided to start training for his championship swimming career. Cliff diving is his new specialty."

She chuckled at her own joke.

"Yeah, well, by the looks of it, you should do some more practicing, Evon," Flip said. "You look like complete shit."

Evon smiled and looked at Ruthie. She called herself a matriarch and she looked every bit the part. Long, brunette hair that was streaked with strands of gray. She was flat-chested, skin sagging enough that you could take a pinch of it with your fingers and extend it away from the rest of her structure. She'd been a bigger woman in the past, that was evident. Even with that, she was still an alluring woman, not much younger than Evon, which made her choice to dress like a teenager so puzzling. She always wore denim that hugged every remaining curve she had and usually paired it with a colorful shirt that was equally as tight. The one she wore now had a band name that he didn't recognize written across the chest.

He realized he'd be staring at that area longer than he should have and brought his eyes back up. She smiled at him and he saw a glint in her hazel eyes.

Slightly embarrassed, he turned his attention to the two men that he'd interacted with on occasion.

Flip was fairly new to him, a rambunctious young man who had a lot left to learn about the world. They hadn't talked much, just in passing from time to time. He had come around while Evon was in the midst of his lowest of lows. Thus, they hadn't built up much of a relationship. Evon was too busy wallowing in the filth he'd created in his mind.

Gideon was a different case, though. When Evon first came to Dreg City, Gideon had already established himself, and the place didn't even have a name yet.

They had enjoyed a few light-hearted conversations and during one of those conversations, in jest, had declared themselves the dregs of Oak Harbor. A moniker for their place of habitation was born, and Evon thought a friendship was as well, but he and Gideon had never quite fully meshed after that.

An attempt was made, though, for Evon realized both were contemplative men and deep, introspective thinkers. However, while Evon had focused on the multitude of follies in the past that destroyed his zeal to live in the present, Gideon ruminated on what the past had meant for his future. Evon tried many times to delve deeper and get inside Gideon's innermost thoughts but he never acquiesced. He wanted to keep whatever happened in his past locked away in a place only *he* could visit.

Evon just chalked it up to age. Young people, at least the ones he'd interacted with, were reticent to speak on anything deeper than the surface level, and just because Gideon was 30-years-old didn't mean there wasn't a child still inside that physically mature body. Being more than a decade senior to Gideon had afforded him those thought processes. The foundation of a common life struggle was formed, but nothing much was built upon it, and just as the present separates itself from the past, so too had Gideon separated from Evon.

"Well," Ruthie said, "hand the money over."

"Oh, yeah, here you go," said Flip as he handed over the stash.

Evon watched Ruthie count it carefully, probably making sure she didn't miss any bills that could've stuck together.

"This'll be a nice addition to what we already have. We're sitting at about $700 total now. Proud of you guys. Not sure how you did it, not sure I even *want* to know, but whatever. It'll make for a nice dinner."

"Right around the corner," said Deon.

"Ah, it all makes sense now. *That's* why you decided to show your ugly mug, Evon," Ruthie said, playfully patting him on the shoulder.

"Well, as nice as sticking around for your cooking sounds, I don't think I'll be able to make it. I've got very important responsibilities to take care of, but I'll try," Evon said.

"That will work for me. All you can do is try. You know you're still family around these parts, Evon. No matter how fucked up you look now," replied Ruthie.

"Were you guys getting ready to do something earlier?" Flip said. "You seemed to be having a pretty damn animated conversation."

"Great observation, Flip. Evon was just regaling me with tales of his past few months. Little bastard won't give me much details, so I'm trying to talk him into taking a night walk. Maybe that will open him up some." Ruthie playfully jabbed Evon in the stomach. "And he still hasn't said yes yet."

Evon let out a hearty laugh. "Fine, fine. Let's go. You can do me the honor of walking me back to my hotel room."

"You mean you came back here after all this time and you're not gonna at least stay the night?"

"No, no, not tonight. Got myself a room at The Dutch Inn. Sleeping out here does a number on my joints now."

"Wait a minute, you're staying at *THE* Dutch Inn?" Ruthie said.

Evon chuckled. "*THE* Dutch Inn, that's right."

"Man, I have some fond memories of that place, that's for sure," Ruthie said sarcastically.

All four of them fell silent for a moment, pensive.

It was pitch black out but the full moon illuminated the area they stood in. A light breeze flew through, bringing with it a November chill, rippling the tent, and making them all shiver.

"*Shit*! It's not getting any warmer out here, guys," Flip said.

"Flip's right," Deon began. "I think we're gonna hunker down for the night."

"Pansies. Evon and I are gonna take on the elements for a little bit," Ruthie lightly jabbed. "Well, shall we?" she said, turning to Evon.

Evon smiled and nodded.

He and Ruthie started to walk out to the street in the direction of The Dutch Inn. He turned around to see

Deon and Flip staring at them and raised a hand to wave goodbye for the night.

Only Flip returned his wave.

"You sure those screwed up legs can make it back to the hotel?" Ruthie asked.

"These screwed up legs made it here, didn't they?" Evon replied.

"Good point. So, spill the beans, buddy. You took some kids car… and then what?"

As they walked along the street, Evon told Ruthie about how he jumped off Deception Pass Bridge, how he woke up immobile in a hospital bed, and about the nice nurse that assisted in his recovery. He briefly mentioned that he found out that it was a pair of boys who had found him, but he left out that he had paid one of them a visit, only to be rebuffed by a divine joke.

"For fuck's sake, you've been through some shit, Evon. Of course, it's your own damn fault. Jumping off the damn bridge like that."

"I don't know, I kind of feel like I was *pushed* off, you know? Like I was *supposed* to have fallen off the bridge at that particular moment to change the course of my life. I can't really explain it, and you'd only know what it felt like if you tried it yourself, you know, if you were in the same situation I was."

"That's not happening anytime soon, I can guarantee you that! I like living a little bit too much. But man, pushed off… you mean like divine intervention?" she asked disbelievingly.

"Yeah, yeah… That's *exactly* what I mean."

"Come on, Evon, that's such bullshit. I mean, I guess you can believe whatever you want, but me? I don't subscribe to that crap. So, God *wanted* you dead? For what?"

"I know it's kind of hard for you to understand. It's not that I think He wanted me dead, because I'm here, right? He knew that I wouldn't end up dying. It was just so that I could take a new direction in life, something I couldn't see that I needed to do. That's why I'm here, talking to you. It's all for a reason."

Ruthie pondered his statement for a moment while they walked.

"Whatever you say, Evon. Still sounds like a crock of shit to me."

"I don't know… He works in mysterious ways…"

They continued to stroll silently, taking in the sights and sounds of their surroundings.

"Anyway, enough about me. What have you been up to these past few months? Enjoying life? Staying clean?" he asked.

"Eh, I've had my ups and downs, but yes, clean for the most part. Those urges are hard to fight off sometimes, you know?"

Evon turned to look at Ruthie as they walked. She was looking forward, not meeting his eyes, smoothly striding against the pavement.

"No, I *don't* know," he said. "Drugs have never been my thing. Drinking? Yes. Sex? At times. But I've never understood how someone could let drugs take control of them like that."

"Well, let me ask you this: isn't alcohol a drug? Can't it take control of you just like heroin?"

The change in Ruthie's tone and the way she demonstrably moved her hands told Evon his response had annoyed her.

"You're asking the wrong person. I drank, but it hardly had control of me. It's easy to stop that and I could've done so at any point I wanted. What had control of me was just overwhelming sadness. Depression. I came to the painful realization that I *really* messed up my life, as did you."

"Look, don't *even* try to compare what I've been through to what happened to you," Ruthie said angrily. "*You* might've chosen to fuck your life up, but what you and I have gone through are two totally different things, Evon. Remember that."

"Maybe you're right, Ruthie. I apologize. We *have* been through different things. There's a big difference between me losing all my money and losing my family and you having sex with men for an income. There's a big difference between having a few drinks and knowing I can stop whenever I want and you shooting needles full of brown stuff into any vein you can find."

"Hey, fuck you, Evon!" Ruthie yelled as she and Evon stopped walking.

"Say whatever you want," Evon said, "but you need to understand that the truth hurts sometimes. Especially now. While you dabble around and take pleasure in your demons, I've been cleared of the desires that had such a firm grip on me. You have no idea what it's li–"

"*I* don't know what it's like? *I* don't know what it's like? Let me tell you something, you asshole. *You* don't know what it's like to be introduced to the word *pussy* when you're fucking 8-years-old because your dad snuck into your room every night he got drunk. *You* don't know what it's like for your older brother to watch your dad shove his fucking fingers inside you and not only do nothing about it but decide it'd be fun to make his little sister give him a blow job when your parents leave."

"Well, look, I–"

"*You* don't know what it's fucking like to tell your mom that you're being fucked by her husband and her son and have her not believe you. *You* don't know what it's like to run away from that hell and have nobody give a shit about if you're okay or not. Don't you *ever* try to tell me I don't know what it's like until you've had to let any random man on these streets do *anything* they want to you, stick their fucking fingers and tongues and dicks wherever the hell they want so you can get a bite to eat."

Evon had been staring directly into Ruthie's eyes as she yelled at him, but removed his gaze to look around. They were the only pedestrians on the street, though a few cars rolled by.

"Oh, and then when you decide that's enough of living like that," Ruthie began, "you head home hoping, fucking *praying* your family would welcome you back with open arms only to be told you're a disgusting bitch, a whore that's no longer allowed to be part of the family. Why do you think heroin was so fun to do? *Huh*? I'll answer that for you. Because it was the only thing that showed me unconditional love, that would never let me down, that took the pain away. Yeah, I had my bouts with man after man to help me pay for it but it was *so* much more worth it than having to sit around crying, wondering why your own flesh and blood would hurt you like they did. So, when you wanna compare your fucking life to mine, you think about whether *you* know what it's like."

They both stood there quiet, alone on the sidewalk. Ruthie was breathing heavily, her chest rising and falling with every tear that escaped her eyes and streamed down her face.

Evon showed no emotion on his face, yet, he felt a swell of it swirl around in his chest. He wasn't sure if it was the same feeling that Ruthie undoubtedly had, but it was a palpable one nonetheless.

The Dutch Inn was just yards away.

"God, Evon, you have me over here crying like a fucking wimp in front of the goddamned Dutch Inn," Ruthie stammered.

She took a wrist to her eyes, then her nose, wiping away tears.

"I didn't mean to–"

"Yeah, yeah. What the fuck ever, man. Well, you did. Let's get you to your room and get you tucked in.

You've already been told a bedtime story for the ages tonight. I need to use the bathroom anyway."

The two began walking again and passed the front door of the hotel. Evon looked inside the small, brightly lit lobby and locked eyes with Hank, who was at the counter reading a magazine. Hank broke their gaze to look at Ruthie, who was walking in front of Evon. A smile spread over his face as he shook his head.

"What room is yours?" Ruthie asked.

"Um, 14. In the back."

They continued on to the back of the hotel. Evon unlocked the door and Ruthie walked in after him.

"Hmph, this shithole still looks about the same, I see," Ruthie said.

Evon pointed to the bathroom and said, "You can clean yourself up in there. I'm going to start getting ready to call it a night."

Ruthie looked at him and nodded as she started toward the bathroom.

"What I told you back there? You repeat to absolutely *no* one. Do you understand me?"

He met her eyes. There was a fire in them, a determination that no amount of tears could ever squelch. He knew she was deadly serious with him: He wasn't to reveal anything she told him to anyone lest he feel her wrath, a wrath she didn't explicitly threaten, but he knew was implied.

"Of course, of course," he nodded. "That stays between you and me."

She closed the door and Evon heard water rushing as she turned on the sink faucet.

Once he was sure that she couldn't hear his movements over the running water, he walked over to the mini fridge, opened it, and pulled out the vial of clear liquid he'd stored there earlier.

Then he walked over to retrieve a syringe from his backpack next to the desk. He sat on the bed, removed the orange protective cap from the needle, and took a deep breath before piercing his arm.

Then he punctured the vial of liquid.

As he pulled back on the plunger, he thought about what he was brought here to do. What he was *saved* for. Everything happened for a reason, and clearly, whether he understood that reason or not, God had presented this moment to Evon. This was not a time to be idle, neither with his mind nor his hands.

He returned the vial to the fridge, and Ruthie came out of the bathroom. She clicked off the light and wiped her damp hands on the legs of her jeans.

"Well, I'm gonna go. I'm sorry for laying it on you thick tonight, but you were asking for it. You gotta get it through your head that not everyone's circumstances are the same. We're all a little fucked up, otherwise we wouldn't be homeless, ya know? Sleeping outside and shit. You understand?"

"I got it, I got it. You live and you learn. I accept yours and ask that you accept my apology."

Evon extended the syringe to Ruthie. "Olive branch?" he said.

"What's that?" she asked.

"A peace offering. Having that heart to heart made me realize I shouldn't judge what one does to deal with their pain. We all cope a little differently. Take it, no judgement."

He raised one hand as if he was giving a scout's honor.

"Evon, why in the hell do *you* have heroin?"

"It's not heroin, it's something even better that I came across. You haven't lived until you've tried this stuff. See?" he said as he showed her his arm. "Already took a little myself."

"Ok… but what *is* it?"

"I forgot what it's called, starts with an A. All I know is that it takes the edge off."

Ruthie stood there and thought over it for a moment before sitting down next to him. The springs in the mattress groaned.

"You're a real piece of work, Evon, I swear. I'm not sharing a needle with you, though."

"Come on, I've watched the seasons change in a *hospital.* It doesn't get more sterile than that."

Ruthie laughed. "You prick, I guess you're right. Alright, I'll try some of this stuff and then I'm heading back to my boys. You got a tourniquet?"

Evon looked around. "Hadn't really thought about that."

"Amateur. Well, do you have a belt?"

"As a matter of fact, I do."

Evon took off the belt he was wearing and handed it over to Ruthie. She started to loop the belt around her arm as Evon watched.

He handed the syringe to her.

"Yeah, let me see that," she said as she stuck the needle in a bulging vein. "Show you how it's done."

Ruthie flashed him a toothy grin, and Evon watched as she pushed down slowly on the plunger.

After a few moments, Ruthie said, "I'm not sure what this shit is but I'm not feeling anything."

Then she turned to look at Evon and opened her mouth to say something but no sound came out.

Her arms slackened and she fell back on the bed with her eyes wide open.

Evon took it as a cue to get up to retrieve something from his backpack: a scalpel.

"I remember now. It's called Atracurium. I couldn't get my hands on anything that would prevent me from getting my hands dirty, but this'll paralyze you. You can still breathe, but not for long. Don't worry though, I'm not going to let you suffer. You've been through far too much, Ruthie."

Evon sat back down and pulled Ruthie's limp body into his arms. She was breathing slowly, but steadily. He noticed that she had managed to squeeze out some tears; they were streaming down her cheeks just as they had before.

"I know, I know. Everything's going to be ok now."

Evon brought the sharp, silver scalpel up to Ruthie's neck and applied pressure.

Blood started to trickle. He pressed harder, slowly slicing through her skin from left to right. Evon felt the warmth of her blood stream over his hands. He watched as rivulets of her tears slid down her neck to mix in with the thick, red blood.

Ruthie's breathing halted and there were no sounds in the hotel room.

"Everything's going to be ok."

NINE

The sudden chill woke Evon.

He slowly blinked his eyes open to greet the sun's rays that had managed to peek in through the curtains. He was lying supine on the bed, and there was a great weight upon him that kept him from sitting up.

It wasn't the weight of knowing he'd taken someone's life for the first time ever; it was the fact that her cold, stiff body was laying on top of him.

He thought about all the mental exhaustion that wracked his body for so many hours for him to have fallen asleep with Ruthie's body still in his arms as he pushed her off him and onto the bed. Evon came to the realization that dead weight on a person did indeed feel heavier than when they were living and breathing.

He took a quick look down at her. Her eyes were wide open, as was her mouth and the fatal neck wound he'd sliced into her. The blood that seeped out and trickled down her neck had smeared a little bit on both of them, probably because of movement while they slept. Long enough for rigor mortis to make a visit.

The clock next to the TV read 11:26 AM.

He hadn't bothered to look at the time before he took Ruthie into his arms, but he knew it wasn't *that* late when he did, so sleeping for well over 12 hours came as a surprise. It was ok, though, because now he was well rested to continue to forge ahead.

He rose to his feet. The bed let out a loud creak, a thank you for relieving it of the duty of holding so much weight.

He looked around to take stock of everything. Nothing was amiss, neither taken nor added, except for a discernible smell that he hadn't noticed before: a hint of urine.

Luckily for his delicate nostrils, that was the only bad smell, as the body in the bed hadn't started full decomposition yet.

He thought he was well past the age of wetting the bed during sleep, so that could only mean one thing.

Evon looked down at Ruthie's rigid corpse and then reached out to touch her legs. He slowly patted up and down until he came upon a slightly damp spot.

She'd soiled herself a bit.

Poor woman, he thought. The excitement of moving on from a sad existence in this world had been too much for her to handle in her last moments.

He wiped his hand against his pants.

Ruthie stared up at him, mouth agape.

"Was there something you wanted to say?" Evon said, knowing she wouldn't reply. "You know, we talked on the phone while I was in the hospital. You said you'd take me to my rehab appointments when I made it into town, that you'd take care of me. We never got a chance to get that far. It was far more important that I took care of you."

He began to caress her face and ran his fingers along the incision he'd cut into her neck. Then, with his two forefingers, he attempted to close her eyelids, but they wouldn't stay shut.

"Have it your way," he said.

Evon proceeded to reach inside her front pockets.

There was nothing in her left one, but in her right pocket he pulled out a small, beat up picture with two smiling, brunette-haired kids on it.

There was a boy and girl, the boy being the elder, with his arms swathed around the younger girl. They both were wearing what looked like Christmas sweaters. Evon didn't know who these kids were and had never seen them before now. He flipped the picture around and saw a scrawled message written on the back: *Dillon and Harrah-Christmas 2013. They love you! Can't wait to see you again! Be safe!*

He wasn't sure who wrote this message, nor was he one-hundred percent certain whose cherubic kids these were, but if he had to bet, he'd say these were Ruthie's children.

She'd never told him about them before but it all made perfect sense. She was fresh out of a career of the oldest profession, and until recently, found herself strung out on whatever temporarily took the pain away. The environments she routinely found herself in were not suitable for young kids; thus, someone else must have custody of young Dillon and Harrah. After recent events, that mystery person would retain custody for quite some time.

Don't worry kids, Mama's in a better place now, Evon thought to himself.

Evon rolled Ruthie onto her stomach and checked her back pockets until he found what he was looking for: Dreg City's bank account balance.

There was a folded-up mass of differing bills that Ruthie held on to as the funds that kept her little portion of the city running.

Before they'd taken off on their walk, Evon knew there was talk of her doing something big for Thanksgiving. The people back there would have to make other arrangements because he needed the money a little more than them right now. He wasn't stealing it but merely borrowing it for a much greater cause.

You will be repaid in spades, Ruthie.

The clock read 11:45. Evon decided it was time for him to carry on with the rest of his day, but first, he needed to secure this room as his base of sorts; there would be no more sleeping with his old friends outside, especially in this weather.

Hank said he could get some more use out of this room if Evon paid no later than 10:00, since check-out was 11:00. It baffled him as to why Hank hadn't come knocking, then. However, it was a good thing, too. He certainly didn't need Hank walking into the scene in the room. He wouldn't understand what had transpired, and even trying to explain it to him in a way that he could comprehend surely would be difficult.

With almost $700 added to his wallet, Evon decided he'd go up front and ask about renting the room for a week. He thought that would be enough time for him to do everything he needed to do, but just in case it wasn't, he certainly had the funds now for even more time.

Evon still had everything on from the night before, including a shirt with blood on it, which he took off and replaced with the one in the heap of clothes he'd piled up earlier. After changing, he took another look at Ruthie's prone body that was face down and headed to the hotel lobby.

Outside, it was cool and nearly cloudless. He wasn't sure if it was the time of day or the time of year but Oak Harbor resembled a ghost town today. The cars that inhabited the roads were few and there weren't really any people out walking either.

Maybe it was just this area of town.

As he walked inside the lobby, Hank said, "Well, look who it is. Have fun with that broad last night?"

"That was no broad, Hank. She was actually a good friend of mine. We were just having a chat."

Hank smiled and said, "Chat. Sure." He let his skepticism linger in the air for a few seconds. "Anyway, what can I do you for this morning?"

"I need to get the room. Again. For about a week. What do I owe you?"

"Hmmm, you're kind of pushing it, buddy. Didn't I tell you to let me know at least an hour in advance? Look at the clock! It's damn near check-out time already!"

Evon turned around to see a clock affixed to the wall right above the door he walked through. It read 10:50.

"The clock in my room actually said I was late, though," Evon said.

"Nah, don't pay attention to that damn thing. I just don't give a shit about changing them over for Daylight Saving. Pssh, fall back my ass!"

"Well, it's good to see that I still have a little bit of time, then."

Hank sneered. "Yeah… I guess I'll make an exception for you, seeing as how there ain't a whole lot of business going on right now. I won't be so nice next time."

"Duly noted."

"Duly noted… Hmph. A week you said, right?"

"Yes, how much do I owe you?"

"Well, can't you do simple math? $34 a night, times seven days?"

Evon sighed. Hank was in a combative, cantankerous mood this morning, but Evon wasn't in the mood to go through this with him again.

"No, Hank, I can't do that simple math right now. Help a guy out."

"Ok. Let's see… Well… Oh dammit, who am I kidding? I can't do that shit either!"

Hank let out a loud chuckle. "Might as well make use of this damn calculator I got right here, huh?"

Evon nodded.

"Ok, so… one week will cost you $238 big ones."

"This includes taxes?"

"Shit. No one ever gets a week here anymore, I don't know. What was the tax for the room you got last night?"

"I don't remember. Can I just give you $300 and call it a deal?"

"Hey, that's fine with me! You want the same room?"

"Yes, and I'd like a little privacy. Don't worry about cleaning or anything. I'll take care of everything."

"Suit yourself! Whatever kind of shit you're gonna be doing for seven days is something I don't wanna have to clean up after anyway. So, I'll hold you to that."

Evon handed over $300 and Hank slowly counted, switching the bills from one hand to the other as he went.

"Two-seventy, two-eighty, two-ninety. Three hundred! Looks like you're all set now that I know you ain't trying to short me! Ha!"

Evon stared blankly at him.

"Hey, lighten up, ya stiff bastard! I'm just busting your chops. Holiday spirit and all that."

"Yeah, yeah…" Evon sighed.

As he turned to walk away, he noticed a stack of newspapers on an end table by the door.

He hadn't read one in ages and had likely missed out on lots of news going on around the town. Now was as good a time as any before continuing his day, he thought. He might even humor himself and read up on business news since that was his cup of tea not too long ago. A brief indulgence in old pleasures wouldn't bring about too much harm.

Evon proceeded to pick one up from the stack.

The *Oak Harbor Sounder*. The headline read: *Veteran's Day Parade Recognizes Lt. Cdr. Craig Bryant.*

"Craig Bryant…" Evon whispered to himself. "Lieutenant Commander…"

Craig Bryant was a close childhood friend of Evon's from back in the day. They had once been as thick as thieves but didn't keep much contact with each other as they'd gotten older.

Evon became entrenched in the tech and business fields and was much more concerned with filling his coffers with money and women, while Craig had become interested in boats, fighting, and macho military stuff.

It was only a few days before Thanksgiving but for some reason Hank was holding on to these old papers that dated back to a day after Veteran's Day.

"Hank," Evon started, "you know these papers aren't recent, right?"

"Yeah, I know. Clocks? Daylight Saving? Sensing a theme?" Hank replied.

Evon shook his head. "Mind if I keep this one?"

"It's all yours, buddy. Take more if you'd like!" Hank said.

Evon flashed a thumbs-up and walked out of the hotel lobby, back to room 14, where Ruthie still needed attending to.

When he opened the door, he stood in the doorway and examined the room.

He wasn't sure why he thought Ruthie might be sitting on the bed smiling, waiting for him to come back, because that was irrational. She was gone now, sitting with their Lord and Savior and smiling from above. She couldn't tell Evon thank you, but he was very certain that she was grateful.

Some people just wanted to go, but they were too afraid to ask someone for help leaving and were too scared to take matters into their own hands. Evon couldn't help *every* person that had this wish, but with this newfound outlook on life, he just knew who they were when he saw them.

Ruthie was the first, and before he was done, she would not be the last.

The room was starting to be overcome with the hovering odor of urine, and before too long, her body would start to decompose. He walked to the half-closed bathroom door and pushed it all the way open. Then, he made his way to the bed to test out his strength.

He started to lift Ruthie's stiff body but pulled back suddenly when he made contact with her skin. It was ice cold, even though the room felt much warmer than her body indicated.

Evon made the decision that lifting her wasn't for the best, especially considering how weak he still was. He grabbed her by the ankles with both hands and slowly slid her off the bed and onto the floor. Her body made a soft thud as it hit the ground. From there he backed into the bathroom, dragging her body along the way. He let go of her legs briefly so that he could pull the curtain back that draped over the tub. Then he picked her legs back up and stepped into the tub, pulling her body into it with him with as much strength as he could muster. Her head and limbs made noisy clunking sounds as they knocked against the porcelain-covered steel.

Her eyes remained open through it all.

Evon stepped out of the tub and pulled the curtain shut, concealing the body, and walked out of the bathroom.

He sat down on the bed and started to shiver. Not because of the room temperature, not because of the contact with Ruthie's frigid remains, but because this was all so new to him. It was an experience he hadn't had before but one that he needed to get used to if he was to do God's work with any kind of fervor.

He spotted his Bible peeking out of his backpack on the floor and thought this was a perfect time to delve into the scripture for answers, for reassurance, for comfort.

Evon turned to Psalms because the words in there had always soothed him, had always made it clear what he was here to do and why. It might even be his favorite book within the Book, though there were other spots in the Bible that were not without some value. What he needed right now, though, was help coming to terms with what he had just done.

There was a slight twang of guilt, no doubt, because Evon, before his literal come-to-Jesus moment, was familiar with some of the verses that every professed Christian knows.

Thou shall not kill, found in Exodus, those who kill shall *be* killed, hidden away in Leviticus, and other verses that made it clear, in no uncertain terms, that taking a life is a sin.

Or is it?

There were plenty of examples of God giving instructions to kill certain people, where it was looked at as a divine intervention of sorts. And what if you were just trying to help? With no malice in your heart? Surely *that* can't be punished.

When He calls upon you to do a great deed, you undoubtedly must act, lest you be punished for going against His will. What Evon set out to do was no different than the work missionaries did, albeit in a much more intensive fashion.

Flipping the pages and analyzing his thoughts led to a passage in Psalms that served to be the answer he was looking for: *Yes, the Lord hears the good man when he calls to Him for help and saves him out of all his troubles. The Lord is close to those whose hearts are breaking; He rescues those who are humbly sorry for their sins.*

This was the biblical embodiment of Ruthie's predicament, Evon thought. Heartbroken over not being able to provide for her offspring, reluctantly giving up custody of them to someone who hadn't gone through the rigor of carrying them in the womb for nine months, fornicating, and ruining the purity of the temple God had provided were all reasons Evon was sure that Ruthie had called out.

The Lord had heard her.

Evon was her rescuer.

TEN

"I've got a funny feeling, Flip. Ruthie still hasn't shown up."

The two men had been sitting on the ground near their tent, engaging in small talk most of the day, until that pang hit Deon's stomach.

"Ok…" Flip said as he surveyed the camp. "Is there a reason she needs to be here right *now*? It hasn't even been a day yet. She's been gone longer before."

"Yeah, I know that, but not when it's so close to the holiday. She said she was planning an extra special day for us."

"Relax, man," Flip said as he got up to walk away.

Deon had seen this before, Ruthie disappearing for longer than usual. Most of the time it never bothered him, as she would show back up after having some alone time. Sometimes that meant just wanting to get away from the goings-on in Dreg City, and who could blame her? There were other times, however, where it meant she had relapsed and was too embarrassed to let anyone see her in that condition.

What made this particular time more worrisome was the fact that Thanksgiving was just around the corner, and Ruthie said she was very excited to eat, drink, and be merry with all of her guys.

The money everyone had collected from receipt duty was more than they'd had in quite some time, and she planned to use those funds to make it a very special holiday.

Maybe Deon was overreacting a bit. Surely, she wouldn't leave everyone hanging, would she? Was she having a little bit too much fun with Evon?

They'd been pretty close before the time Dreg City became his home. Maybe they were still doing some catching up, although in his new condition, Deon didn't think Evon could be doing much more than engaging in lengthy conversations. The guy looked like a mess now. His facial appearance had certainly taken a hit, with the way scars had crisscrossed his face and neck. Deon even noticed that his mouth was devoid of the pearly whites that had been there before, replaced by empty space and remnants of what had once been.

Beyond his physical change, Deon was sure that something else in Evon had changed. Falling, jumping, floating, whatever he did off that bridge did much more than make him *look* different. The action alone would be enough to make a profound effect on someone's life. Living to tell about it and then shrugging it off? Deon felt that Evon's soul most certainly underwent a transformation that could be felt from anyone that came close enough.

But as uneasy as Evon made Deon feel, he couldn't afford to be worried about him right now. If Ruthie didn't come back soon, he'd have to step into a role that made him uncomfortable. One that he wasn't really ready to embrace at this point in life. Being invisible to the world wasn't the only place he wanted to remain unseen. Here in the camp, he was content to just coast, to just float along while someone else handled the big responsibilities. But even considering all of that, he would not sit back and watch his family of dregs get their hopes up for this holiday only to have them dashed because of the absence of their matriarch. This was a time for action.

Thanksgiving was in a few days. That meant meals would be needed. Deon couldn't cook worth a damn and neither could Flip, as far as he knew. He was sure there was someone within the camp that could, but it was a moot point unless there was food to actually cook. And *that* was a moot point unless there was money to actually buy the food with.

Flip was like a lost puppy on most occasions, spending more time by Deon's side than away. While Deon was pondering what he needed to do, Flip was a few yards away now, talking to an older woman that Deon knew but didn't *know*. He'd seen her around and talked to her in passing, but just like a good portion of the people here, he never really took the time to get to know her.

Even though everyone here liked to talk and act as if they were a close-knit family, the reality was slightly different. Everyone was cordial with each other, for the most part, but there were cliques that formed, factions that separated themselves from the rest of the pack, as was natural in any society.

She was heavily bundled up, even though today felt unseasonably warm under the partly sunny sky. The two were laughing about something, inaudible to Deon. He didn't want to interrupt but he maintained eye contact with Flip, hoping he'd look up for just a moment to lock eyes and come to an unspoken understanding that his presence was needed again.

After a few moments, Flip did just that. When they had each other's attention, Flip squinted in a puzzling way and Deon motioned with his hand to come over. Flip said a few parting words to the woman he was speaking to and walked over to Deon.

"What's up, Gideon?" Flip said as he sat down, slightly annoyed. "Is this still about Ruthie?"

He took his eyes off Deon when he didn't answer right away and stared out into the street. He caught a glimpse of a black four-door that drove by with a loud engine. Steam billowed out from its exhaust pipe as it trailed away, leaving his line of sight.

"I say we give her a little more time. Thanksgiving is a few days away. Let the woman live a little," Flip said.

Deon thought about it for a few seconds more and then looked down at the ground, shaking his head.

"No, Flip. Usually I'd agree with you but not this time. We can let her finish whatever it is she's doing with Evon, but that doesn't mean we can't do something to help our situation in the meantime."

"Is that what this is *really* about?"

"What do you mean?"

"Evon. Is this about her running off with Evon? Because if it is then I see what you mean."

"You feel it too? That there's something… *off* about him?"

"Yeah, he looks like a fucking weirdo now. And you just know he's gotta be off his rocker. I mean, who the hell jumps off Deception Pass Bridge? That idiot is lucky to even be alive right now. Anyway, if you're worried about if he's doing anything with Ruthie other than eyeballing her teeth, wishing he had some, I suggest you chill. She's a grown woman. She can take care of herself."

"Ok, ok," Deon started, "but I think we should still get some more money just to be safe. That way, we can get something for the guys here just in case she doesn't show up in time."

"Yeah, I don't think that's such a bad idea. What do you think we should do?"

"Receipt duty. We're gonna need all hands on deck, too."

"Shit, Gideon, most of us have already been doing that stuff pretty recently! It's gonna look suspicious as hell for us to be doing it again so soon!"

"Flip, what the hell else do you expect us to do? If you've got any better ideas, I'd love to hear them."

"Fuck, man, you know I'm gonna defer to you on these things."

"I thought so. We'll make it work, Flip. We're just going to have to keep our rotations up and not show up at places we've been to recently. We'll also need to keep the items we return low, just a few, the most expensive ones, but we'll need everyone here that can to go out and do it."

Flip nodded. "So, you want me to go deliver the message to everyone?"

"Yes. Don't scare them but let them know it's kind of urgent."

"Ok. What if people start asking if it has anything to do with Ruthie, though?"

"Well, tell them no, that Ruthie's ok but we just need extra money to be safe. Most of them don't know how much she had in the account anyway, so they'll buy it."

"Now?"

"Now."

Flip patted Deon on the back, then got up and walked away to let everyone know what needed to be done. As Deon watched him deliver the message, he wondered once again about Ruthie, hoping everything was ok. People always say to trust your intuition, that when you get a feeling deep inside your gut that something isn't quite right, you should trust that feeling and do something about it. Fight, flight, cover, discover, *something.* Just act on it. And Deon would. Because now he had to.

***

Deon and Flip entered Rand's Grocery on Huron Street amidst a wave of shoppers trying to fulfill Thanksgiving dinner options.

These were the days that Deon knew grocers absolutely loved. The seasonal food items that no one even thinks about except for maybe one or two days out of the year go flying off the shelves at ballooned prices that served two purposes: one, to fill the stomachs of family members who won't be heard from after December, and two, to fill the coffers of distributors.

Deon and Flip had to weave their way through busy aisles full of people pushing carts filled with all the traditional fare: frozen turkeys, cans of vegetables, bags of potatoes–both sweet and plain.

They stalked the aisles, grabbing the most expensive items.

After they were finished getting everything they needed, which came up to an adequate sum, they headed for the customer service counter to proceed with the refund process.

"You're up, Gideon. I'm pretty sure I did the talking last time," Flip said with a smirk.

He was right. The other day he made the mistake of betting against Deon's intellect and had to do the talking to the last clerk. Deon wasn't worried about it though, because he'd done it many times before. At this point it was a skill, and a well-honed one at that.

Flip fell back and started taking in the crowd of hurried shoppers while Deon approached the customer service counter with his cart.

There were three clerks behind it: to the left, a tall, razor-thin, blonde, older woman who was helping an elderly gentleman with some sort of electronic; on the right, a portly young man who was bent over, intently writing something down on a piece of paper; and in the middle was a shorter woman who looked younger than she probably was. Her hair was light brown, bone-straight, and shoulder length. Her body was fit and very attractive and Deon felt himself staring at her a lot longer than he should've been.

The woman had an annoyed look on her face, as if she was already prepared to deal with the lie Deon had prepared for her but would have to accept anyway.

This particular day worked well for him because these clerks had likely worked long, tiring days already and wouldn't question him too much about the things he was returning. They just wanted to get him in and get him out. The faster they did that, the faster they'd be rid of a pesky customer so they could stare at the clock, counting down the minutes until they could leave.

She flashed him a forced grin and said, "I can help the next customer."

Deon turned to look behind him. He was the next customer. He pushed his cart up to the counter and fished out the receipt he had in his jacket pocket.

"I, uh, need to return this stuff and get a refund. The wife went to the store earlier without telling me and when I got home with all this stuff, we already had what we needed. We still need to work on our communication I guess," Deon said, showing her a playful smile and scratching the back of his head.

The clerk stared at Deon, meeting his eyes directly. She didn't seem to be in the mood for fun relationship stories, nor did she seem enthused to have to ring all the contents of his cart back through the system.

"Can I see your receipt please?" she asked, and held out her left hand, knowing that he'd have to oblige.

Deon looked down and noticed her hand. It looked, soft, delicate, and well-manicured, as if it hadn't ever seen a minute of strenuous work.

"Yeah, here you go," Deon said as he handed her the crumpled receipt.

She took it out of his hand and scanned over it, eyes darting back and forth, occasionally looking up to peer inside the cart to make sure the items matched.

"It's a full refund you want? Not just returning *some* items?" she asked.

"Um, yes," Deon nervously replied, "This food's no good to us now. We're not trying to be too greedy, Thanksgiving be damned."

"Yeah…" she started, "You know, I had someone tell me a similar story about their wife just the other day."

Deon started to get even more nervous. He felt his body start to flush and wondered if someone else in the camp had used the same story. Forget it, he thought, he was here now and needed to see it through. The worst the clerk could do is say no and tell him to leave the store.

He shrugged and said, "Guess there's a lot of ambitious wives out there this time of year."

The clerk gave him a disbelieving smirk. "I need you to hand me the items from the cart so I can scan them," she said, motioning to the cart.

Deon nodded and started to hand her the items one by one.

She was quiet and stern as she scanned each item. Only the beeping sound after each scan and the rattling off of some keys she pressed on her register broke up the silence.

After a few moments, he looked behind him and noticed Flip staring and smiling at him. Deon wasn't sure how long Flip had been staring but he gave him a thumbs-up. Flip returned it and Deon turned back around to continue to help the clerk out.

As he handed her the last of the items in the cart, his eyes caught a glimpse of a girl sitting in a recessed area behind the counter. It looked to be an area that employees used to relax and store their items when they clocked in for work.

The girl wasn't very young, Deon thought. She was probably a teenager, which made what she was doing kind of odd. She was coloring something, which Deon knew because she was holding a pink marker in her hand. However, she wasn't holding it between her thumb and forefinger, as was customary; she was gripping it in her fist, like holding the handle of a knife. Her tongue wagged out of her mouth, making contact with her long, blonde hair, and Deon could tell she was determined to color the hell out of whatever was on the piece of paper in front of her.

"My daughter."

Deon snapped out of his trance. "Excuse me?"

"My daughter? You were staring back there like you wanted to know who was there. It's my daughter," the clerk said.

"Oh, I didn't mean anything by it if that's what you were wondering," Deon replied.

The clerk let out a soft laugh. "I'd certainly hope not! She's way too young for you and you have a wife waiting on you at home with a *lot* of groceries."

Deon felt himself blushing.

"School let out a little early today?" he asked.

"Try a little early this *week*. The damn school gives them a break *all* week for Thanksgiving whether parents can adjust to the shitty scheduling or not. So, Sunny is gonna join mama at work for a little bit."

"Sunny? That's her name? There's no babysitter for her?" Deon asked.

"No, I don't let just anybody come around my girl. She's…special."

By the way the clerk said it and what he observed the girl doing, Deon knew exactly what kind of special the clerk meant.

"Well, regardless, she's a good lookin' kid and I'm sure she's a pleasure to be around," Deon said.

"Thank you for that," she said. "I don't know what I would do without her. Anyway, I'm done processing your refund, husband of a wife who doesn't communicate very well."

Deon laughed as the clerk handed him a lump of cash and coins.

"I'm Deon," he said.

The clerk smiled and pointed to the nametag that was pinned to her shirt.

"Chastity."

ELEVEN

Evon sat at the measly, bumpy desk that he had pulled up to the edge of the bed.

He had been reading his Bible for a few hours, letting the heat of the sun he allowed to seep in from the slight crack in the curtains warm his skin.

To some people, sitting in one spot in complete silence for an extended period of time reading a book, let alone the Bible, would be tedious, boring. But to him it was a moment he relished and took comfort in. It was perfecting a craft that he was woefully underprepared for. He couldn't expect to adequately help the ones he loved if he couldn't even help himself. Indulging in the word was truly like food for his soul, nourishment, and like John 4:34 said, "*Nourishment comes from doing the will of God*."

He had lost track of time, doing so much reading, and when he finally looked over at the hour-too-fast clock, the time said 5:47, meaning it was almost five o'clock.

He decided a temporary break from the Bible would be good because diminishing returns would start to naturally occur.

Next to the TV lay the old newspaper he'd convinced Hank to let him have and he thought he'd explore that front-page article a little more, especially since his old buddy and Lieutenant Commander Craig Bryant was on it.

Craig was being honored and recognized by the *Sounder* for being an Oak Harbor native and serving so admirably in the Navy for decades. There he was, emblazoned on the front, in all his glory, waving and smiling to the parade crowd. He was in full Navy regalia, from his head to his toes. He was a tall, handsome man, not much different than Evon had been back in the day. Although, Craig had beefed up considerably since the last time Evon had seen him.

Just like Evon, though, Craig loved philandering with women, and there was no doubt that being in the Navy all these years made the practice even more fun and even more accessible.

Evon thought of a time when they were riding the bus in the morning on the way to middle school. Craig was always a leader, and Evon took more of a follower role, so when Craig thought it would be fun to slide on their backs under the seats of the bus to look up girls' skirts, Evon went right along with it.

The shrieks of the girls and some of the feigned embarrassment they displayed sure was a lot of fun to experience back in those days but it almost disgusted him to acknowledge that now.

There was also a time in high school, when physically they were more mature, where they would hang out by the lockers to watch the girls go into the bathroom that was nearby. Craig would tell Evon to be a lookout, while he followed the girls into the bathroom. The girl's bathroom was different than the boy's because there were no urinals to stand at, only stalls. So, when Craig followed them in there, he'd wait until he heard the stall close and lock, then he'd get into an adjacent one and stand on the toilet so he could peer over while the girls would be handling their business.

They couldn't just stop in the middle of doing what they were doing, so they would just yell at Craig while he laughed his head off. After that, he'd run out of the bathroom, hysterically telling Evon about all he'd seen.

This was a common practice at Luckeroth High, and it was well understood that you were not to raise a ruckus about what Craig Bryant did. He was the celebrated quarterback, high-profile point guard, and track and field star that got his way from his peers and most importantly, the teachers and principal. If you wanted to tell on him and get him to stop the shenanigans, you did so at your own risk. Males got bullied and relentlessly ridiculed, females lost any hope they'd had of becoming the future Mrs. Bryant.

Evon was glad he left that all in the past.

Scanning the article, Evon couldn't find any mention of a wife or kids. That could mean Craig hadn't grown out of his ways and was thoroughly enjoying the single life, or that the newspaper just neglected to add that detail.

Evon thought that while he was back in town he could spend a little time catching up with his old friend. A respite from what he was *really* in town to do might not be a bad idea, although if Craig thought he could get Evon to take part in any form of their past activities, he would have to respectfully decline.

Looking through the paper further, Evon couldn't find any contact information for Craig, but the article mentioned how he had recently retired and was looking forward to spending time helping to serve early Thanksgiving meals to needy vets at the Opportunity Center.

Evon would start hitting the proverbial pavement there since it was so close to the holiday.

On the small, wooden nightstand next to the bed there was a lamp and a telephone, which looked to be in disrepair with all the chips and cracks in it.

Evon picked it up.

There was a dial tone.

Underneath on the shelf partition was a thick, beat up phone book with rips, tears, and dog ears throughout. Evon thumbed through it and eventually found the number for the Opportunity Center.

He started dialing it, hoping it wasn't a busy part of the day, and put the phone up to his ear. It started to ring on the other end, and after several rings, he was met with an automated message in a woman's voice. He waited for the right number to press to reach who he needed to talk to and listened as the other end rang once more, presumably for an employee there to pick up.

Before anyone on the other end picked up, he heard a sudden muffled *thump* come from the direction of the bathroom. Evon turned his head and stared in that direction, wondering what it was.

"Thank you for calling the Opportunity Center. This is Amy. How can I help you today?"

Evon hung up the phone and got up from the bed, walking slowly in the direction of the bathroom.

He'd been inside the hotel room by himself all day, he was sure of that, and he had locked the door behind him when he went to talk to Hank earlier. There was no way that anything, not a person, nor an animal, could've gotten inside his room without him noticing when he returned.

That left only one unimaginable possibility that made Evon extremely uneasy.

He turned the doorknob and pushed the door open slightly and was met with a powerful odor that was unmistakable. Although he had never smelled a decaying body, he was certain that was the smell that greeted him.

He pushed the door in further and flipped on the bathroom light as he crept inside. Nothing was amiss that he could notice and the shower curtain that he had closed to conceal Ruthie's body was still shut.

He pulled back on the curtain slowly and saw that Ruthie wasn't miraculously alive again but was still laying on her back in the tub. The only thing different was that her body wasn't stiff anymore and her head had relaxed and was pressed up against the right side of the tub. Evon thought *that* was what had made the sound: bone meeting steel.

After being reassured that everything was ok, his senses came back to him and the putrid smell that would only get worse had forced him out of the bathroom.

He would have to deal with that at some point, but now wasn't the time. He made his way back to the phone and pressed redial so that he could speak to Amy again. There was no need to listen to all the automated options again, so he just pressed five to speed up the process.

"Thank you for calling the Opportunity Center. This is Michelle. What can I assist you with?"

"Um, hi," Evon said. "I was talking to Amy a few minutes ago and lost my connection, but I'm sure yo—"

"Yes, Amy went on break."

"Right. Uh, yes, I was looking to get some contact information for a Craig Bryant?"

"May I ask your relation?"

"Yes, I'm an old friend. I just wanted to get in contact with him to touch base. It's been awhile, and I'm back in town for a little bit."

"I'm sorry, sir, but we don't give out client information to anyone but immediate family members."

"No, no. He's not a client there. He's the Lieutenant Commander? The one that's volunteering for you guys for the annual Thanksgiving dinner?"

"Oh! My apologies, sir! Do you mind if I put you on hold for just a few moments?"

"Not at all. That's fine."

"And what was your name again, sir?"

"Evon. Evon Brisk."

"Thank you. One moment please."

Evon waited for a short time while he was serenaded by Christmas tunes. It was odd, but some people couldn't wait until even after Thanksgiving to get into the Christmas spirit.

Michelle returned to the line.

"Thank you for holding, sir. Mr. Bryant is actually here right now. He's in the kitchen speaking with the coordinator of the veteran's meal. He said he would love to speak to you if you wouldn't mind holding on for just a few more minutes."

Evon was surprised but happy that he had called apparently at just the right time.

"Uh, yeah! That would be great! I'll just hold on," he replied.

"I'll let him know! One moment, please," Michelle said.

Evon waited once more. Even though he was elated to be able to speak to an old friend after such a long time, he got an uneasy feeling. Things had changed to a large degree in their lives. It wasn't the high school days anymore.

Evon had tasted success beyond his wildest dreams and had experienced the failure of his worst nightmares. Even though he was at a good place now, having received a new lease and purpose in life, Craig had obviously reached the pinnacle of a successful life and wasn't coming down. What would Evon say to him after all these years?

The Christmas music abruptly stopped playing.

"Hello?" a man's voice said on the other end.

"Hello?" Evon replied.

"Who the *fuck* is this?" he sharply whispered.

"Uh, this is Evon Brisk? I was hoping to talk to Cra—"

"Ha ha! Evon Brisk, you son of a bitch!" the man's husky voice bellowed. "I had to be sure it was you! Man! What the fuck? How have you been? What have you been up to?"

A smile spread across Evon's face. "Aw, man, it's good to hear from you! I've just been enjoying life. I was in town again and read about you in the paper. Memories, man. Thought I'd reach out."

"Damn, that's crazy! I mean, where the fuck have you *been*? It's been *years*!"

"I've been around, you know…"

"No, I don't know, you prick. Ha ha!"

Evon laughed. "Well, hey, I see you're doing major things, Lieutenant Commander Bryant."

"Hey, thanks man. Hard work, dedication. Just wanted to help my country. That shit is over with though now, man. It's time to start a new chapter in my life. What that is, I have no fucking clue right now! It's been a long time, Evon. Haven't seen you on the news or anything. You still making money with that little tech company of yours? Or is the new chapter you've started chapter eleven?" he asked, laughing at his own cleverness.

"Very funny, Craig. No, things have definitely changed in my life. For the better, I think."

"For the better, huh? I'm not sure what could be better than making millions of dollars, but whatever you say Evon."

"Stuff happens, you know."

"Oh, believe me, I *know*. But hey look, this has been great and all, and I hate to cut this little reunion short, but I got these people waiting on me so we can finish planning for the dinner in a couple of days. What're you doing for the holiday?"

"Um, I'm not sure. Hadn't really thought about it to be honest," Evon said.

"You're not here with family or anything?"

"No."

"Well shit man, we can't have that! Why don't you come over to my place and help me cook? Of course, you'll get to actually *eat* afterwards. Then we can really catch up on what's been going on instead of this quick, shotgun bullshit you pulled."

"That actually sounds good, Craig. It would be nice to properly catch up."

"Great. You got something to write with? I'll give you my number and address."

Evon looked around the hotel room. There was nothing to write with or on in sight.

"Just, uh, tell me and I'll remember it," Evon said.

"Ah shit, man. Hold on," Craig said.

Evon heard the phone receiver being put down and some muffled words were exchanged between Craig and someone else in the background, although he couldn't make out what.

He thought going over to meet with Craig would be a distraction but perhaps a welcomed one. He'd get to eat some good food and take pleasure in some of the simple things in life, something he'd forgotten to do for many years.

"Yes ma'am," Craig said to someone. "Evon, you still there?"

"Yes, I'm still here."

"Good. Ok, 675-9800. That's my phone number. Got that?"

"Yep."

"Ok. 11708 West Beach Road. That's my address. Huge beige and brown house. Can't miss it."

"Got it."

"Ok. And do me a favor, will ya? Call before you show up or I'll kick your ass."

"I can do that."

"Great! Good to know you respond well to threats! Alright man, well I look forward to seeing you again. Be well."

"You do the same, Lieutenant."

"Ha, cut the bullshit, Evon. Just Craig to you."

Evon fixed his lips to reply but the phone hung up.

He hung up on his end and sat on the bed for a few moments, committing Craig's phone number and address to memory.

It was now 6:22 and all that talk about Thanksgiving meals was making him hungry. He realized he hadn't eaten in quite some time, longer than he would've liked, but with everything that had occurred over the past few days, thoughts of food had taken a backseat.

Until he was able to go to Craig's place, he was going to have to eat the next best thing and that was food out of the vending machine in the lobby. It wasn't the best but it provided Evon with everything he needed for now: nourishment.

TWELVE

A day had passed since Deon, Flip, and the rest of the camp had gone on an extended, emergency receipt duty run. The returns had been decent, good enough to at least have a feast of some significance for everyone. There wasn't enough disposable income to do anything special along the lines of what Ruthie had in mind, but at least everyone would be fed and wouldn't have to fight for portions at the Opportunity Center.

The happy, loving, and bright feelings of Thanksgiving were only a day away. On its eve, however, the feelings and sky were drearily gray. A mixture of several cloud formations filled the sky. The slight hint of sunlight peeking through was there to remind everyone that the day had enough hours left in it for them to make meaning of it. Looking up, Deon wondered if rain or snow was on its way to make life in Dreg City less tolerable at a time when it would be at its most unwelcome.

The colors of the fall could be seen in all the leaves that were being whipped around by the late

November breeze. As Deon and Flip walked, a whirlwind of red, orange, and yellow leaves danced and weaved as if trying to escape from the crush of their boots.

They sauntered through the homeless enclave asking each individual what they would like to see for their group Thanksgiving meal. The answers they received showed just how much their area of town was a microcosm of Oak Harbor at large.

There was Flo, who wanted food that reminded her of being home in the Philippines again. Gonzalo Guzman, who required everyone to call him by his full name, wanted Mexican food or he was going to be pissed. Of course, he was just joking, though. Gonzalo Guzman looked like the gruffest, most dangerous image of a Mexican a mind could conjure up but was truly harmless and downright cherubic. The oddest request Deon got was for chitterlings. That came from the old, black couple, the Washingtons, affectionately known as the Dollars because when they first showed up there they liked to remind everyone that they didn't have a dollar to their name. The only reason Deon even knew that chitterlings were something people actually ate and not a nickname for something more palatable, was because his dad had mentioned them when he talked about Thanksgivings with his grandparents who lived in Oklahoma.

All the specialty requests that he got were of no consequence anyway. The majority of the people there wanted the more traditional Thanksgiving fare, and with limited funds, he couldn't make an exception for a select few. Had they been in possession of what Ruthie was holding on to, it wouldn't have been a problem.

After making sure they had input from everyone and the money they needed was accounted for, Deon and Flip made their way to Rand's Grocery to gather the goods.

When they arrived, the scene resembled the one they'd left before: people darting in and out trying to beat the clocks in their heads as well as whatever was prepared to fall from the sky, cars screeching to a halt to let half-aware shoppers walk toward their parked cars, and kids shrieking with delight at the thought of getting to eat pumpkin pie enveloped by whipped cream.

The aisles had become amusement parks. People played Bumper Cars with their carts. They dodged getting their toes ran over. "Excuse me's, "no, you're ok's, and "go right ahead's rang out from the shoppers. The looks on their faces were stressed, annoyed, impatient, but they all knew better than to verbalize anything that would go against being in the holiday spirit.

Deon and Flip each grabbed a cart and filled them as far as the money they had would allow for, then they made their way to the checkout lanes so they could escape the asylum the grocery store had become.

Every lane had a line that seemed like it would take hours to endure, but they had no other choice and settled into one, standing behind a rotund gentleman who was holding a frozen turkey in his arms. Deon thought about offering the man a cart so that he could save his skin from frostbite but decided against it.

"Check the list *and* your basket, Flip. Let's make damn sure we got everything so we don't have to come back here," Evon said.

"Roger that. But I got a question for you, Gideon: How in the hell are we gonna carry all this shit back?" Flip asked.

"Shit, I didn't even think about that."

"Uh huh, that 30-year-old wisdom, right?" Flip snickered.

"Well, look, we'll just have to take the carts back with us. It'll be tough but it's been done before."

"You know damn well that Rand's has people walking all throughout the parking lot looking for shit like that, right?"

"Yeah, I think we're partly responsible for that, but unless you have another idea, I don't think we have any other choice."

Flip didn't offer an alternative and silence fell between them.

The line in front of them was moving slowly but surely. The fat man with the turkey was uncomfortably shifting the frozen bird from one arm to another.

Deon could hear laughter and the beeping of the scanner as food was being slid across and bagged. He turned to look at Flip who was looking at his part of the list to make sure they'd gotten everything.

"Everything checks out ok on my end," Flip said.

"Good."

As the line continued to advance, Deon started thinking about the best route they could take with the carts to avoid unwanted attention. They'd gotten this far just to recoup the money and then to buy the food. They couldn't afford to be tripped up when it mattered the most. They had lots of people depending on them right now.

"Man, what the hell? Cooking some of this shit?" Flip asked.

"What do you mean?"

"I mean, some of this food can't just be cooked over a stoked fire. Hell, there might even be rain on the way. You got a plan for that?"

"Yeah, I do. Remember? We can go to the Opp Center and use their stuff and bring it back. Shouldn't be that difficult."

"If you say so."

The guy with the frozen turkey put it on the conveyer belt. He whisked away some of the water and ice chips that were gathering on his arms and started talking to the woman who was ringing everything up.

Deon recognized her: it was Chastity.

What the hell was she doing up here and not at the customer service area? Deon wondered.

He turned around to face Flip, hunching down.

"*Shit!*" he whispered.

"What?" Flip asked.

"It's the woman from the other day. The one at the refund desk. The excuse I told her about wanting a refund is apparently a popular one to use. We're lucky she just let it slide. What's it look like with me buying some of the same shit I just returned?"

"Well, this isn't good. What do you wanna do? Do you wanna get out of this line and go to another one?"

Deon lifted his head up to look around to see where they could move to. Every other line that was available was just as long as the one they were in. It would set them back another few minutes if they left now.

"Have a good one," Chastity told the frozen turkey guy. That meant Deon and Flip were next. They hadn't even moved any of their food onto the conveyer belt yet.

"Well… look who it is. Did your wife actually forget some stuff, Deon?"

Deon turned to face Chastity, locking with her eyes, and he instantly started to feel throughout his body the warmth that came with being utterly embarrassed.

Flip shrugged and started to take things out of their carts and load them onto the belt.

"Yeah, she, uh… we, uh forgot a few things," Deon said.

"A *few* things? If those are both of your carts behind you, I don't consider that a few things," Chastity said.

Deon stood there staring at her. He was speechless and embarrassed that he'd been caught in a lie. By an employee that he'd become acquainted with, no less.

"Well, you've gotten this far. Help your friend there," she said.

Flip looked up with a grin and a wave.

Chastity began scanning the food and slid it over to a teenaged boy standing next to her who proceeded to bag the groceries.

"So, this is what you do, huh? This is your line of work? Swindle grocery stores when you don't have money so you can buy food? Who the hell are you buying all this stuff for anyway? Surely not just for you two."

Fearing that she would make a scene, he said, "Could you keep it down, *please*?"

"Chill, if I wanted to get you in trouble, believe me, you'd *be* in trouble, Deon. Is that even your real name? Or just something you throw out there, you know, in case you get caught?"

"It's actually Gideon," Flip interjected.

"Gideon, huh?" Chastity asked.

"Yeah," Deon said.

They all fell silent while she continued to scan the items. Around them, the cacophony of voices, cart wheels, scanner beeps, and bags being filled continued.

Chastity stared at Deon as she rang up the last of the items, scrutinizing his appearance.

"You're wearing the same exact clothes as the other day."

Flip looked at Deon. He didn't reply.

"If I had to guess, I'd say you and your buddy–"

"Flip," Flip said.

"Philip," Deon corrected.

"Whatever your name is, I'm guessing you guys stay at the Opportunity Center? But then what would you need all this damn food for?"

"That's because we don't actually live there, lady," Flip answered.

Deon stepped in to make sure Flip didn't incite a confrontation.

"We live in our own little portion of town. Not sure you've heard of it. Dr—"

"Dreg City. I've lived here long enough to have heard of it. Never had the pleasure of visiting though."

"It's not the best place to be but we make it work," Deon said.

"I'm sure," Chastity replied. "Anyway, your total is $261.19, which I know you have at least part of because of what I gave you the last time we saw each other. And push your carts forward so he can load your food."

The boy bagging their groceries smiled at them, having been acknowledged for his hard work.

Deon tugged on the front of the cart and wheeled it over to the kid, then dug in his front pants pocket and retrieved a lump of cash. He counted out $261 but he didn't have any coins to make up the rest of the total. He turned to Flip, who flashed a grin and reached inside his own pocket and came back up with a shiny quarter.

"Saving your ass, Gideon," he said with a smirk.

Deon snatched the quarter out of Flip's hand and handed the money to Chastity. She tried to hand him back the remaining six cents in change but he waved it off.

"Oh, so now you're turning *down* money!" she said.

Deon blushed as she handed him the receipt.

"I got a funny feeling you won't be needing this either. Check this out, I get off work in about ten minutes. Why don't you and your friend here wait up front for me. I'll give you a ride back to wherever it is you call home because I am *not* letting you guys get away with the carts."

Deon and Flip looked at each other, silently pleading each other to be the one that answered.

"Alright, we'll be up front," Deon said as they walked away with their carts.

***

Gideon and Philip sat on a bench by the entrance and watched shoppers come and go. A few minutes later, Chastity walked up and Deon recognized who was with her: it was her daughter. From his vantage point the last time he saw her, he wasn't able to discern all of her features. The blonde hair was there alright, straight and formless, unsuccessfully covering up her larger than normal ears. However, this time he was also able to see that she had bright, blue eyes that were unnaturally shaped, which made her look even more distinct. She was a little on the chubby side, too, filling out a pink, flowery designed t-shirt and black leggings. Standing next to her mother, it looked like she was the same height but might outgrow her in the years to come.

"Thanks for waiting, boys," Chastity said. "Follow me out to my car and I'll give you a ride. Free of charge."

Sunny stood there silently but waved at them and smiled while putting on a thin, red coat she was holding in her hands.

They all started to walk out to the busy parking lot and stopped at a late-model, silver Range Rover. Deon and Flip exchanged glances at each other. Chastity pulled out a set of keys and pressed a button on a black key fob. The hydraulics let out a squeal of air and the tailgate opened up high above them.

"Food back here, you guys in the back seat," Chastity said.

They took turns placing the bags in the back and Deon noticed Sunny standing there smiling at them, silently watching.

"Can I help?" she asked.

Deon hadn't heard her speak before and was surprised by her childlike voice that was different than what her size might indicate it should be.

"Um, sure? I think you might have to ask your mom, though," he said.

"Okay!" she squealed before dashing up to the driver side to talk to her mother.

"Dude, who is that?" Flip asked.

"That's her daughter."

"No shit, I guessed that, but she was just staring at you and smiling, like you guys had history or something."

"Flip, she's like a teenager or something. Any history we have only traces back to yesterday when I first saw her. And it isn't a shared history if that's the case. We hadn't spoken until just now. I don't know why she's so smiley but it doesn't bother me. She's just eager to help, I guess."

Sunny skipped back to the tailgate.

"My mommy said I can help!" she said proudly.

"Great! Hey, what's your name? I'm Philip," Flip said.

Sunny looked quizzically at him.

"Flip? Like a front flip!"

Deon shook his head, half amused, half amazed that even this stranger girl could pick up Flip's speech impediment and accurately come up with what his name actually sounded like.

"Sure, just call me Flip," he said.

"I'm Sunny!" she said excitedly.

"Well, nice to meet you, Sunny. This is my friend Gideon," Flip said gesturing to Deon.

"Giddyup!" she exclaimed. "Mr. Flip and Mr. Giddyup!"

Chastity walked back toward them.

"You guys done yet? What's the hold up?" she asked.

"We were just introducing ourselves to Sunny here," Deon said.

"Mommy, this is Mr. Flip and Mr. Giddyup!"

Chastity chuckled.

"Interesting! So now you're telling my daughter code names, huh? Hurry up and get those bags loaded, would you? It's not getting any warmer out here."

Deon agreed, and with Flip's and Sunny's help, they quickly loaded the rest of the groceries and hopped in the back of the Rover while Sunny got in on the passenger side.

Chastity shifted the car into reverse and started to back out of her parking spot in the lot, preparing to pull out into the bustling traffic.

"Seatbelts on," she said. "Set a good example for my daughter."

Sunny smiled at her mother.

"Remember, I've only *heard* of your secret location. I don't exactly know where it is, Giddyup," Chastity said and Sunny laughed at hearing the name she came up with.

"Actually, it's not too far from here," Deon said.

"Alright. Just give me directions."

As they rode down the street, Deon issuing out directions to Chastity, he took time to look up front at Sunny.

From where he was sitting, he could see her reflection in her window. She never looked away, always remaining quietly and steadfastly focused on the world outside her window. A smile was spread across her face and it had been that way since they'd gotten inside the car as far as Deon could tell.

There was a sense of serenity in her, despite the chaotic blur of images her eyes were taking in as they drove down the street.

Deon had just formally met her only minutes ago, but he couldn't help but feel the urge to connect with her more, which was silly, he thought. He had his life and she had hers, which was by all accounts very good if the car they were riding in was any indication.

Still, that feeling was there, which he would have to vanquish once their car ride was over.

They stopped at a red light.

Chastity looked back at Deon and Flip through the rear-view mirror. Flip was silently looking out of his window, while Deon was staring up at Sunny's.

"Where to now, Deon?"

Stirred out of his trance, he said, "Oh, I'm sorry. After this light, take a left and then a right."

Sunny continued to look out of the window, undeterred by the pause in the action.

The light turned green and they continued driving forward.

As they got closer, as if their thoughts were connected, Deon and Flip instinctively started to unfasten their seatbelts.

"Right here," Deon said.

Chastity stopped and started to take stock of the camp.

Sunny looked up as well.

"Hmph," Chastity started, "kind of hidden, kind of in plain sight."

Blue tarps were set up as crude tents all around. Some had cardboard and duct tape for fortification. Milk crates and grocery store carts littered the area. Some were used as seats, which several people there displayed. There were a few barrels set up with a fire ablaze and people standing next to them, warming themselves. The wind whipped around leaves and discarded paper. Empty bottles and cans tried their hardest to join the rest of the debris in the wind but couldn't meet the weight limit for the ride. All around were people standing, sitting, walking, with somber looks on their faces.

It might have come across as a sad and humbling scene to any outside observer, but Deon knew this was true contentment, reservation. They didn't have much but what they did have was truly theirs.

"*This* is where you live?" Chastity asked.

"Yep," he replied.

He and Flip opened their doors and got out of the Range Rover. Chastity popped open the tailgate so they could retrieve their groceries. She and Sunny joined them in the back.

"But how in the hell are you gonna *eat* this stuff you bought?" Chastity asked.

"We'll make it work. We always do. Plus, the Opp Center will let us use some of their appliances, so I don't think we'll have any problems."

Some of the people in the camp started to perk up and pay attention to them lifting bags out of the back of the car.

Sunny stood there, smiling.

They finished unloading all the bags. Flip shouted and motioned for some of the residents to come over and help. Deon slammed the tailgate shut.

"Well, thanks for everything," he said, facing Chastity. "And thank *you*, Sunny."

She ran up and gave Deon a big hug that knocked him backwards. He wasn't prepared for her surprising weight to be thrown at him. He thought Chastity might be bothered that her daughter embraced a relative stranger, but she just looked on and smiled while Flip and some of the people he asked for help made off with some of the bags.

"Look, I'm in the holiday spirit. Why don't you let everyone here have this food here and you and Flip come over to my place for Thanksgiving. My treat."

It only took a second for Deon to consider the offer and come up with a response.

"Thanks, but no thanks. You've done enough. It's really not a big deal eating with everyone here. Like I said, we make it work. We don't need the extra charity."

"You don't know me very well, Deon," she said as she walked to the front of the car, Sunny following suit. "I *rarely* take no for an answer and I certainly won't today. Plus, I've got some making up to do anyway. I'll be back here tomorrow morning to pick you guys up."

Chastity and Sunny got inside the car and shut their doors.

Deon walked up to the driver-side window and Chastity lowered it.

"You don't know *me* that well. It's really not necessary," he pleaded.

"Sunny would *love* to have her new friends over, isn't that right?" she said looking over at Sunny.

Sunny flashed a bright grin and nodded her head to the point where it looked like the only thing keeping it attached to her neck was a string.

"Then it's settled," Chastity said as she backed up into the street, forcing him to move away from the car.

"Wait!" he shouted.

She pulled away, ignoring him.

Sunny looked back at him through the tinted back window and waved.

It was settled. He would be seeing them again tomorrow.

THIRTEEN

The sky began to darken. The clouds that were dimly illuminated by the sun earlier were starting to give way to the evening and a brightness that only the moon could provide. Nary a star nor a creature that inhabited the sky was visible quite yet, which served Evon well because he would need the remaining light to be able to read the street signs ably enough.

As was requested, he called Craig to let him know he was on his way, lest he risk a jovial physical altercation upon arriving. Before leaving, he made sure he had his backpack and that his hotel room was locked tight. He tried the doorknob several times and slammed his shoulder into the door hard enough to test if it would budge.

He was good to go.

He could've solicited a ride, either from Craig himself, a taxi, or maybe even from Hank, but luckily his location near City Center was within his walking threshold to Craig's West Beach Road address in Penn Cove Park.

Sure, it would take a few hours, which was quite a long walk for someone in his condition, but he didn't mind. It would serve as a form of physical therapy and would undoubtedly work up an appetite. It wasn't Thanksgiving Day yet, for the real feast would come tomorrow, but if he was going to help prepare food then he expected Craig to hold up his end of the deal and allow a taste test of the menu.

After winding through the smaller streets in town while trying to avoid getting on the North Cascades Highway, he made his way onto Fort Nugent Road, which if his memory served him correctly, would lead him directly to Craig's residence.

It was a lonely walk, aside from being accompanied by the many cars filled with people traveling to wherever they planned to take part in the next day's festivities. But it was a scenic one to say the least.

The road was lined with the sprawling, late fall remnants of Garry oak with its gray-brown mosaic of a trunk that defined the city of Oak Harbor. Mixed in were vibrant evergreen trees and other plant life that would have to slumber through the next seasonal cycle before they were allowed to shine once again.

Modest and fancy homes alike found a way to elbow their way into the picture as well. It was evident that this area belonged to nature, first and foremost, and human inhabitants decided that their westward expansion to the sea wouldn't be denied.

Though his eyes couldn't spot any discernible animal in the sky, Evon did notice an abundance of Douglas squirrels running about the ground, taking their chances to cross the road to gather food. He knew what type of squirrels they were because lying in a hospital bed without much to do leads to boredom. Boredom leads to looking up random facts. And here he was, being able to identify the little, dark brown rodent with the carrot-colored—though streaked with gray—underbelly, and black, bushy tail.

He had read that they weren't all that friendly to humans and would quickly dart off when one was in its vicinity. Yet, as he walked alongside the road, he neared a group of them hunting in the grass nearby and they didn't seem to mind his presence.

That comfortability faded as he got closer and closer because they started making loud squeaks that were like a dog's chew toy being incessantly squeezed. He figured out they were an alarm meant to scatter the group when all but one of the group ran for the trees.

A railing separated the sidewalk he occupied and the grassy, tree-lined area that this lone squirrel's friends high-tailed it to. The one that was left crawled underneath the railing and onto the sidewalk directly in front of Evon.

They both stopped and stared at each other. There Evon was, staring into the black, beady eyes of this rodent and that same rodent staring into his dark brown eyes, although, at this late hour, they would appear to be black and empty aside from the glint of the streetlights. The squirrel twitched its tail. Then its nose. Meanwhile, it never looked away from Evon; instead, its gaze was as piercing as it could be for any four-legged creature. Evon wondered, could an animal such as this understand the human condition? Could this woodland quadruped sense the purpose both of their creator had imbued him with? It would be silly to attempt to ask, for it would elicit no response.

He took a step toward the squirrel and it sped out into the road. A driver in a navy-blue pickup truck was headed in their direction and instantly recognized the dilemma on his hands: keep speeding forward, taking the chance of running over and ultimately killing the squirrel or dangerously alter his driving path in order to avoid hitting it.

In the split second he had to think, the driver chose the latter and Evon saw him through the windshield yank his steering wheel to the left.

The tires let out a squeal as they adjusted to the sudden change of direction on the pavement. Although the squirrel had been given a chance to get out of the way, it still managed to run in the exact direction the truck had moved to and a muffled *pop* rang out through the air.

The driver corrected his path and continued down the road. Evon looked on as the red taillights faded in the distance and then he looked both ways before crossing over and bending down next to the crushed squirrel.

In the short amount of time between their silent exchange and the furry creature's demise by a more dominant four-legged beast, its fine fur had changed colors to the crimson of freshly spilled blood. Its form was no longer three-dimensional, but rather a two and a half, and the twitch it had displayed in its nose and tail had coursed through its legs in a final throe.

To Evon, that begged a question: why hadn't this squirrel run off with its friends? Don't they see many of their kind suffer the same fate? Not flourishing through life but rather caught in the perpetual grasp of pavement, only to be relieved by weather or a scavenging predator? To him, the answer was clear. The moment they had shared was an unspoken acknowledgement by the squirrel to Evon that he indeed knew what he was still on this earth to do. That squirrel had indeed seen many horrific scenes of its ilk crossing roads only to meet untimely deaths by uncaring machines and had decided to take its own life with Evon serving as the catalyst.

Its legs still twitched and it was still suffering whether it knew it or not. Evon stood up from his kneeling position and noticed the squirrel's head still intact. Its eyes seemed to roll back into its skull, mouth dangling open with trickles of blood spilling out onto the blacktop of Fort Nugent Road. Evon raised his right leg and rested his foot onto the squirrel's head and applied pressure until he felt the pop through his shoe. The twitching stopped and he continued to walk toward Craig's house.

***

He finally reached the home of his childhood friend, Craig Bryant. He was a little worse for the wear, but he knew he'd be able to rest his body shortly.

As he walked up the long, paved driveway, he came upon an expansive front yard that had barely any green remaining. There weren't many trees either, and the ones that were there were small in stature compared to the ones he'd seen on his way. This was in stark contrast to the house next door whose yard was very much obscured by the vast number of tall trees, hiding the home from the curious eyes of passersby traveling on the road.

To someone who could see the forest for the trees, this revealed a lot about people: either they wanted to be watched or they wanted to be the watcher. Craig's neighbor was content to be hidden but ever watchful over his property, while Craig had no problem inviting anonymous stares from the roadway.

Evon stood near a mailbox and stared at a slab of stone near the entrance that was illuminated by a lone spotlight protruding from the ground: 11708 etched in black numerals.

As Craig had described, the house was predominately beige, with the window accents being dark brown by his best estimates considering how dark it had become outside. Along the bottom of the large home was a stone exterior that in all likelihood wrapped around the entire house. A two-car garage stuck out from the front of the home. The terra cotta roof on both the home and the garage was a series of triangles of varying heights. Every window that he could see was lit up in a bright, yellow glow. Where Craig's home was positioned, adjacent to the sea, it was as if the building was a lighthouse, guiding the way for wayward travelers.

Evon tilted his head back to look up at the sky. When he started his journey to the house, it was too bright to see any stars. Now, the wispy clouds had broken up and revealed a speckled night scene. Both the heavens and the serenity that came with the knowledge that you were just a small part of something bigger and more significant was alluring, calming, almost. It was a moment he wished he could appreciate longer, if the weather was warmer and the silence wasn't broken up by Craig's booming voice.

"What the fuck are you doing out there? Get your ass in here!" he shouted from his steps.

There were three steps that led to a wide porch; potted plants lined each side. Craig stood in the open doorway, arms crossed. Evon brought his gaze down from the clouds.

"Enjoying the view," he said.

Where Craig stood, Evon was blanketed in darkness and it would've taken some effort to get a good look at him, but Evon could see Craig just fine. He was wearing a periwinkle, long-sleeved button-up and tan khakis with a razor-sharp crease. The porchlight shined off his bald head as well as his mocha-colored dress shoes.

"Come here, man. Let me see what you're looking like these days," Craig said.

Evon slowly took some steps forward, bracing himself for the reaction he knew he would receive. While Craig had a few physical changes from the last time they'd seen each other, the last image Evon had was one that he now resembled.

Evon on the other hand had changed profoundly and whatever Craig thought he might have looked like would not match the figure that approached his front porch.

Evon was now standing just feet away, awash in the lights coming from the home. They stood there in silence taking stock of each other. Evon's hands were at his side. Craig uncrossed him arms, shoving his hands into his pants pockets. He clicked his tongue and looked Evon up and down, otherwise expressionless. Evon noticed the aroma of cooking food wafting out from indoors. His mouth started to water, pangs rumbled in his stomach.

"Man… you look like shit," Craig said.

Evon dropped his head. "I know, I look a little a different than you probably remember."

"Different? Different is an understatement. Evon, you look like *shit.* I mean, you look like you've been through hell."

"Might as well have been."

"And look at your fucking clothes! I see you're a fan of Summer Creases."

"I'm sorry?"

"Wrinkles, creases. Some are here, some are there…"

"Sorry I can't be as pressed as you right now."

Craig started to look around, tapping his right foot. "Where's your car?"

"Don't have one."

"Someone drop you off?"

"No. I walked."

"Walked? Walked from where?"

"Not too far from City Center, the Dreg's."

"Jesus Christ, Evon! What the hell? You should've let me know and I could've given you a ride!"

"It's not a big deal, really. I made it here ok, didn't I? I needed the walk anyway."

"You need something, alright. God, look at your face, man! Who the hell have you been fighting and losing to?"

"Life."

"Life… Get your ass in here, Evon. You've got some explaining to do."

Craig gestured and Evon followed him up the steps and into his home. He took off his backpack upon entering and set it down by the door.

Besides being reminded about the smell of the food, he was instantly struck by the architectural beauty. Every wall was pearly white. Beneath his feet was the finest wood flooring, buffed and shined to the point where it looked like every step was an invite to a slip and fall. The ceiling extended high, seemingly without limits. There were two levels to the home. Evon looked to his right at the staircase that led to the second level, which included a balcony from which to look down on everything below. The railings were wrought-iron, ornately decorated with geometric shapes.

"I've got a massive, finished basement, too," Craig said, as if he were one step ahead of Evon's thoughts.

He looked up to see there was a large skylight above the living room to his left. Tables and glass decorations of various colors and shapes flanked big, white couches. The large sofa faced a set of doors that led to what looked like a deck. A smaller loveseat faced a dormant fireplace and flat TV that was affixed to the wall with two paintings hanging on either side of it. They seemed to be displaying a field of red and yellow roses. Nothing else.

Directly forward was a dining area. The round table and chairs were wooden and probably not cheap. They looked to be solid and the craftsmanship was impeccable. In the middle sat a yellow bowl of fake fruit, maybe the only unremarkable set of items in Craig's ostentatious home.

"Pretty fucking impressive, huh?" Craig said.

"Your plastic fruit?

"Ha, you asshole. No, I mean my three bed, three bath, 3,333-square-foot home. And yes, I know that's a lot of threes."

"Well, yes, it's a very impressive home. Although, I haven't seen the rest of it yet."

"Yeah, got the pond as my backyard. Not quite the deep blue, but it'll do. Come check out the kitchen."

Evon followed him into the kitchen. He was greeted by fine wood cabinetry, marble flooring, granite countertops, and stainless-steel appliances. The entire place was gaudy, no doubt. Something Evon would've taken delight in years ago.

"Close to a $1,000,000 home," Craig said.

"That's pretty expensive! How are you paying for this with the kind of pay you were getting from the Navy?" asked Evon.

"By being smart, Evon," Craig said, tapping the side of his head with a finger. "I could be like everyone else around here and grab myself a Whidbey Whale *easily* if I wanted to settle, but fuck that. What would I look like being shacked up with a woman like that? Nah, man, I hooked up with this hot executive out of Seattle. She handles 60% of the expenses, I cover the other 40% here, and why not? I deserve to be cut some slack being who I am. She's got plenty of money anyway."

"The paper never mentioned a significant other. And you didn't tell me about her when we talked on the phone."

"Didn't have time to. Plus, I didn't know you'd call out of nowhere, dickhead."

Evon looked down at Craig's left hand. "Where's your ring?"

"Shit, thanks for reminding me. Took it off to start preparing some of this damn food. Jillian would give me shit if she saw me without it on. It's on the counter over there. Grab it for me, would you?"

Evon walked to the counter by the fridge where Craig pointed. Lying next to a knife was a standard issue gold band.

"That's her name? Jillian?"

"Yeah, man. Hot piece of fucking ass. Not like the buns I've had on the ships. Had to get one a little younger than me, too. Thirty-nine. Lucky to find one that doesn't mind being with an old salt like me, ha. She should be back in a little bit. We were missing a few items we needed for dinner. Shopping is a bag of dicks for me, but she loves that shit."

Evon handed Craig his ring and watched as he slid it over his ring finger. His stomach started to growl and he was sure Craig had heard it.

Craig chuckled and patted Evon on the back. "Say no more. I'll fix you a plate of the lasagna we heated up. Not letting you eat any of the Thanksgiving food just yet. I was gonna put your ass to work with a cutting board and a knife but since you walked over here and look like shit on a shingle, I'll cut you some slack. Tomorrow, though, I'm putting you to work!"

Evon smiled. "That sounds great, Craig."

"Yeah, yeah. Don't mention it. But you *do* need to tell me what the fuck has been going on with you since the last time we hung out."

Evon nodded. As Craig pulled the pan of lasagna out of the oven and cut three generous portions, one presumably for Jillian, he started telling him about his journey thus far.

They stood in the kitchen conversing, taking turns to eat or talk. After a few minutes, Craig grabbed two glasses from the cabinet and filled them with crushed ice and water from his refrigerator. He motioned Evon over to the dining room where they sat and continued with their conversation. Evon had to reach back quite a way in his memory to fill Craig in on everything he'd missed, but it was almost therapeutic. He hadn't had a real conversation with very many people since he'd come back in town, aside from his brief run-in with Ruthie, and they wouldn't be able to speak to each other again for a while.

Evon got to the part where he became fed up with life and decided to jump off a bridge to end his sorrows. Craig was cutting into what remained of his large piece of lasagna and stabbed a piece of it with his fork. He slid it around on the plate, sopped up cheese and tomato sauce and was lifting it toward his mouth but suddenly dropped the fork back down on the plate with a clatter.

"Let me get this straight. You jumped off fucking Deception Pass Bridge because you weren't getting any pussy, lost your kid, and blew your fortune?"

"You put it in such simple terms, Craig. It was a little more complex than that."

"Maybe, but it didn't have to be. Could've contacted me. You know we go back."

"That's kind of hard to do when you're on battleships, floating around on the sea. Besides, I didn't have any contact info for you once you went to Annapolis. Kind of thought we went our separate ways after that."

"Ha, ha, aw, man… Annapolis… Fun times, Evon. I never did tell you about all that shit, did I?"

"Nope, you sure didn't! But please do so I can eat my cold lasagna."

"Ha, fuck off. Here, I'll warm it up for you. Gotta check on all the other food anyway."

Craig grabbed Evon's plate and got up from the table to head to the microwave.

"So, what all do you wanna know?" he shouted from the kitchen.

"I don't know. I guess you could fill in the gaps from when I saw you last."

Craig slid the plate in the microwave. "I'm gonna give it a good nuke for you. That way it'll remain hot for you for my life story. Let's see… we last hung out in the summer after graduation, right? Well, you know how it was in school. I was the shit and you kind of just hung around to get a whiff."

"Very funny."

"Ha, ha, well, it was true. But of course, being the shit attracts attention, for better or for worse. The teachers and the coaches there would always stop me in the hall or try to whisper to me in class about how I'm ruining my future or whatever. That I had leadership qualities that would benefit me in the future if I just quit being such an asshole. Remember ol' coach Pat Schmidt? 'Fat shit' is what I always called him. But anyway, he pulled me aside at football practice one day our senior year and told me I should consider a career in the military, which was complete bullshit to me. Everyone knew damn well I wasn't a guy who liked to take orders, but I didn't really have any plans for the future after high school so I looked into it over Christmas break. I wasn't into doing grunt work in the Army. I didn't give two shits about flying around for the Air Force. So, being that I grew up in Seattle and was always close to water, I figured I'd look into the Coast Guard or the Navy. Well, obviously you know which one I chose."

The microwave beeped and Craig walked out to hand Evon his hot plate of half-eaten lasagna.

"Man… How was it up there? In Annapolis?" Evon said. "I've heard school there is pretty tough."

"Nah, not for someone like me. Besides, you gotta do what you gotta do if you wanna be an officer. I didn't just wanna be a regular ol' Joe Navy, you know? I wanted the opportunity to do something more once I got out. What that is? I have no fucking idea yet."

"So, *the* Craig Bryant I knew in high school, which we'd both agree was an unsavory guy to say the least, traded the west coast for the east and suddenly became a law abiding, stand-up, straight-laced guy, right?"

Craig let out a hearty guffaw.

"Well, I wouldn't say all that. C'mon, man, you know how that shit goes when you're new at a place like that."

"No, I really don't."

"Well, let me tell ya! You gotta earn your stripes! I've done the whole bit, from being a Ricky Ninja, to hot-dogging it on the ship, to skating on work for some other poor dickhead to pick up the slack. Those things are what made me the fabulous man that stands before you."

"That's a stretch."

"Oh, shut up. What do you know?"

"I know that you retired, so something must've happened that broke up all the fun you were having."

"Yeah, you're damn right something happened. That damn Glenn Defense, Fat Leonard scandal hit the Navy. I had some pretty damn intimate knowledge of all the bribery and cover-ups that were going on with that situation and wasn't about to let the hammer come down on me, forget that. That, and me being stonewalled as I tried to climb the ladder? JARTGO."

"What was that?"

"JARTGO, man. Just another reason to get out. Keep up!"

"Kind of hard when you're speaking in tongues."

"Whatever. Eat your damn food while I check on this other stuff."

Evon looked on as Craig walked away to fiddle through the kitchen; checking inside the oven, moving pots around on the stove, wiping up spills on the countertops.

A smile spread across his face. Even though Craig had become even more debauched than he was in high school, Evon still enjoyed his company. He would never again indulge himself in the things that were probably fun to Craig, but he couldn't deny that his jovial spirit and friendship, even after all these years, was something that made him feel good inside.

As he forked a piece of lasagna into his mouth, he turned his attention to the front door and the sound of keys scraping on the other side. Someone out there was fumbling away at the lock. He knew this had to be Jillian.

The door slowly opened and the sound of the keys and grocery bags sang in unison as she walked in. Craig looked back at Evon quizzically and he nodded toward the door to let Craig know what he was looking at. Jillian slid off her coat, revealing an outfit similar to her husband's, like they started out their day coordinating their attire. The only difference in hers was that her blouse was a darker shade of blue and rolled at the forearms. Her tan slacks were thinner and skin-tight, but shorter, not quite covering up all of her ankle. On her feet were matte-black heels, which Evon saw made her taller than Craig when he came out of the kitchen and locked her in an embrace.

They pecked a few kisses at each other before Craig playfully slapped her behind. She laughed a little bit and pushed him away with one hand, handing him the bags she carried inside with the other.

As he walked to the kitchen, that's when she turned to notice Evon sitting at the dining table, staring at their interaction. She stared at Evon, startled at his being there, as if he materialized out of thin air.

"Oh," Jillian said. "And who's our guest?"

"Babe, that's my childhood friend, Evon," Craig yelled from the kitchen. "I know he looks like chewed up foreskin, but he's harmless."

Jillian nodded and walked over to Evon, extending her hand to shake. "Nice to meet you, Evon. I'm Jillian. If my husband is complimenting you with such flowery language, I guess you can't be all that bad."

"Thank you, Jill. You're obvi—"

"*Jillian.*"

"My apologies. Jillian. You're obviously more graceful than that guy in the kitchen."

She removed her hand from Evon's grasp. "Yeah," she sighed, "he is a handful. So, how long are you staying?"

"I, am… actually not sure. I could leave whenever."

"Fuck that," Craig yelled from the kitchen. "Your dumb ass walked all the way over here, damn near in the middle of the night at that. I'm not letting you walk *back*, at least not until after dinner tomorrow."

"Don't you have to go do your volunteer gig, though?" Evon replied.

"I do, but you can just kick it here until Jillian and I get back. There's a bedroom and bathroom in the basement and other things to entertain yourself with, which I suggest your sorry ass take advantage of."

"Craig, knock it off!" Jillian snapped.

"Hey, just saying! There's a laptop down there, too. For all your Netflix or porno viewing pleasure. If you're into that shit," he said as he walked toward his wife.

Jillian playfully punched his shoulder and nudged him back into the kitchen.

"I know he's your friend but he can be such an ass sometimes!" Jillian said. "Yes, you can stay the night here and everything you need is downstairs. If you need anything else, just let us know, ok?" Jillian walked into the kitchen and helped Craig rummage through the grocery bags.

Evon looked on as they took out items and spoke to each other, although he couldn't hear what was being said. He was enjoying his warm lasagna, actually being able to taste it now that it wasn't surface-of-the-sun hot.

Every few minutes or so, Jillian would look over at him with a blank stare. When they'd make eye contact, she would subtly smile.

A few minutes went by before she finally left the kitchen. She told Craig that she was going upstairs to take a shower and get into some more comfortable clothes, then she'd come back down to help him finish up in the kitchen.

Craig walked out with a drink in his hand and sat down with Evon, who was firmly planted at the table. He had finished his meal, but being that he was in foreign territory, he didn't feel comfortable getting up to wander around.

"Nice, isn't she?" Craig asked.

"Mhmm," Evon mumbled.

"She can be a real bitch sometimes, though."

"Oh? Is that so? Didn't you say she was hot earlier?"

"Yeah, man. Look, I was describing what's on the *outside*. Gotten kinda stale on the *inside*, if you know what I mean."

"I have an idea."

Craig swirled the drink around in his cup. The ice clanked off the glass, breaking up the relative silence that had fallen over the room.

"Yeah, and a guy's got needs, if you know what I mean," said Craig.

"So… you masturbate? I guess that's not that big of a deal."

"Heh, you're a piece of work. I guess I *could* jack off, but why do that when I can have the real thing?"

"You thinking about cheating?"

"*Thinking* about it? I've already stepped out quite a few times, actually. And it's not cheating if you don't get caught. Besides, what she doesn't know won't hurt her. I know you won't understand because you haven't gotten any ass in a while, and probably won't, based on how you look right now, but trust me when I say: it's just harmless fun."

A door creaked open upstairs and Evon and Craig fell silent again as Jillian came down the stairs. Her hair was still wet from the shower and she had slipped into a pair of jeans and a sweater that very much complimented her figure. A pair of white and black tennis shoes replaced her heels from earlier.

"*Scuttlebutt*," Craig whispered to Evon, looking him sternly in the eye and making a "zip your lips" gesture with his fingers.

"Mighty quiet down here," Jillian said.

"Yeah, we've been talking about the dinner at the Opportunity Center tomorrow. It's just sad to think about all those people out there, you know?"

"Yeah, you're right. Anyway, I'm headed back out, babe. Left my damn wallet at the store. Be right back."

Jillian came over and placed a kiss on Craig's cheek.

"You know where I'll be!" he said.

"Love you!" she said.

"Love you, too!" Craig returned.

She smiled and waved goodbye to Evon and rushed out the door.

Evon heard the garage door open and the rumble of an engine starting. He looked out of the window next to the door and watched the headlights of a car that he couldn't make out back out of the driveway and crawl down the road.

Craig got up from his seat. "Scuttlebutt, you hear me?"

"I hear you. I guess I'm having a hard time understanding why relationships have to come to cheating. That goes against everything you vow at the altar, don't you think?"

Evon arose from his seat and followed Craig into the kitchen.

"Look, man, if you're preparing a lecture, save it. It's just sex. There's no feelings involved. I love my wife for what she brings to the table, but she's *boring*! Divorcing isn't an option. Too much to lose, too much of a lifestyle change. The other one feels the same way."

"The other one?"

"Yes, the chick I'm fucking. She's married, too. Her husband is like Jillian, only with a dick he doesn't know how to use, which is fine by me."

Evon shook his head and couldn't help but feel a twang of sadness creep in. It wasn't *his* wife but what was being done was an affront to what is supposed to be a holy unity, he thought.

But this was his friend. And this was a friendship that withstood the test of time; otherwise, he wouldn't be in his home right now. Things happen for a reason and conventional wisdom dictated that he was *supposed* to be right here, right now. He didn't like hearing about Craig's extramarital activity but he sat through it anyway.

"So, how long do you plan on doing this?" Evon inquired.

"I don't know. I really don't see an end in the near future at least. Unless I get caught. Then, of course, I'll have to make sure Jillian doesn't leave me. But even the broad I'm with now can be replaced. She's not exempt. What I *do* know is this: if Jillian doesn't learn how to please me at some point, I'll have to do what I have to do until I no longer have a sex drive! Ha, ha."

"Adultery."

"What?"

"It's not just cheating, what you're doing. It's not like a video game or something, Craig. It's adultery. In the Bible…"

"I know what the fuck the Bible says, so cut the bullshit. And correct me if I'm wrong, but I don't think we all do exactly as the Bible says one-hundred percent of the time, right? We're all sinners, if that's where you're going. If I'm being punished for everything, then call me a masochist because it's feeling pretty damn good right now. I'll come to terms and ask forgiveness on my deathbed, just like everyone else does. Until then, best believe I'm gonna enjoy the life I got."

Stillness fell over the room, and despite his best intentions to try ignoring it, Evon felt a palpable tension, too. He was already aware that he and Craig were on two separate wavelengths in life but not to this extreme. He loved his friend but the night had changed from a fun reunion into an uncomfortable one.

"Look, man, I know we're a little different now," Craig said. "You live your life and I'll live mine. Don't worry about me. Whatever happens, happens. You know? Anyway, I'm gonna grab a beer and park it in front of the tube for a few. You want one?"

Evon returned a blank stare.

"Well, more for me."

Craig walked over to the fridge where he clutched a bottle of beer from the inside. He twisted the top off and stood with the door open, scanning the contents inside.

"Is there a bathroom I can use?" Evon asked.

Craig finished the swig of beer he took. "Yeah," he said, pointing in the direction of the bathroom.

Evon walked into the living room momentarily so he could retrieve his backpack and walked down the hallway into the bathroom Craig had pointed him to.

Once inside, he flipped on the light and shut the door, which noisily creaked. Their bathroom was aromatic, smelling of fruits and flowers of an unknown origin. This was typical of bathrooms; it masked all the smells that would otherwise make it an unpleasant place to spend too much time.

The toilet seat lid was up and Evon lowered it so he would have a place to sit down. This might take some time, he thought.

He unzipped his backpack and grabbed his Bible from inside. The night's events had presented a dilemma to him of which he was conflicted about how to proceed.

Here was his best friend, at least from his childhood, bragging about committing a mortal sin. The degree to which Craig seemed to take delight in it sickened Evon, but more than that, it hurt him and made him incredibly sad.

On the other hand, there was Jillian, whom Evon didn't know much about except that she didn't like being called Jill. The other thing he knew in his heart of hearts was that she was a good wife. Who else could put up with Craig like she was so admirably doing? Evon was sure that she tried to make Craig happy in every way she could but all Craig thought about was pleasures of the flesh. His excursions into another household and another man's wife would have to come to a head at some point because those kinds of secrets don't stay long hidden. If there was ever a scenario where the saying "what's hidden in the dark eventually comes to light" was appropriate for, this was it. When it did, there would be a great many people heartbroken. Households ruptured. Souls tormented.

Evon flipped open his Bible to scan through the book of Leviticus where he knew he was sure to find what he was looking for.

Reading through the Bible while he sat in a hospital bed recuperating, he'd come across many passages about adultery. Matthew, Mark, Luke, and John certainly had a lot to say about it. To say it was highly frowned upon was an understatement, considering the level of sin it was. It didn't take much time to find it in

Leviticus: *If a man commits adultery with another man's wife, both the man and woman shall be…*

Evon closed his eyes and closed the Book.

He didn't know the other woman, but Craig?

He heard footsteps approaching the door and opened his eyes. A rap of knuckles hit the wooden door.

"You ok in there?" Craig asked.

"Yeah, yeah. I'm ok."

"In there taking a shit or something?"

"Something like that."

"Well, make sure you spray in there and wash your damn hands, you smelly bastard."

"Gotcha!"

He continued listening until he heard Craig walk away and was sure he wasn't listening on the other side.

Rash decisions got made when people didn't take the time to think things through, which was why he needed to stay in the bathroom a little while longer.

Why was he here? Given a second chance at life?

He was given the answer from his Creator months ago, and this shouldn't be a time to doubt the realization. That realization was that when God told you to do something, you don't question His wisdom. Spread throughout His word were innumerable examples of His orders being handed down and what could happen when you obeyed.

Or disobeyed.

Evon had obeyed before and he knew he'd be rewarded. This was different, though. Whereas Ruthie was shackled by a grasp of pain that needed to be relieved, Craig wasn't the one in pain in this situation. It was his wife, Jillian.

He had just met her, though, and he knew God meant for Evon to heal her by proxy, which meant the unthinkable for Evon. It was hard to come to terms with and even harder knowing that he was temporarily severing a connection, but the Lord saves His toughest tasks for His steeliest of servants.

He dug through his backpack and took out a fresh syringe and a vial of Atracurium from his reserves. After taking off the cap, he poked the needle through the protective barrier on the vial and pulled back on the plunger. Evon got up from the toilet, lifted the lid, tossed in the cap from the needle, and flushed it. He turned on the sink and let the water run for a few seconds while he put everything else he didn't need back in his backpack.

He would leave the pack in the bathroom for now and come back to retrieve it later.

He swung the door inward quickly because opening it slowly would've drawn out the clamorous screech in its joints; he didn't want to attract Craig's attention.

With the syringe in hand, he slowly crept to the loveseat Craig was sitting on. Evon was thankful that the finishes in the house were so high quality, so gaudy, because the hardwood floors didn't make a sound.

Craig had his back to Evon. There was a beer in his left hand, a remote in his right. He was too preoccupied with taking sips of his drink and flipping channels to feel the presence of Evon standing over him.

"I'm sorry," Evon said.

"Sorry for what? Did you fucking clog up my toilet? Goddammit, Evon—"

Before he could finish, Evon jabbed the needle into the right side of his neck and pressed in on the plunger.

"What the fuck?" Craig screamed out as his beer fell to the floor.

He wildly swung his arms backwards, sending the remote crashing to the floor and swiped at his neck, trying to knock away Evon's hand.

Evon hadn't finished depressing the plunger all the way before Craig arose from the couch and angrily pushed Evon away. The needle was still protruding from his neck, the muscles having contracted and firmly taken grasp of it. Craig yanked the needle out of his neck and held it in his hands, puzzlingly inspecting it before tossing it on the floor.

"*What the fuck did you stick in me*?" he shouted.

Craig approached Evon, who stood still, waiting for the injection to take effect.

"Huh? I asked you a question!" Craig howled.

He grabbed Evon by his shirt with both hands and threw him against the wall. He let go momentarily before grabbing him again and throwing him toward the couch. Evon stumbled trying to keep his balance and sent a ceramic decorative saucer smashing onto the floor.

"Goddammit, fucking answer me!" Craig bellowed.

He wiped his neck where the needle had been and held it in front of his face to inspect it. There was a small smear of blood.

Time seemed to be at a standstill; Evon needed it to quicken its pace. This was proving to be more difficult and taking much longer than it had with Ruthie.

Craig came forward with fists clenched and swung at Evon, landing a blow on his eye. Stunned, Evon fell backwards onto the coffee table, taking more glass fixtures down with him.

He reached up at his eye instinctively and Craig rushed toward him. He sat on top of Evon's chest, grabbing him by the throat and raining down punches in a frenzy.

Evon tried his hardest to thrash about and dodge the barrage, but he was still caught by many of them.

Why wasn't that stuff taking effect yet? he thought.

As he was processing that thought and thinking that maybe he made a mistake in how he approached this latest task, he felt Craig's grip on his throat loosen. Then it slipped off. Craig tried to grab it again but weakly flailed doing so. The punches had turned into taps, then stopped completely. He shook his head as violently as he could as if trying to rid himself of cobwebs. He tried to say something but the only thing that came out was a guttural mewl.

Evon removed his hands from where they were shielding his face and locked eyes with Craig. He looked like he wanted to form a pained expression but couldn't.

His mouth slackened, drool forming and spilling out, then he dropped down on top of Evon. Craig was still breathing, as was expected, but all other movements had ceased. Evon pushed Craig off him and onto the floor. Craig was lying prone, one arm tucked underneath him. Evon stood up, taking in the scene in the living room. They had created quite a muddle. A beer bottle lay on its side on the floor, its contents slowly dripping out. The coffee table was broken with glass and ceramics all around. The sofa had been pushed from its original position.

He looked down at Craig and knew he had to finish his work. With Ruthie, he'd finished her off with the scalpel to quickly relieve her.

Craig, however, wouldn't be afforded the same mercy because what was being done wasn't for him, it was for Jillian, to spare her the pain that her husband's infidelities were causing her unknowingly.

Craig was wearing a black, roped-leather belt. Evon bent down and rolled him onto his back. He offered no resistance; he just laid there with his eyes closed, but he was still breathing. Evon knew he wasn't asleep, just paralyzed.

"I know you can hear me," Evon said. "This is your time to repent. Jillian won't be in any more pain, rest assured. Even though this isn't about you, neither will you."

He unfastened the belt Craig was wearing and rolled him back onto his stomach. He sat down on the small of Craig's back and crisscrossed the belt around his neck, lifting his head up. He pulled tightly with both hands, leaning back with the full force of his weight. This put a strain on his already damaged back that was made worse by the fall he took tonight, but he had to endure through it just a little bit longer.

He was feeling for Craig's breathing to stop but he hadn't succumbed yet. That's when he heard the front doorknob being twisted open.

Evon must've blanked out and lost his sense of time because he hadn't heard the car return, and from his position in the living room, he couldn't have seen the headlights anyway. This was a predicament he hadn't even thought about, but now it was too late.

The door opened and in walked Jillian. She immediately looked right in their direction but seemed to be confused about what was going on because she hesitated before walking any further. She and Evon caught each other's stares, and he stood up, dropping the belt.

"What the hell is going on in here?" she said, a tinge of fear in her voice.

Evon reached out both hands. "I can explain," he said. "He was cheating on you. He was hurting you."

"*What the hell did you do*?" Jillian screamed in horror as she looked down at her husband.

Evon stood silent.

"Oh, my God…" Jillian said.

She quickly reached for the door.

"Wait!" Evon said.

Jillian swung open the door and rushed outside, Evon hurriedly following right after. By the time she'd reached the black Explorer parked in their driveway, she was fumbling for the key fob, trying to get it open. Evon grabbed her arm and she yanked away. The keys dropped to the ground as she took off across their yard.

"*Help! Somebody, help!*" she screamed.

Evon ran after her as fast as his legs would manage and caught up with her. He grabbed her arm again and she thrashed wildly.

"*Get the fuck off me!*"

"*Shhh… shut up! Stop screaming!*"

She ignored Evon's request and continued to scream. He wrapped his other arm around her and tackled her to the ground. He put his knee on the back of her head, forcing her face into the grass. Her screaming became muffled as he looked around trying to see if she had alerted the attention of any of the neighbors. When he was satisfied that she hadn't, he bent down next to her ear.

"Will you stop now? Will you let me explain? I *had* to do it!" he whispered.

Jillian still struggled underneath him, kicking her legs around trying to make contact with him enough to get him off her.

"*Stop it!*" he forcefully yelled at her.

Jillian stopped.

Evon got off her and she rose up, gasping for air. He made sure to clutch her arm as they sat next to each other in the grass.

"Now, come back inside so I can explain, *please*."

They both stood up, Evon's hand firmly gripped around her wrist, and quickly walked back toward the front door. He looked back briefly to scan the surrounding homes, halfway surprised that they hadn't alerted any neighbors. That was fine by him; he certainly wasn't going to stay outside to wait for anyone. He led the way with Jillian reluctantly following and offering some drag, although not the same kind of resistance she offered moments earlier. When they neared the back of the Explorer, Jillian noticed her keys on the ground and yanked her arm away from Evon to pick them up. Surprised by her sudden strength, he didn't react fast enough to stop her from pressing the button on the key fob that lifted the tailgate.

Jillian jumped inside and quickly closed the tailgate with a thud. She pressed the button that locked all the doors and crawled her way through until she reached the driver's seat. Evon rushed over and tried to yank open the door, only to be denied entry. He frantically started to bang on the driver's side window.

"Jillian, unlock the door, now," he said calmly.

She ignored his demand but kept her eyes on him while frantically struggling to put the key into the ignition.

Evon started to panic and began punching the window. He couldn't let her drive off. Not now. When the pain from the blows became unbearable, he stopped to look around for something to help him stop her. That's when he noticed the large, decorative rocks by the front door. He quickly ran over and picked one up.

Jillian finally inserted the key and started to turn it over when Evon returned to the car window. She got the Explorer started and put her foot on the brake to put the car in reverse right as Evon finally burst through, shattering the glass. He dropped the rock and snatched her hand off the steering wheel with one hand while pressing the unlock button on the door with his other.

Jillian started screaming again as Evon yanked open the door. He pulled on her arm until she was completely out of the car. She tried to pull away, continuing to sound a bloodcurdling alarm to anyone who might be able to help. Evon got ahold of her sweater as she frantically pulled herself away.

She wriggled just enough that Evon didn't have a firm grasp on any part of her body, just the sweater. It started to tear until finally he lost his grip and Jillian took off running once more.

Evon chased after her. When he caught up, he took hold of her with both arms and lifted her in the air. If she wouldn't follow him back inside, he would have to carry her back in. She kicked and screamed and flung wild punches trying to get loose from his grasp, but he had tapped into another level of strength and was able to withstand her attack.

She tried digging her nails into his skin but that didn't hurt him; it only made him clench her tighter. As they neared the front door again, Evon made sure to kick the car door closed.

They finally reached the front door and while still holding onto Jillian, he backed into it to shut it.

Jillian still fought mightily to get out of his grip. His strength reserves began to fade, and when he felt he could no longer maintain his hold, he took her to the ground, falling on top of her.

Jillian had a fighting spirit about her and she refused to stop screaming, even as tears streamed down her face.

Evon straddled her and tried to pin her arms above her head but she continuously fought him off. She lifted her knees up and managed to land a blow to his groin.

This shocked him and he instinctively let go of her arms to reel back from the sudden pain.

She started to slide backwards across the smooth wood flooring, never taking her eyes off him. Before she got too far, Evon reached out and grabbed her right ankle. She kicked loose and he came away with just her shoe.

He reached again and was able to get the cuff of her jeans. He pulled her toward him, the floor offering no resistance and making it easy for her to glide back to him. Evon lunged and got back on top of her. He reeled back his right arm and struck Jillian in the mouth.

Her head violently rapped against the floor and she groaned while bringing her hands up to her face because of the jolt of pain. Evon wrenched her hands away from her face and grabbed onto her throat with both hands. Only then did he notice how much blood was leaking from the hand he hit the window with.

With a new-found ferocity coursing through him, he began to choke Jillian. Her eyes got wide and started to bulge. Her hands scratched and clawed at Evon's hands as she tried to remove them from her neck. Her nails dug into his skin, making him bleed even more.

Evon had gone to a different place. Not feeling any pain. Not aware of his surroundings. Tapping into more strength than he ever thought he had. Jillian's legs shook and trembled as she tried to escape. A pained expression spread across her face as Evon squeezed harder still until finally, her hands released from his and fell to her sides.

In the moment, Evon blacked out, but when he finally snapped back and became present, he looked into her eyes, which were bloodshot. Blood from his hand was smeared across her neck and cheek. He stood up and continued to stare at Jillian's unmoving body. She was a mess from head to toe. There were blades of grass in her brunette hair, blood smudged into the pale skin of her neck and chest, and she had urinated on herself during the struggle.

She would not offer any more resistance.

Evon walked over to look at Craig's body. It was still face down and frozen in place, meaning Evon had fulfilled his duty.

Craig was the only one that was supposed to go tonight; Jillian was the one that wasn't supposed to be hurt any further.

But she didn't understand, didn't *want* to understand. She just kept screaming. Evon wasn't the bad guy. He was just trying to help, but a brief moment of rage at her unwillingness to cooperate led her to her demise earlier than either of them probably expected.

He finally started to take notice of the pain that soared through his body. The numbing effects of adrenaline had worn off. His back hurt. His legs hurt. His hand was cut up. This wasn't supposed to be a painful situation tonight. It was supposed to be a carefree, amicable get-together, but when you're called into action by Him, you act.

The living room was in complete disarray now, but Evon wasn't about to start to clean it up. The only thing he wanted to cleanse was his body at this moment. Craig *did* tell him that he could use their amenities while they were gone. Well, they were gone.

Evon decided now was as good a time as any to hop in the shower that Craig offered. Then he would rest. He pondered skipping a slumber and just leaving the house after showering, but Craig was right about what he said earlier: it was too dark outside.

FOURTEEN

The phone rang.

Or phones.

Yes, a chorus of different ringtones going off back to back.

Evon opened his eyes, lying completely still.

There went the rings again, undeniable this time.

He scanned the room. He was in Craig's basement, in the bedroom, in the bed.

He felt a chill fall over him as he sat up. He'd failed to cover himself with a blanket.

He had also failed to cover himself with any clothes.

He didn't remember lying down naked, but apparently after he finished showering, clothes were the furthest thing from his mind.

He stood up, shaking clearer thoughts into his head, and walked to the bathroom where he stood in front of the mirror staring at himself, at the scars that marked his flesh from the numerous operations in Seattle.

He ran his fingers along the raised parts of his skin that traveled across his neck and chest. They were relatively old and had healed. The ones on his hands and forearms? They were battle scars, fresh reminders of what happened last night.

The phones continued to ring upstairs.

He walked out of the bathroom and upstairs into the living room, still completely naked.

Jillian was still there on the wood flooring, right in front of the main entrance. Craig was still face down in the living room amongst his broken decorations.

There was a white cordless phone, that seemed to be out of place, affixed to the wall by the entrance to the kitchen. Phone cords connected it to the black answering machine sitting just below it on a small table. It rang again. Evon wouldn't be picking it up.

When it finally stopped, the caller left a message that played loudly over the answering machine: "This is Shelly down at the Opportunity Center. It's now 10:28 and we haven't heard from you. We've called several times and just wanted to make sure you were going to honor your commitment to serve Thanksgiving dinner. We hope everything is okay. Please call us back as soon as you can to update us on what's going on. I will call the cell number that is listed just in case you're not home. Again, please contact us at your earliest convenience. If you're already on your way down here and are just running late, please disregard this message. Thank you."

The call ended and immediately after, Evon heard a cell phone ring. It was lying on the granite countertop in the kitchen. He assumed it was Craig's phone.

People were looking for him on this special day but he wouldn't be showing up, nor would Jillian.

This meant that Evon needed to vacate the premises with some urgency. But before he could do that, he would need clothes.

Putting back on the clothes he'd worn here wasn't something he wanted to do. He went back downstairs and rummaged through the bedroom where he slept. He looked inside drawers, closets, and baskets. No clothes could be found there.

He came back upstairs and ascended another flight of steps to get to the second floor. He opened each door until he found the bedroom where the married couple once slept.

It was immaculate inside, which shouldn't have surprised him since they now did their sleeping in the living room.

There was a large walk-in closet to his right. Evon peered inside to find anything he could wear that would fit. After considering the array of options, he settled upon a pair of black jeans that looked unworn and a navy-blue shirt that had the U.S. Navy insignia on it. The shirt fit snuggly but the jeans had just enough room in them to be comfortable.

Evon considered the weather and decided to take an olive-green bomber jacket, too. His makeover was almost complete, but he needed something for his head and feet as well, so he decided to grab a Supersonics cap and a pair of weathered, wheat-colored boots.

He looked into a large mirror that was attached to the back of their bedroom door; he was satisfied with his new appearance.

After finishing, Evon went back downstairs to the main level. He looked at a clock hanging on the wall: 11:01. He'd spent entirely too much time shuffling through the closet and needed to leave the home fast.

Even though he was calm and had his capacities about him, the last thing he needed was to be met by police when people from the Opportunity Center inevitably sent someone over for a wellness check. The police, or anyone else for that matter, wouldn't understand the scene that occurred here. They were governed by *man's* law. Evon followed those of a much higher order.

Evon entered the bathroom to gather his backpack from where he left it the night before. Moving to the kitchen, he pocketed Craig's cell phone, weighing the merits of borrowing it. But after a few minutes of letting it stew in his pocket, he decided against it. It would be an impromptu tracking device and he didn't need that, either.

He went back down into the basement and grabbed the silver laptop that Craig said he could use. The charger was attached and he took that, too. He stopped to look around, making absolutely sure he had everything he needed. He came across his pile of soiled clothes that were on the bathroom floor. He considered balling them up and taking them with him but decided against it; there would be no consequence to them being left and discovered.

After his business was finished downstairs, he went back to the kitchen because he would need a small meal and something to drink for his trek back to the hotel. He felt like the best thing to do was walk back. He could take the Explorer, but that, too, would be a mistake.

The kitchen had a faint aroma of all the food that had been prepared for this holiday but would not be eaten. There were pots on the stove, cold to the touch, filled with yams, corn, green beans, and other delicacies. Still in the oven was the turkey and ham Craig kept checking on. On the center island were empty grocery bags and the desserts that had been prepared.

Evon opened the refrigerator and decided to take an unopened pack of sliced oven-roasted turkey. On the shelf underneath were bottles of water. He grabbed five of them. He went around the kitchen opening every cabinet until he reached one where the bread was kept. He took two loaves down and stuffed all the contents into his backpack. It was now time to leave.

As he walked to the front door, the phone rang again. He knew who it was and he ignored it as he walked outside, closing the door behind him.

He heard the soft rumbling of an engine and looked at the Explorer that was in the driveway. He walked over to it, placing a hand on its warm hood as he stepped on some of the broken window glass that fell out. He looked inside. The keys were still in the ignition and the car had run idle all through the night. Evon reached in and turned off the car, pocketing the keys.

Although this was a different situation, it made him think of the time where he did the same thing with that Mustang on that rainy, April day months ago. He had no intentions of taking this car, though.

He took a moment to assess the weather, breathing in a deep breath. Many a song was written about Thanksgiving Day. About how the wind should sting the toes and bite the nose. But it was calm out, barely a breeze. It was cool out, too, but not unbearably so. The sky wasn't without clouds but they weren't the types that foretold of impending rain or snow. The sun wasn't exactly shining; instead, it was a muted light, one that struggled to force its way through the clouds and reflect off the nearby ocean.

No cars were driving on the road, which was a good thing. Evon didn't want anyone to notice him leaving and being able to provide a detailed description when they were asked by the investigators, who would surely come at some point in the day.

Feeling satisfied that all his business was complete on West Beach Road, he thought it was a good time to finally leave. It was more crucial than ever before to finish what he *really* came back to town to do because time was of the essence and Sunny was waiting for her daddy.

FIFTEEN

Deon and Flip were sitting down on a couple of rickety milk crates when Chastity pulled up in her silver Rover. They had their coats on, even though the weather was tolerable enough on this Thanksgiving Day; a rare occurrence in these parts.

She stopped her car in the same spot as the day before, only this time she didn't get out. Even though she and Deon made eye contact, acknowledging that she had arrived, she decided to noisily blare her car horn several times.

Deon peered over to the passenger seat, where Sunny was getting a kick out of her mother's antics. Everyone in the camp looked on at the commotion, but once deciding it wasn't worth their concern, returned to their previous activities.

Chastity rolled down her window. "You guys ready?"

Flip started to walk toward the car.

"As ready as we'll ever be!" Deon said as he followed Flip.

He got in on the side closest to Sunny, Flip got in on the other.

"Flip and Giddyup!" Sunny exclaimed.

"And hi to you, too, Sunny," Deon said.

"Ready for some home cooked grub?" Chastity asked.

"Yeah, especially since we're not having to cook anything," Flip said.

"Good! Well, let's get outta here! You guys have a curfew?" Chastity joked.

Deon and Flip returned silence.

"Well… alright then, on we go!" Chastity replied.

She put the Range Rover in reverse and they backed out onto the road.

"Where I live is going to take a few minutes to get to, so hunker down. You guys wanna listen to any tunes or something?"

"I think we'll be just fine," Deon replied. "Sometimes silence is good, you know?"

"Sure…" Chastity said.

As Deon had noticed before, Sunny was buckled in up front, transfixed to the views just outside her window in seemingly utter amazement of the world that passed them by.

He'd deliberately sat behind her again so he could, maybe through osmosis, and without any words being spoken, understand what it was that made her so happy.

He could tell there was something different about her, and his best guess was that she had some developmental… uniqueness. Chastity even hinted at such when they'd first met in the grocery store, but she didn't go so far as to confirm it. He wasn't going to ask about it though; he didn't feel like it was his place to do so. Maybe he'd subtly nudge Chastity toward telling him about it once they'd gotten a little more comfortable with each other later.

Deon wondered if Chastity let Sunny dress herself because she was wearing black leggings, which weren't all that alarming considering that they were standard fare for today's youth, but she was also wearing pink flip-flops which didn't in any way fit the accepted dress for the season.

Uncanny.

She did have on a neon-green hoodie, though, so there was that.

Deon took his attention off her so that he could stare out the window, taking in the images instead of trying to live vicariously through her during the ride.

They passed by buildings he was very familiar with, having traversed the city, scavenging and exploring. He saw old buildings that were decades older than he was, new ones with all-glass fronts that returned the reflection of the cars and onlookers as they moved past. The number of pedestrians out at this time was scant. Traffic was almost non-existent. Thanksgiving was a day that the vast majority of Oak Harbor residents took seriously and stayed indoors embracing the company of family and friends.

This made him think of the past Thanksgivings he had as a kid. It was always special to him because he was lucky enough to get *two.* His white mother's side of the family did things a little different than Deon's black father's side.

Back when he was a kid, things weren't unlike how they were now. Schools gave the kids and families roughly a week off from classes to accommodate travel plans and have time to digest the food that came from several days of feasting. Deon's family would always travel by car to Oklahoma, which took them almost two complete days of driving, to spend two days with his father's side, before coming back to Seattle to spend some time with his mother's side.

The food offered as Thanksgiving dinner was unique to both sides. The dishes varied to such a degree that you would think you were having two entirely different holidays.

The atmosphere matched the variation in dishes, too, because his mom's family wasn't exactly warm to Deon's father; yet, they were more than friendly to Deon.

He didn't feel any resentment toward the chilly reception his mother's side's gave to his father, but Deon never forgot it, either. He vowed to never be that cold to people who were different than him. Although he had some bumps along the way as he grew up, he thought he did a dutiful job of fulfilling that vow.

His reminiscing of the past was interrupted by a sudden change in driving conditions. The sound from the undercarriage transitioned from the soft whirring of tires on a smooth, paved road to the rumbling sound of dirt and loose gravel being kicked up.

He didn't know the exact moment the surrounding environment had changed, but it had as well. Gone were the trappings of the inner city; the retail shops, the grocery stores he had frequented on so many occasions, the sidewalks, the street lamps, the stoplights. They had all been replaced by a long, dirt and gravel road, barren oaks, full pines, and tall weeds and grasses. Deon couldn't identify any building but one: a quaint, bile-green, one-story home. There was a long driveway that led from the road to the lonely domain. Chastity pulled onto it and crept slowly toward the house.

Deon looked around and was able to discern some poles with power lines connected to the home. The unflattering green he identified on the home was vinyl siding. The roof was covered with flat, gray shingles. A brick, unfinished chimney poked out from the top, with burnt-orange rust stains adorning the gutters that were attached to the roof. The front and back yards were wide and open, with barely any trees growing close to the home. The few that existed were small in stature. He imagined that this afforded whoever's home this was a wide-open area in which to roam. There was a small, faded-red shed roughly twenty yards from the right side of the house; it looked to be barely standing and in disrepair.

Chastity brought the Rover to a halt.

"Are we picking somebody else up? Or are we stopping at someone else's home for dinner?" Deon confusedly asked as he unfastened his seatbelt.

"This is *my* home," Chastity replied. Then, looking over at Sunny, said, "*Our* home."

Sunny returned a toothy grin.

Chastity turned off the ignition. Everyone filed out of the car.

"So, you and your daughter live out here all by yourselves? All this land is yours?" Flip asked.

"Yep," she replied.

Deon thought having all this land gave Sunny lots of space to run around and be active, if she was even that type of child. Deon guessed she was a more passive kid, content to stare at and scrutinize the beauty of nature rather than physically experience it.

"Ok… so… what about this Range Rover?" he said, pointing to the car. "This doesn't exactly scream quiet, country living."

"It's called quiet, frugal living. I can be flashy with the car but be cozy and just comfortable enough with the home."

"And you work at a freakin' grocery store," Flip said.

"That's right," she said. "We've got more than enough money to live on for a while, but I need something to do with my time while Sunny here is at school."

She grabbed Sunny's hand and walked toward the front door.

"Did you hit the lottery or something?" Deon asked.

She paused a moment before replying. "You could say that."

"Well, which is it?"

"I *really* don't wanna talk about it right now, Deon. Is that ok?"

He dropped the subject and they walked inside.

What greeted them was a scene out of a senior citizen's dream.

There was a floral-patterned wallpaper plastered all throughout the living room, and a thick, brown carpet covered the floor. The sole couch in the room was checkered with shades of burgundy and dark green and was festooned with several throw pillows that had images of wolves and other wildlife on them.

In front of it was a cream-colored wooden coffee table with a glass top. Along the wall was a spot that had brick behind it where a black stovepipe fireplace with tile underneath jutted into the ceiling. The windows were adorned with white, lacy curtains that let light almost completely filter through the house. Against the wall adjacent to what Deon guessed was the opening to the kitchen was a black metal TV stand upon which stood a medium-sized flat screen TV. In various spots all over the wall were framed pictures of animals, along with pictures of Sunny and Chastity in different, smiling poses.

Sunny ran up to the TV and turned it on before plopping down on the couch.

Chastity walked into the kitchen, amidst the smell of already prepared food floating through the air.

Deon and Flip followed suit.

"You don't get scared living out here all alone?" Deon asked.

"Not at all. I picked it for a reason. I can clearly see and hear anything and anybody that comes to disturb our peace and quiet from yards away."

"But you're only one woman," Flip said. "And don't get me wrong, but I don't think your daughter offers much when it comes to defense."

"She doesn't have to," Chastity said. "I've got a bodyguard that will protect us if worse comes to worse."

Deon and Flip looked at each other.

"A bodyguard?" Deon asked.

"Yes. He's black and *very*, very powerful."

The two men looked around.

"Is he here?" Flip asked.

"Yep, he's in the back. In my bedroom."

Deon stared at her incredulously. "What's his name?"

"Thirty-eight Special," she answered.

Flip and Deon exchanged glances again, satisfied with the answer and certain that Chastity was well-prepared to fend off any kind of attack with a weapon such as that.

"And you two are asking all these questions because…"

"Oh! No, no," Flip started. "You don't think we—"

"We're just curious, not testing if you could protect yourself from an assault from two bums, if that's what you're thinking," Deon interjected.

"Uh huh. Now that that's out the way," she started, "dinner is almost ready. I had to go out and get a few more things earlier to be able to feed you guys. I originally only had enough for Sunny and I. She doesn't ever clean her plate, though, so the food is gonna last us a few days anyway. You guys can make yourselves at home. I'm gonna finish up a few things in here and then we'll be all set!" She paused for a moment. "Kind of more like a brunch than a dinner, huh?" she said.

Flip walked out of the kitchen and sat down with Sunny, who was watching some kid's show on TV.

Deon stayed in the kitchen with Chastity. He wanted to spark up a conversation to get some answers to the questions that had been nagging at him.

Chastity was lifting lids off some pots, letting steam waft up to her face as she stirred some of the contents.

"So… you like living out here in the country?"

"Yeah. It's not so bad. It's serene, less busy. Away from all the craziness that goes on out there. I know it doesn't seem like it but it's scenic out here, too. All the pretty trees, the wild animals that walk through here sometimes. Sunny really likes it. I have to explain to her sometimes that she can't go out and play with *those* kinds of animals, though. She doesn't understand that they're not like the ones she reads about in those damn kiddie books or sees on tv."

"About Sunny..." Deon started.

"Yeah?"

"She's... different, isn't she?"

Chastity sighed and turned away from the stove to face him. "What's it to you?"

"I was just wondering. If you don't want to talk about it then it's ok."

She turned back to the stove.

"Well, like I said when we first met, Sunny is special. She has Fragile-X Syndrome."

"What the hell is that?"

In a mocking tone of a doctor, Chastity said, "Fragile-X Syndrome is a genetic disorder characterized by mild intellectual disabilities and may include abnormal facial features as well as symptoms that align with those found in children with autism. That's how the doctor and all the papers broke it down to me when I found out. That's part of the reason I moved us out here and away from the Emerald City. I think she'd thrive a little better in a smaller environment. Oh, and this Fragile-X shit? You see it a lot more in boys. Very rare in girls."

"Why is that?"

"Because girls have two X chromosomes. That extra one compensates for the damaged one."

A pall of silence fell on the kitchen, the only audible sounds were that of sizzling food, Chastity stirring and scraping, and sounds from the TV in the other room.

Deon noticed a solitary tear streaking down Chastity's face.

"I guess I got lucky," she said.

"I didn't mean to strike a nerve."

"No, no, it's ok. Like I said, I'm lucky. She's been a little surprise in every sense of the word."

She reached into the oven to retrieve a turkey that had been inside warming and sat it down in the middle of the glass kitchen table.

"Was she… not planned?" Deon asked.

She grabbed a large carving knife and began to slice up the turkey.

"No. She wasn't planned."

"Just kind of a wild night or something?"

Chastity slammed the knife down on the counter. "You know, you ask a lot of questions, don't you?" she burst.

"I'm sorry! I'm sorry. I can take a hint."

Embarrassed, Deon started for the living room as she picked up the knife to finish slicing away at the turkey. He didn't mean to set her off, it was just that his initial curiosity led to a string of other questions.

"Come and get it!" she yelled, some agitation in her voice.

Sunny jumped up and squealed with excitement as she sprinted for the kitchen only a few feet away. Deon stayed put and waited for Flip to join him.

There just so happened to be four chairs at the kitchen table, enough for everyone to be seated. All four were of different makes and models: one was small, pink, and plastic, presumably for Sunny's use only; one was made of wood with a dark stain that hadn't been spread evenly over the entire chair; and the other two were a mixture of flimsy metal and tattered seat cushions; Deon and Flip chose those.

Chastity reached into her cabinets and pulled out four plates, one of which was plastic and pink. It was partitioned into three sections, definitely made for small children.

Flip elbowed Deon in the side. "That one's yours," he whispered.

With Flip to his right, closest to the sink, and Sunny to his left, closest to the fridge, Deon was well positioned to study Chastity who would sit directly across from him once she got done making the plates.

She made Sunny's first, cutting her a small slice of turkey and ham. She filled the smaller sections of the plate with sides; green beans and candied yams. She drizzled some brown gravy over the top of Sunny's turkey and handed her the plate with a small fork.

"Dig in, honey."

Sunny did as she was told and busily went about her plate of food, starting with the yams.

Chastity grabbed another plate.

"Do you guys have the appetite for a little bit of everything?"

"Yes, ma'am," Flip said.

"Please, with the ma'am stuff," she scoffed. "I'm only thirty-three."

"*Thirty-three*? Deon here is only thirty himself!"

"Knock it off, man!"

"Speaking of which, where's your husband at?" Flip asked Chastity.

She ignored him and continued to fill their two plates with food.

"Hello?"

"I heard you loud and clear. I'm choosing not to answer. Is that ok?"

Flip nodded and looked at Deon who gestured for him to zip it.

While she was finishing their plates, Deon looked over at Sunny as she gobbled down her food. She seemed ravenous, as if she hadn't eaten in a while. They caught each other's eyes and Sunny smiled at him while chewing a mouth full of everything on her plate. Deon smiled back.

"Mommy! I need a drink!" she shouted.

"Baby, I'm making our friends' plates right now. Wait just a minute."

Sunny didn't reply; she just kept on chewing away.

Deon got up from his seat.

"What would you like?" he asked her.

"Coke!"

He nodded and opened their fridge.

Amongst the bottles of water and jugs of tea, milk, and orange juice, the only other soft drinks that were there were various fruit flavors and root beer.

"Um… I'm not sure you guys have any Coke left," he told Chastity.

"Just grab something brown and fizzy. That's Coke to her," she said.

Deon grabbed a can of root beer and popped the tab open. He handed it to Sunny who told him thank you and took several long gulps to wash down her food.

He sat back down and waited for Chastity to get done making their plates.

"Mommy, I need a drink, too!" Flip said.

This evoked a loud chuckle from Sunny that was broken up by a rumbling burp.

Chastity brought over their plates and sat them down in front of each of them.

"*Excuse you*!" she said to her daughter. "Flip, you be a big boy and get a drink yourself."

After getting up to grab an orange-flavored soda, he sat down and dug into his plate along with Deon.

The kitchen was utterly silent except for the sounds of Sunny chewing and slurping.

Chastity sat down with her plate of food, which had miniscule portions in comparison to the plates she'd made for the two men in the house.

She dabbled about with her food, occasionally looking over to Sunny to see where she was at with her brunch. When she noticed that Sunny had cleaned her plate, going against the comment she'd made earlier, Chastity asked her if she wanted anymore food. When Sunny said yes, Chastity paused her eating and made sure her daughter had more added to her plate. This time it was a little more turkey and a small scoop of mashed potatoes and corn. Sunny wasted no time devouring her second serving.

Everyone continued eating for several minutes in the silence that had enveloped the dining table. Sunny pushed along a single kernel of corn on her plate. Deon and Flip had cleaned theirs completely and were feeling very thankful for Chastity and even more so that they didn't have to cook—something they would have done for the entire homeless camp had Chastity not extended her offer. Chastity sat at her end of the table with her fingers interlocked, resting in front of her plate.

"Does anyone have any room for dessert? All I've got is pumpkin pie. And no, it's not homemade."

Sunny's hand shot up high in the air.

"Me and Flip and Giddyup want some!" she yelped.

"Yeah, and extra whipped cream!" Flip bellowed after her.

They gave each other high fives as Chastity looked on and smiled.

After they all scarfed down their pie that was mostly whipped topping, Flip asked Chastity if he could make himself at home by lying on the couch to take a nap, to which she obliged. They'd been there for more than an hour at this point, which was more than enough time to let the tryptophan flood through the bloodstreams. Deon thought he might want a nap as well, but of course, that would mean he'd be on the floor on the old carpet since Flip snatched the more comfortable spot.

He and Sunny sat at the table while Chastity poured herself a glass of red wine.

"Well, we know what Flip is gonna be doing for a while. What are you getting ready to do?" he asked her.

"*This* mother is gonna retire to her room for a little bit," she said, raising her glass in a toast.

"But what about Sunny and me?"

"I can pour you a drink if you'd like, and Sunny can have another Coke, how 'bout that?"

Deon started to reply but was interrupted.

"I know, I know. You're not talking about the drink. I think Sunny has taken a liking to you, so I'm sure you'll figure something out. Go play in her room with her or something, but *I'm* gonna take advantage of any free time I can get!"

"Wait," Deon said, "you're ok with that? Me hanging out with Sunny?"

"Yes, because I have a feeling. Mother's intuition. I know you remember my bodyguard and I know you're not stupid. Besides, Sunny knows what to do in case you try anything."

"I would nev–," he started before Sunny got up from the table, grabbed him by the hand, and with all her might, dragged him down a short, narrow hall to her room. A few steps away was an open door that revealed a bigger, modest looking room that could only be Chastity's.

She followed them down the hall and peeked into Sunny's room.

"My room is right here," she said, pointing to her room. "If you need anything, *don't*."

Chastity partially closed the door, leaving open a crack, before walking away and doing the same with her own bedroom door.

Pink was a theme with Sunny, for the walls of her room were painted that way. It was a departure from what he could see of the rest of the house, with the wallpaper plastered throughout. She had a twin-size bed that was pushed up against the wall next to the only window; it was no surprise what color the sheets and blanket were.

Nearest to the door was a small desk that had a lamp on top. Deon tilted his head to look inside and saw paper, an assortment of pencils, crayons, and markers. A recent piece of art she'd finished was next to the lamp and seemed to show a crudely drawn brown, four-legged animal that was chewing on a tuft of grass. Or maybe it was a bush. He couldn't really tell for sure, but it was some kind of vegetation and it was green.

He picked up the artwork and asked her what it was. She said it was a bear eating berries.

That cleared things up.

Sunny sat down on her bed and pulled out a tablet that was tucked away under one of the two pillows she had. Deon stood there in the middle of the diminutive room, feeling like his head was too close to the low ceiling.

While she happily tapped away at some game on her tablet, he continued to look around. To his left there was a closet that had a long, embroidered curtain draped over it to hide the contents. Against the wall to his right was a short, six-drawer dresser that had a mirror. Two of the drawers were half pulled out with jumbled up clothes hanging out.

Sunny started laughing to herself. She was having a blast with whatever game she was playing on the tablet, leaving Deon without any entertainment himself.

"Hey, Sunny, how old are you?"

She took her hands away from the tablet and held up a five and a one.

Deon knew she wasn't suggesting he add the fingers, making her six-years-old, but he instead deduced that she was actually fifteen.

"So… what kinds of things do you like to do?" he asked awkwardly, not knowing exactly how to talk to a teenaged girl, let alone one with Fragile-X.

She held up the tablet to show him what she was playing and smiled. "I like games on my tablet!" she exclaimed.

"Well, that's pretty cool! What kinds of games are on there?"

She didn't answer.

Deon walked over and sat down on the bed next to her. It let out a loud groan, protesting his weight.

"Can I see?" he asked, reaching for the tablet.

She pulled away, never losing her grip on the device, nor the wide grin on her face.

He sat there with her for a few minutes, leaning over to watch her play various games. There was one where she was trying to assemble a set of colorful pipes to let water drain to the bottom. Another game tasked her with smashing fruit as fast as she could.

Having nothing to do himself except be a spectator, Deon got up and walked over to her art desk.

"Do you like to draw? I'm sure we can have fun doing that."

He was hoping to prompt her into something else or it was going to be a long day until Chastity was sober enough to drive him and Flip home. Sunny set her tablet down and rushed over to the art desk with him.

"Yeah! I like drawing sometimes."

Now he felt like he was getting somewhere.

"Awesome! I like drawing too," he said. "Maybe we can draw together. How does that sound?"

Sunny pulled out the chair at the desk and sat down. Deon knelt down beside her.

The desk had an opening that drawing materials fit into, and she pulled out a big, white sheet of paper, laying it down in a landscape position. She grabbed a series of colored pencils and began drawing.

Deon had hoped he could pull her away from her tablet so they could draw together but once again, he found himself having to live vicariously through the deft hand movements of a fifteen-year-old girl. He could complain and try to nudge his way in, but he'd been denied before and had learned his lesson to let her do her thing. When she wanted his participation, she would surely ask.

She started with a yellow pencil in her right hand, outlining what appeared to be a bright, yellow sun in the top right-hand corner. She made sure to give it an abundant number of rays, drawing out long, straight lines from its center. She filled in the outline with yellow, then grabbed an orange pencil to blend in the colors. It wasn't the best-looking sun he'd ever seen but then again, he wasn't much of an artist himself to offer much in the way of a critique.

Next, she grabbed a green pencil with her left hand and scribbled green lines along the bottom of the page. She continued doing this until there was barely any white space on the bottom margin to be seen. She put down the green colored pencil and picked out a brown one. Deon could guess what she'd draw next.

Sure enough, Sunny drew a tree on the left-hand side, topping it off with some green for the leaves. She exchanged that pencil for a red one and made small, round shapes overlapping the leaves.

Apples.

After finishing her small orchard, she moved on to drawing some figures standing on top of the grass. They turned out to be a man and a woman positioned next to each other. They didn't hold hands or even look at each other. Their empty faces stared directly at their creator and her bystander.

After giving them clothes so they didn't resemble the famous couple of Eden, she set about giving them facial features. On the woman, she placed a big smile with a black color. On the man, she gave a frown.

Satisfied with her creation, she put the pencils down and stared at the paper.

"Aren't you going to put in any clouds or pretty flowers?" Deon asked.

She shook her head no.

"Ok. Well, tell me, who are these people in the picture?"

"That's me!" she said, pointing to the sun in the right corner.

"Oh yeah, because you're Sunny, right?" he said, lightly patting her on the back. "And *these* two people?"

"That's my mommy and daddy," she said.

"Oh, ok. Well, obviously I know your mom. She looks happy here. Probably because she gets to eat some apples, huh?"

Sunny let out a hearty chuckle.

"I don't know your dad, but he looks kinda sad, like he doesn't get to eat any apples, ha-ha. What's his name anyway?"

"He's sad because he doesn't feel good," she said. "His name is daddy, but mommy calls him Evon."

SIXTEEN

Deon burst into Chastity's room.

"*Hey*! What the hell are you doing?" she cried out.

Deon shut the door behind him. He was thinking their exchange would get very heated and he didn't want to upset Sunny or cause too much of a commotion.

"Were you ever gonna tell me that Evon Brisk was the father of your child?"

Chastity was propped up in her bed, watching TV. She sat down the glass of wine that was in her hand and dropped her head.

"What all did she tell you?" she asked.

"Just that Evon is her dad and he was sick and that you didn't like him."

"Wait, how do you even know him? And what's it matter to you anyway?"

"The guy used to hang around in Dreg City all the time. He disappeared for a while and then he came back a few days ago. I was told he jumped off Deception Pass Bridge and tried to kill himself."

"I knew he'd fallen on hard times but not that he hung out with *you* guys. And I know he jumped off that damn bridge. Who do you think they called to come look at him in the hospital just in case he died?"

"Were you guys *married*?"

"Yeah, we were. Briefly. One of the biggest mistakes I've ever made. And before you ask, irreconcilable differences. He had to pay me alimony. I got it in one lump sum so I could just be done with him. I didn't even want to let him visit Sunny at first but she loves her dad. Then one day, he just dropped off the face of the planet. The last time I saw him he was in a coma in Seattle."

"Well, he awoke from that coma but he damn sure didn't seem like his old self. He came and ran off with one of our friends..." *Shit. Ruthie*, Deon thought. "You haven't seen him around? At *all*?" he asked.

"No! I told you already, Sunny and I visited him in the hospital and that was months ago!"

Deon felt a pang of guilt hit him, like a blow straight to the gut.

Here he was indulging himself with a hot meal, in a warm home, in the company of others while Ruthie was still out there.

Who knew where she was or what she was doing, but she wasn't where she belonged. She was supposed to be enjoying this day surrounded by people who cared about her. He and Flip had brushed off the fact that she'd been gone so long without a trace—even when they felt something was off—and hadn't even tried to go looking for her.

That nonchalance would stop now.

"We need to go," he said.

"Go where? You want me to take you back home?"

"Yes! We need to go back there, *now*."

"In case you haven't noticed, I'm not drunk but I *have* been drinking," she said, pointing to the half-finished glass of wine and the bottle she'd brought into the room with her.

Deon felt ashamed for making that kind of demand, it was selfish and dangerous, but there was no other alternative and he wasn't going to wait for her to sober up.

"Look, I don't care right now. Do whatever you need to do to get yourself in enough shape to get us there, but we're leaving."

Deon exited the room and walked into the living room. Flip was lying in the fetal position on the couch, sound asleep. Deon grabbed him by the shoulder and shook him awake.

"Flip, get up. We're leaving. We're leaving right now."

Flip sat up and tried to shake off his slumber but was slightly confused.

"Man, what the hell? What's going on? I've been asleep that damn long?"

"No, it's only been a little bit, but we gotta go."

Chastity walked out of her room.

"You gonna tell me what's going on?" Flip asked.

Deon pointed to Chastity. "What's going on is that *she's* Evon's ex-wife!"

"Evon from the camp?"

"Yes! And the Evon that still hasn't come back with Ruthie, which is why we're leaving."

Flip reached for his shoes that he'd slipped off before he laid down.

Sunny came out of her bedroom holding the artwork that was the catalyst to Deon's newfound sense of urgency.

"Mommy! Look what I drawed!" she said.

"That's nice, baby. Put that back in your room. We're gonna take our friends back home. It's time for them to leave," Chastity said. "Look, at least take some food back with you."

Deon waved her off; he no longer had an appetite.

When everyone was ready, they went outside and got into Chastity's Rover. They put their seatbelts on and she drove back in the direction they'd come.

The whole way there, Deon sat on needles, half-paranoid that Chastity would arouse the suspicions of any police, half-anxious to get back so he and Flip could pin down Ruthie's whereabouts.

Deon noticed that Chastity was driving carefully and more slowly than she had when she'd picked them up. He felt bad that he was forcing her to take such a huge risk by getting behind the wheel of a car considering what she'd imbibed, but he was deadly serious about getting out of there one way or the other.

There was a palpable tension in the car, thick enough for a proverbial knife to cut through.

As before, Sunny didn't take her attention off what was going on outside, but this time Deon noticed that she was no longer smiling. She was in tune to the anxiety that flowed from the seat behind her and her face showed it.

After some time, they arrived back in the Dregs, all without attracting the attention of any of Oak Harbor's finest.

Deon and Flip unfastened their seatbelts and prepared to get out.

"Look, I don't know what's going on or what's got you all riled up about Evon, but I hope everything's ok," Chastity said before they exited.

She reached into her glove compartment box and retrieved a small notepad and pen. She wrote her phone number and address on a sheet and handed it to Deon.

"If you need anything, please, let me know. Ok?"

Deon nodded, folded the piece of paper without looking at it, and put it in his back pocket. "Before I forget, thanks for the meal."

"Ditto!" Flip shouted as he walked away from the car.

"Mommy, can I go with Giddyup? *Please*?" Sunny asked.

"No, Sunny. You're coming back home with mommy."

Sunny looked away, dejected.

"I don't own a phone myself, but if I need to get ahold of you, I'll find a way," Deon said. "I'm really sorry to have to cut things short so abruptly, but me and Flip have some serious business to attend to. Considering that, I wouldn't feel right staying at your place just hanging out. Maybe I'll tell you about it later, but now's not the time."

"Well, you were doing just fine until I left you alone with Sunny."

"Yeah," he said. "I know."

***

Deon and Flip filtered through the camp, interrupting the meals and questioning the patrons about whether they'd seen Evon or Ruthie return. Every answer they got was a "no," but the question itself raised the hackles on everyone they'd asked.

They assured everyone, even though it was a comforting lie, that they didn't need to be alarmed.

Yet.

Satisfied that they'd exhausted their search in the Dregs, Deon and Flip had only one other place that they knew they could look: The Dutch Inn. They remembered hearing Ruthie and Evon talking about this before they walked away the other day. It would only make sense to check there, but it was a few blocks away and they weren't sure how much help they'd get on a holiday. However, the alternative was sitting on their hands impatiently, an option that was quickly dismissed.

During their walk there, Deon and Flip were quiet, pensive, knowing that the situation they faced was getting serious. He was guilt-ridden over the fact that they'd enjoyed themselves, albeit momentarily, while Ruthie was still out there somewhere, probably needing help.

Deon tried to tell himself to calm down, that he'd arrive at the inn, find Ruthie, and she'd chide him for being such a worry-wart. Then, they could go on about their day. Maybe he could even find a phone and call Chastity and ask her to pick them all up for another round of her cooking. But in the event that they came up emptyhanded, he wasn't sure what other course of action he'd take.

Standing about thirty-yards away, they arrived in the vicinity of The Dutch Inn. It looked dead. It was devoid of any discernible human activity and there wasn't a car in sight in the small parking lot.

He worried that it was closed for some reason and they would have to anxiously wait until the next day to return, but he motioned for Flip to march ahead with him as they decided to at least peer inside the windows of the lobby.

As they got closer, they noticed that there wasn't a sign that said the place was either open or closed, but they did see a portly man walking around inside.

Deon tried the door. The place was open.

He told Flip to wait outside while he talked to the man inside. He figured he'd be more willing to talk to an older person.

When he walked inside, the man was moving some chairs around the lobby and looked to be doing some general cleaning.

"Hey there, can I help ya?" he said.

"Yes, sir. I'm hoping you can help me find a couple of friends of mine that went missing?"

"Missing? Hmmm… Well, I guess I'll try to help you out as best as I can, although I'm not the detective type. Were they staying here or something?"

"Yeah, it's an older guy who looked kind of… scarred up and walked funny. He probably had a woman with him. She's kind of older too, but looks pretty normal compared to the other guy."

The man scratched his hairless chin and then snickered to himself.

"*That* guy… yeah, I know who you're talkin' about. Kind of a weird fella, wanted to argue with me about the damn price of the rooms. He came back here the other night and had some woman with him, probably the one you're talkin' about."

"That's what I thought. Is he still around? It's pretty urgent that I get ahold of them."

"I'm pretty sure he is. He hasn't checked out yet, so he's probably in his room or something I imagine."

"What room is he in?" Deon asked.

"Ah, hold on real quick."

The man walked behind the counter and looked at a peg board attached to the wall. There were several keys hanging from it, but there were some empty spots.

"Yep, he's in room 14. In the back," he said pointing with his thumb.

"Thank you, sir. Really, thank you."

"Hey, not a problem! Glad I can help out!"

Deon walked back outside where Flip was pacing back and forth.

"So?" Flip asked.

"The guy in there said they were definitely here the other night, and Evon hasn't checked out, so he's still here. They're in room 14. Nothing left for us to do but to go check it out."

"Right behind you."

Deon and Flip walked to the back of the hotel. Deon felt anxious, and he knew Flip had to feel the same way, too.

He was hoping everything was ok, that he'd knock on the door, Evon would let him in, and they'd walk back home with Ruthie. No problems, no arguments, no hassles. That was the *hope*.

They reached room 14 and Deon knocked on the door. It was a solid door and didn't reverberate much.

They waited for a little bit, looking around at their surroundings. When they received no answer, Deon decided to knock for a second time, harder, more urgently.

There was one window for the room and Flip put his face up to the glass to try to peer inside, but there were curtains obstructing his view.

"Should we try again?" Flip asked.

Deon stood silent. He felt his heart rate start to pick up. His hands started to dampen and he wiped them on his pants.

"You knock on the window while I do the door," Deon said.

Flip balled his fist and pounded on the window with the flat side. The window shook and vibrated against the force of his hand. Deon did the same thing against the door but a lot more forcefully than the first two times.

He put his ear up to the door, hoping he'd hear someone coming or some rustling inside, but could hear nothing through the wood.

They repeated the process for several minutes, but they were starting to realize it was a fruitless endeavor.

"Dammit! Flip, you stay here in case someone answers the door," Deon said. "I'm gonna go up front and see if that guy will let us inside."

"You really think he'd let us in someone else's hotel room? Even if we do know them?"

"I don't know, but we're obviously not getting anywhere at this rate."

Flip stayed by the room door, hunched over, peering as hard as he could through the window as if the harder he stared, the better the chance the curtains might magically move.

When Deon got back to the lobby, he asked the man inside if he could come open the door.

"No. As a matter of fact, *hell,* no, buddy," he said emphatically. "I can tell you where your friends are at, but no chance of me letting you in there unless you're the police, my friend. I can't just open doors to my guest's rooms to anybody who asks. That's a good way to lose business, business I'm barely getting in the first place. Nope, I don't give a damn if you know 'em or not."

"Sir, I don't think you understand. This might be serious!"

"I don't think *you* understand. I'm not opening that door. But I'll tell you what, you have a few options: leave and come back later, sit here and wait for your friends, or, if it's so damn serious, call the police. Short of those, I don't know what to tell ya."

Frustrated at being stonewalled by both the locked room and the innkeeper, Deon walked out of the lobby to see if Flip had any new developments. When he got back to the room, Flip was ramming his shoulder into the door, grimacing and grunting loudly with every attempt.

"Flip, what the hell are you doing?"

"Pounding on the goddamn door and window wasn't working. Maybe we need to force ourselves in."

Deon grabbed his shoulder and yanked him away from the door.

"Just stop. The guy up front said he's not gonna let us in. Said we could either come back, wait, or call the cops."

"Well, what do you think we should do? I sure as hell don't wanna wait around all day, but if we leave and come back, we might miss him again."

"That just leaves getting the cops involved, but I have a funny feeling they won't be too helpful."

"Yeah? And what makes you think that?"

"Because, Flip," Deon started, "Look at us. We're fucking homeless. *They're* fucking homeless. Cops don't really give a shit about homeless people turning up missing because it's to be expected. We're just junkies and bums to them. They'll just chalk it up to being part of the lifestyle. Hell, you know as well as I do that they probably want us all to just disappear, makes life easier for them. That leaves us as the only ones who will get any wheels in motion."

"So then, what should we do?"

Deon started to walk away.

"We're gonna have to take matters into our own hands. But first, we need to head back to the Dregs."

SEVENTEEN

During his walk back from Craig's house, Evon strode along the side of the road proudly, with his chest out and his head held high. Doing anything less not only meant that he was ashamed or abashed, which he wasn't, but it also would draw attention to himself from passersby. Being hunched over and closing your body off meant you were trying to protect yourself, fight something off, become smaller, and none of these described his current state.

To say that he wasn't somewhat paranoid, though, when he saw several cop cars drive by in the opposite direction, would be disingenuous. That reminded him to dig inside his pocket and toss the car keys into the bushes.

He would never be able to know if the policemen were on their usual patrols or if they'd been alerted to Craig and Jillian's absence, but either of those possibilities wasn't what bothered him. It was the prospect of being stopped and apprehended for any kind of questioning that made his stroll that much swifter.

He knew he had time for his final act of mercy by proxy, so he wasn't worried about what the cops would eventually find at the house on West Beach Road. He wasn't in the national fingerprint system, so the fingerprints he'd distributed all over the house would be inconsequential. He knew that Michelle from the Opportunity Center was aware of his full name, but if the police asked her questions about the last person Craig talked to, they would be hard pressed to trace his whereabouts. Evon didn't give his name to Hank; he'd never asked for identification when Evon rented the room.

The best-case scenario, as far as the police force's investigation was concerned, meant it would take them weeks, if not months to tie up the loose ends that he left them. By then, it would be too late. Evon would have succeeded and would be long gone from Oak Harbor.

As he neared The Dutch Inn, he stopped to survey the surroundings to make sure nothing was amiss. Confident that he shouldn't be on edge, he approached his room and went inside.

The fetid smell that rushed into his nostrils was powerful enough to make him recoil. It was a repulsiveness that was foreign to him initially, but one that his stomach knew instinctively to make itself nauseous. He knew without a doubt this could only come from one source, and he didn't need to do any further investigating for added reassurance; the bathroom door would remain closed.

The conditions inside his room were ones too unbearable to work in, so he decided he would rent another room from Hank. He would deal with his original room later.

He locked the door and walked into the lobby where Hank was there doing busy work, probably to stave off the boredom that came with working on a day like this.

"Hey you!" Hank said. "Were you just in your room?"

"No, I just got back from a walk."

"Yeah, that's what I figured. You probably would've heard your friends that came back there to check on you."

"Excuse me?"

"Oh, yeah, some friends of yours came here looking for you and that chick you had with you the other night. I gave 'em your room number to see if you were asleep or something, but you didn't answer, which makes sense now. They asked for a key to get in; must've been worried about you guys or whatever."

"*You let them into the room*?"

"Fuck no! Do I look like I'd violate my guest's privacy like that? I'm trying to *keep* business, not lose it. I told them what they could do instead, but I wasn't gonna do that. No way, no how."

"Well good. Good…"

"Anyway though, sounds like it was a false alarm and everything's good! Everything *is* good, right?"

"Yeah," Evon said. "Everything is fine. My friend is just sleeping. Life's been hard on her."

"Oh, alright. I ain't even gonna ask."

"My friends… who were they? I have a lot of them and just want to know who to thank for coming to make sure I was alright."

"They didn't give their names, and stupid me, I didn't even think to ask, but it was a black guy, who didn't look too old, and he had this skinny white kid with him. Or at least he looked like a kid, he was definitely younger."

Evon knew exactly who they were and that was a problem.

"Hey, Hank? I'm gonna need to rent another room. Just for a night. I'll be having a guest over later and want to give them their own space."

"You'll get no push back from me, buddy! Say no more. Vacant rooms aren't good for the bottom line! Ha! Sure you don't want to get a *few* rooms?" Hank said gleefully.

"Thanks for the offer, but just one will do. For now at least."

"Well, you know how much it is. I'll gladly take your money."

Evon reached into a pocket on his backpack and handed Hank the rent for one night. He told him to keep the change.

"I need this room to be a little further down from mine, please."

"Sure, whatever you want!"

Hank reached onto a pegboard that held all the keys to the vacant rooms and grabbed a dull, silver one to give to Evon.

"You gonna be up here for a while, Hank?"

"Shit, yeah! Gotta keep it open for anybody else that might run through here."

Evon gave him a thumbs-up and walked back to the new room he'd rented for the night.

It was relatively refreshing to smell the stale linger of cigarettes and cleaning agents that occupied the room before Evon walked in, along with the burst of fresh, outside air that accompanied him. It was much more pleasant than what he'd left behind in room 14.

He didn't care about the comfort of the bed or whether the clocks were set to the correct time. He had no use for either of those things. The television, though, would serve him well because he thought it would be a good idea to keep his eye on any news developments. It was a respected Lieutenant Commander and his big-wig wife who he'd vanquished, although one was more just than the other. He turned the TV on and turned it to a local news channel. He would leave it on while he worked.

Evon got the laptop and charger out of the backpack and plugged it into a socket.

Luckily, for the search he was about to embark on, Hank's place offered free internet, as painfully slow as it was.

Sunny.

This is who he'd come back to Oak Harbor for.

His daughter.

He knew she was here waiting for him to return to her life because he relied on the enhanced instincts God had given him. That was the only way he was able to tell who he needed to free of their earthly torment and report to their Creator for an everlasting pain-free life. He'd been successful with three thus far, even though he had no intent on dealing with them upon returning, but he knew he would be judged more heavily by the last task ordered of him.

This world wasn't for Sunny any more now than it was from the day she was born. People born with afflictions like hers only suffered through life. To Evon, he would be doing her a grave injustice by letting her suffer any further. This wasn't a friend, the friend's wife, or even a fellow Dreg. This was his *daughter*. His own flesh and blood, and as such, what he needed to do had a substantially increased importance. Failure was not an option, in fact, it wasn't even something he spent much time thinking about. He knew he'd be successful one last time.

The laptop was updating its operating system, which meant he'd have to be patient for a few more minutes. While he waited, he pulled out the card Sunny made for him while he laid in a coma.

Git wel daddy.

Defective.

Weak.

Simple.

He put the card down on the bed when the laptop sounded that it was ready to be put to work.

Evon couldn't complete his assignment without finding where Chastity was keeping and prolonging the pain of his daughter. That was the first part of the equation.

Fortunately for him, he still had his wits about him when it came to technology, having been a part of the boom in the industry before the dominoes started to fall in his life. It was the use of this technology that would assist in his search.

A good friend of his, Ian Gipson, had developed an online person-search website back in the day. Since they hung out in the same circles, Ian had come to him for help and advice on how best to get the service working. Algorithms and such.

One of the perks that came from that was that Ian had given Evon unlimited account access to work on the beta and deliver his thoughts to Ian. It was ages ago, before the internet and applications got on the bullet train to progress, but Evon thought it wise to try that website he'd perused so many times before.

The laptop restarted itself twice more before he opened up the browser and typed in the address that he still remembered. The site loaded slowly. It looked completely different than he last recalled, but that was a good thing. He smiled at the thought that Ian had come so far in the tech industry and Evon took a little pride in knowing that he had some hand in that. It was comforting to know that *someone* he knew was thriving in the industry, even after all this time.

On the right-hand side, there were two boxes that asked for a username and a password. He put in his name as the username and entered the password: *Sunny5k135*, then hit login.

He was denied access.

He re-entered the information but was rebuffed twice more. It appeared to him that either he'd forgotten his login details or Ian wasn't as good of a friend as he thought.

Undeterred, he pondered for a minute on what route he should take next, and that's when it hit him.

He was making this unnecessarily difficult.

There were much simpler ways to search for Sunny, and one of those ways was all the rage in this day and age: Facebook.

Before he'd fallen on hard times, he watched the boom of social media, half jealous that he didn't focus more of his attention on that growing demography instead of just developing some of the tools to create those sites.

He wasn't a fan of social media because of the invasion of privacies that he himself held dear, and he questioned those who chose to use those services. It was one thing to get online and have fun, watch videos, engage in frivolous banter with keyboard warriors, and things of that nature. It was quite another thing to upload pictures and videos of your toddlers using the bathroom, or playing in the bathtub, or standing in front of their schools on their first day.

Evon wasn't heartless; he knew that the people who did these things did so with the best intentions. He understood they were just being proud parents and wanted the world to take notice, to receive that virtual pat on the back, but he didn't think they understood just how inviting they were being to people who were much less virtuous than he.

And now, these same exact services that he loathed would help him find his daughter.

He didn't have a Facebook account, but it was relatively easy to create one.

He had no plans on using it other than for the purpose of locating Sunny, so there was no need to upload any pictures or make any status updates.

In the search function, he put in his ex-wife's name. She appeared immediately: Chastity Brisk. He was glad that she decided to keep his last name. It made it easier to find her online. He wasn't interested in adding her as a friend, though. He'd tried adding her as a wife and eternal partner 15 years ago and that didn't work out very well for him.

He clicked on her profile and scanned it for updates and pictures. There was a lot to be found: how she was frustrated with life, various memes, and recipes for meals that looked easier to make online than reality would prove. But there were very few pictures, which struck him as odd considering the lifestyle he knew she once lived.

He noticed one picture that appeared to show Chastity wearing a forest-green polo with a nametag attached to her chest. She was standing in front of a grocery store, smiling. *First day at my new job!* the caption read. The photo didn't show the name of the store, but it did show the likes and congratulatory comments of Chastity's many friends.

He moved on to another picture. This one showed Chastity proudly hugging Sunny, who was smiling as if her life depended on it, in front of a quaint, light-green colored home. The caption for this one read: *Just bought a new home! SO excited to start a new life with my baby girl! House party details coming soon! LOL*

It was a grainy and slightly blurry picture, likely taken with a cellphone by someone with a shaky hand. Evon zoomed in on the numbers he could see on the front of the house: 1001.

This didn't help him. There could be several homes out there with that address. What he needed were more details. He needed the street name this house could be found on. Then and only then could he take the next step in God's plan.

He continued to filter through the pictures on Chastity's Facebook page and came across some she'd been tagged in. One in particular looked similar to the one he'd just got done scrutinizing, minus a smiling Sunny.

He clicked on it.

She posed with one hand on her hip, the other dangling at her side. Her hair was styled the same. She was wearing the same pair of figure-hugging, blue, stonewashed jeans. The red and black flannel top that complimented her figure was the same. Even the smile she flashed in the previous photo was the same.

This photo was taken on the same day.

The person who tagged her in the photo was a woman who worked for a real estate agency. Evon found the caption: *Another happy Oak Harbor resident! If you were interested in the house at 1001 W. Frostad Road, contact me for other properties that are still available!*

Bingo.

Evon's heart began to race as he committed the address to memory.

He closed the laptop and thought about what he was about to do, and he knew he would need some materials to successfully complete the job.

This wasn't a new idea that he'd stumbled upon, he thought about it during his long walk back from Craig's house. He was conveniently located next to where he could procure those tools: Hank's garage.

Evon got up from the bed and walked outside. He stood still for a moment and listened. Just *listened.* There were no voices, no footsteps, no cars driving by. All was clear.

Behind the hotel was the limp chain-link fence that separated it from Hank's car repair enterprise. There was a section of the fence that had seen better days and it no longer fortified the boundary between the two buildings.

Evon approached it, taking a second to look back at room 14. He climbed through the damaged portion of the fence and sauntered through the collection of cars Hank had outside waiting for their turn to be fixed and returned to their respective owners.

Hank's big, metal, stained garage doors were closed and locked, but he was pleased to find out that the walk-in door adjacent to them was not.

He walked inside and immediately spotted the things he needed, grateful that he wouldn't have to rummage through the shop to find the vital tools. He picked up two of them, one in each hand. He was satisfied with their weight, it meant that they would serve him well.

Evon quickly walked back to his room undetected and set the materials down on the floor. He sat on the edge of the bed with his Bible in hand and tore out some sections he had bookmarked earlier, then started to cry. They were happy tears, not ones filled with sorrow. It was the first time he'd cried since his revelation in that lonely hospital bed.

Tonight would be the night where everything would come to fruition.

EIGHTEEN

There was an uneasiness that had befallen Deon. It was borne of his intuition that something just wasn't right. He didn't know exactly what—he couldn't quite put his finger on it—but it was something. It was a myth that only women had great intuitiveness because he certainly had it at the moment. He only hoped that it wasn't activated too late.

Why would Evon not be at the hotel he said he'd be at just days earlier?

Furthermore, even if Evon *had* taken off temporarily, where, then, was Ruthie? Surely if Evon had left with the intention of coming back later in the day, since he hadn't checked out yet, then Ruthie wouldn't stay there alone and certainly would've heard the banging on the door and window.

None of this made any sense to Deon, as hard as he tried. But what else could he do? The innkeeper had given him three options and he had made his decision with Flip to take one of those options, but he needed to add to it. He wasn't content to just leave the premises without having the foresight that he was eventually going to search for Evon himself.

The most logical thing to figure out first was where Evon would even go. He looked to be in bad shape, so he wouldn't be going far. That ensured that the search area wouldn't be too wide and that it most certainly wouldn't extend past the city limits of Oak Harbor.

He'd rented out a hotel room and hadn't checked out, meaning that he had every intention to return. He hadn't shown his face around Dreg City since he left, either, and his ex-wife and daughter hadn't seen him in months.

Frustration and worry was starting to build.

Deon didn't even care about Evon. They'd had their past relationship, if it could even be considered as much, and he was content with its deterioration. Considering how much Deon felt Evon had changed, he saw no reason to try to fix what they'd once had; he just wanted to know where Ruthie was and to know that she was safe. She was a much more important person to him at this point in his life. There were people here that cared about her just as much, and even though she never said it, she needed them, too. Deon knew that she thrived off being someone who people actually depended on, and there was no doubt that it kept her straight-laced.

If the shoe was on the other foot, he felt comfortable knowing that Ruthie would be doing the same thing for him, searching when she felt he was in danger.

It was early afternoon now and it had become considerably cloudier than it was in the morning. The November sun was visible, but barely so. The thick, dark clouds tried their best to obscure the rays from providing warmth to the living creatures below and they were doing a damn good job of it. The atmosphere hadn't become intolerable yet, but it would be before the day was over, and shelter or more clothing layers would be needed.

It seemed as if time was moving along at a crawl, and it was easy to lose sight of the fact that it was still Thanksgiving Day. Just hours before, Deon and Flip were eating a hot meal inside the warm home of a relative stranger. Just hours earlier, Flip was asleep on a surface far more comfortable than what he was accustomed to. Just hours earlier, Deon was in the company of Sunny with the Fragile-X and learning just how legitimate the notion of the six degrees of separation really was.

As slow as the day felt like it was moving, Deon welcomed the molasses-like movement because it meant he still had enough time left to think, to figure things out, to come up with a new plan of action. Had the seconds and minutes ticked any faster, the pressure would start to build and the decisions wouldn't be as calculated.

Now, he and Flip were back amongst their family of closely-knit vagabonds. Before he'd left, Deon had tasked one of the older couples with taking care of meal preparations and delegation of anything they saw fit in his place in order to make the day as enjoyable as possible. He was greatly relieved to see that they took their duties seriously and everything appeared to be running very smoothly, even in the middle of his imposing dread.

Some of the residents offered meals to him and Flip, figuring that their own had been interrupted, but they politely declined.

"Are you thinking what I'm thinking?" Flip said, interrupting Deon's thoughts.

"Yeah, probably," Deon said.

"*Really*? You think we should've taken that plate of leftovers Chastity offered us, too?"

Deon gave Flip an icy glare.

"Maybe not," Flip said.

"Seriously, Flip, food is the last thing I'm thinking of."

"Damn, lighten up, Gideon. I was just screwing around. If it's not food on your brain, then what *were* you thinking about?"

"I don't know, man. Ruthie. Evon. Shit just doesn't feel right, you know? Like, there's something we're missing that we need to figure out, fast."

"I got you. Yeah, I wonder where they took off to. I mean, it's *Thanksgiving*, you know? Didn't you say the fat dude at the hotel said Evon still had the room?"

"That's what he said."

"Well, shit, maybe we just need to head back. It's been a few hours. They're probably back there now."

"Could be, but what if we walk there again just to find out he still isn't there or we missed him again? It'll just be a game of tag."

"I guess you're right. Well, you said we should look for him ourselves, too. So, what's the plan? Where the hell do we even start?"

"Good question. I'm still thinking about that, Flip. I'm really not sure at this point. I mean, where the hell could we look that we haven't already? The only other place I can even think of him going to is Chastity's, but they divorced years ago according to her."

"Yeah, I don't know what all was said about him, but I got the feeling he's one person that isn't invited to any house parties, so he's not headed back there."

"I agree. So then, *where*?" Deon said frustrated.

"You don't know, I sure as hell don't know, so I guess we just sit here with our thumbs up our asses until the answers come."

"Unless you have a better plan…"

Deon hated sitting around passive and waiting for an epiphany to hit him, but that's all he could do for the time being. He was full of questions and the answers weren't coming easy.

As they sat, ruminating together, a dusty-brown squirrel appeared and scurried in front of them. It dipped through and dodged the people walking about, trying to find its way back out into its natural environment. Deon could see it stop and stand on its hind legs, twitching its nose and bushy tail. Maybe it wanted to find a meal of nuts and kernels for itself. Or perhaps it was getting a feel for the impending change in the weather; wild animals were much better at being in tune with their surroundings than humans.

NINETEEN

Evon paced back and forth in the hotel room, wired from his new sense of purpose. He'd let a few hours go by, repeatedly reading passages from his Bible. His hands had become so moistened from the excitement and nervousness that they stuck to the pages as he turned them.

He was human. His physical reactions to his mental and emotional state proved it so.

He considered going out to Chastity and Sunny's home before nightfall to scope out the scenery and be totally prepared, but decided against it once the rain started to come down.

It began softly, as a light sprinkling. He looked outside of his window when he first heard the pitter-patter against the roof. The dark clouds had drizzled a glaze of rain over the street and buildings outside. The gentle shower wasn't going to be enough to prevent him from leaving the confines of his room, but when it started to turn into a deluge, he changed his mind. Being that he only had one set of the clothes, the ones he had on, he would be soaked and not in any shape to do anything that night.

Evon stopped pacing. It would be wise to take comfort in the calming effects that a quiet downpour offers. He looked out the window again to see the sheets of rain blanketing the outside world. Streaks of it ran down the glass and formed rivers that flowed off the edge of the small stone sill, falling into puddles on the cracked concrete below.

This reminded him of something, of how everything happens for a reason and why God's subjects shouldn't challenge the plans that He has set forth.

Everything happens for a reason.

Sometimes humans get out of their own way and manage to understand those reasons. Sometimes it's beyond their abilities. Evon stopped trying to make sense of the *why* during his stay in Seattle's hospital because it was a fruitless endeavor, but he thought of the *how* for many days and nights, culminating with today.

Git wel daddy…

I *am* well, Sunny, he thought. I *am* well. *But how to get to you…*

This was the third such occurrence in which transportation other than his legs was needed, but he wouldn't borrow another car. His funds were extremely low now and he had to make sure they weren't spent on any unforeseen circumstances. It would be more convenient for him to go to Sunny alone, but if a car he acquired needed more fuel than he could pay for or if it broke down for any reason that would leave him stranded, he might be behind the proverbial eight ball.

That was a risk he wasn't willing to take. Not now. Not at the moment in which he'd finally be able to make good on his ultimate plan.

The option that appealed to him the most was asking for a ride under the cloak of darkness; he would ask Hank for that ride. Evon was in his good graces, having let him keep the change on his payments for the rooms and even renting the rooms in the first place considering how bereft he was of other customers. There wasn't a doubt in his mind that Hank would agree to take him there, within reason. That meant Evon needed to go there before it was too late for Hank to be willing to help but late enough where he wouldn't be bothered with any undue obstacles.

The TV was still on in the background; he kept it on to be kept abreast of any news that might concern him. To his surprise, the local news hadn't mentioned a word about the welfare of the Bryants. Instead, they displayed Thanksgiving statistics, Black Friday news, and other national happenings. His activities at the Bryant residence hadn't registered yet, and that suited him just fine. In time, they'd make the Oak Harbor news and so would he. Although that wasn't his goal, he knew it would be a byproduct of what would occur later in the night.

Ignoring the non-events on the TV screen, he picked up his weathered Bible and turned to the back where he'd kept several torn passages tucked away for safe keeping. They were carefully selected and tailored to his plans for the night. He read what they said and a smile spread across his face. He folded them and put them into his back pocket for later then looked around his hotel room, scanning for anything he might take with him when he went to see his daughter. He decided it wasn't necessary to take any additional materials with him, so he picked up the digital clock on the nightstand by the bed to set the alarm.

He would nap for a short while before heading out. A fresh tank of energy was necessary for later. He knew that Hank had a propensity for not caring about the correct time on the clocks in the rooms, but it didn't matter. Evon knew the hotel would be open until 11 P.M. tonight, the time Hank scrawled in marker on the red and white store hours sign attached to the front of the lobby; they would leave shortly after that time.

***

The beeping of the alarm forced Evon to sit up. It was 10 P.M. Or it could've been 9:00 if it was indeed fast like the clock in his other room. It didn't matter to him, though, because he planned to get up no later than an hour earlier than close anyway. An extra hour of preparation was inconsequential.

He rolled out of bed and stretched his arms high above him to let out a loud yawn. He'd fallen asleep with his clothes and shoes on and had what he needed in his back pocket. He walked to the window and pulled back the curtains. The rain was still steady, although its force was significantly weakened. No gale was evident, as the rainfall came straight down from the clouds.

He saw a few cars drive by, their faint yellow headlights piercing the darkness that had befallen Oak Harbor. He heard the muffled splashing sounds the tires made against the wet pavement as they traveled to their destinations. He, too, would be traveling shortly.

Evon turned off the light in his room and walked out, locking the door behind him. He slid the room key in his right front pocket, where the key for his other room had been placed. He walked to the lobby and peered through the window where he saw that Hank was sitting behind the front counter with his legs kicked up. He appeared to be sleeping, which Evon couldn't fault him for. The guy undoubtedly worked hard at both his respective businesses when he had the time and doing it alone probably took its toll on him more often than not.

As Evon walked in, the sound of the door opening startled Hank.

"I wasn't sleeping," he said as Evon approached him. Hank looked at a wristwatch he had on. "Shit, got about an hour before I close this puppy down and take my ass home for the day."

"Mind if I ask you for a favor, Hank?"

"I guess. Doesn't mean I have to agree to it, but shoot."

"Remember the guest I told you about earlier? The one I needed the extra room for? I'm in need of a ride to go pick them up. Think you could help me out with that?"

"Damn, man. At this time of night? They can't get themselves over here?"

"Well, it's a younger family member. I fell asleep and let time get away from me; otherwise, I would've asked earlier."

Hank leaned to the side to look over Evon's shoulder, scratching the back of his head with one hand.

"How's the rain out there?"

"Not too bad," Evon replied.

Hank consulted his watch again.

"This can't wait until tomorrow?"

"No, it really can't. They were looking forward to spending the holiday with me."

"Well, I'm not sure if you noticed but there ain't much holiday left."

"Yeah… I mean, I guess if you'd be willing to let me borrow your car so I could do it myself…"

"Let me stop you right there; that ain't happening." Evon stood silent. "Shit, man. Look, let's just go ahead and knock it out now. Then I can come straight back here and close and head home."

"Are you sure?"

"Yeah, yeah. I'll just put the 'I'm on a break' sign up. I'm not getting any business now anyway. I'd be shocked if anyone came while I was gone."

"Alright, then. I really appreciate it, Hank."

"Eh, don't sweat it. You ready to go?"

"Yep, I'm all set."

"What part of town do they live?"

Evon tapped the side of his head with his finger. "I got the address right here."

After Hank temporarily closed and locked the doors, he grabbed a light jacket and walked with Evon over to the garage behind the hotel. That's where he kept his silver Ford Ranger. It looked like it was an older model. Along the base and by the wheels, there were spots where rust and wear and tear had worn chunks out of the old truck. Inside, the once black leather had been cracked and turned into a dark gray by a sustained beating of the sun's rays. The floor was littered with balled up wrappers and receipts, along with debris that had made its way in from outside.

"Don't mind the mess," Hank said.

They got in and closed the doors, which let out loud, creaky groans. Hank put the key in the ignition and tried to start the truck. It fought him for a few seconds before finally starting. He flipped on the headlights and started the windshield wipers that whisked back and forth, straining and squeaking against the glass.

"Sorry, man. Not the best ride in town, but she's goddamn reliable. Address?"

Evon gave him Sunny's address and they pulled out onto the street.

"I haven't been out that way in a long time. Nothing out there but a few houses and a whole lot of nature. Anyway, you like music?" Hank asked.

"Sure, I don't mind it. It's been awhile since I last enjoyed some."

Hank switched on the radio and turned the dial to an oldies station. An old song by Kenny Loggins came on.

"*Holy shit!* Haven't heard this in a while!" Hank exclaimed as he turned up the volume.

They weaved in and out of the streets, mostly alone on the roadways as Hank bobbed his head and tapped the steering wheel while singing along with the songs that came on.

Evon remained silent, pensive. He enjoyed listening to the music, not as much as Hank, but it provided a soundtrack for the scenes playing in his head.

They left the main part of the city and started down a dark, lonely road. It was difficult to see, but the scant lighting provided just enough illumination to show him a display of oaks and vast, open areas of grass and shrubbery. Small rocks kicked up and pinged off the undercarriage. The ride became bumpy, the wheels fighting for traction on the pockmarked path. Hank slowed his acceleration.

"Dammit, I can't really see the house numbers. Can you?" Hank asked.

Evon scanned around as best he could. Hank was right, there weren't very many homes out in this area, but he knew what Sunny's home looked like from the front and would be able to easily identify it if he got close to it.

Hank slowed down even more, almost to a crawl. That's when Evon spotted the house. It was unmistakable. It was the house he'd seen Chastity and Sunny posing in front of on Chastity's Facebook page.

"Right there," he said pointing to the house.

Hank slowly pressed down on the brakes until they came to a full stop.

Evon looked out the passenger window at the house, the rain trying its best to obscure his vision. There was an SUV parked in the driveway. It was dark outside, so he couldn't tell if it was gray, maybe silver.

"They know you were on your way?" Hank asked.

"Yeah," Evon said, never taking his eyes off the front of the house.

"I'll go ahead and honk and let 'em know we're here then."

Evon whipped around.

"*No*! Do *not* honk. I'll be right back. Just wait here for a little bit, please. Turn off your headlights until I come back."

"Ok… Have it your way."

Hank did as he was told and put the truck in park.

"I'll be right back," Evon said as a he exited the truck.

After shutting the door, he glared through the window at Hank to get an unspoken confirmation that he indeed fully understood the directions he was given; Hank issued him a reassuring nod.

As he approached the house, he thought about the best way to go about retrieving Sunny. It would be foolish to try going through the front door, obviously, and he needed to be as discreet as humanly possible. Luckily, the rain worked in his favor because it would help to mask any sounds produced outside. It was already deadly silent out in this part of the city without the aid of rain, but it would be a boon tonight.

He pondered going around the back to see if there was a rear entry, but that presented the same problems as going through the front; it would be too easy to be detected if he didn't know how the rooms were positioned inside.

That meant the smart move would be to do a perimeter check around the house to see if he could locate Sunny's room.

He looked back toward Hank to see if he was watching him. From what he could tell, he was too immersed in whatever songs were playing to pay attention to Evon.

He was starting to feel the wetness soak through his hair and clothes, despite the protection of his hat and jacket. Hank might not be too happy about it when he got back in the truck, but Evon didn't mind. It made him feel alive in a moment he needed the feeling the most.

He started his search by walking around the east side of the house, looking for windows.

Of all the useful materials he'd gathered from the hospital, he wished that he'd taken the flashlight; it would've made the search much easier.

Evon pressed his face up against the first window he came to, cupping the sides of his face with his hands to fight off the rain and to get a better view. It was tough to see anything clearly, but what he could see was what looked like a living room. The only thing he could make out through the curtains was a small red indicator light of something electronic, a table, and the outline of a couch.

This wasn't where Sunny slept.

He continued to walk around the house until he came across a window that provided a view into Chastity's kitchen. No curtains obscured his view and he was able to faintly see appliances and a dining table.

It was starting to feel like time was at a standstill, as focused as he was. If it wasn't for the realization that the rain was indeed soaking him to the core, he'd swear the downpour was suspended in mid-air just for him, just for this moment.

As Evon continued to walk through the damp grass and shallow puddles that had formed, he looked out at the trees and vegetation that were on the outskirts of Chastity's property. He wondered what kinds of animals were out amongst them, creeping and sauntering through the trees, peering out at the world they were forced to share.

He reached the back of the house.

There was a white door that stood in stark contrast from the rest of the pea-green color. He decided to bypass looking through the window on the door, but there was a smaller, lower window he was more interested in on that side. Evon bent down and slowly approached it. There were white blinds inside that covered this window, but higher up there was an opening where the blinds had been bent and damaged, allowing someone to look out without moving them. Or to look inside.

Evon stood up from his crouching position and got on the tips of his toes, putting his hands against the house for balance. He put his eye up against the glass as quietly as he could so as not to make the window rattle and inspected the inside. It was a bedroom, that was for sure, but it was too dark to make out anything in the room except for a bed that wasn't that large and the faint glow of electronic lights. He looked as hard as he could at the bed to try to discern a figure, but try as he might, the darkness would not remove its veil.

Whereas before when he felt time slowed down for him, he started to feel the pressure of the need to speed things along; Hank wouldn't wait forever. If Evon took too long, he was positive that Hank would blare that truck horn and then Evon would be left with options he wasn't prepared for. This was supposed to be a smooth operation under the cover of the night, not a hasty getaway as if making off from a bank heist with an unassuming getaway driver.

Imbued with a sense of urgency, he made his way around to the other side of the house, which was devoid of any windows except one. As he got closer he was pleased to see that there were indeed curtains, but they were pulled back. No blinds were in his field of vision, either, allowing him to clearly see, with the little light there was made available, a bright, pink bedroom.

He put his face to the window and saw everything in the room: a closed door, a dresser with clothes sneaking out of it, a desk and chair, a closet, and a small bed with a figure wrapped up in a blanket.

Sunny.

Evon's heart began to race. He wanted to rush inside to be with his daughter, but that would be a hasty move, even considering his desire to quickly vacate the premises. Instead, he carefully examined the window for any locks or alarms he should be aware of. The last thing he needed was an unseen home protection alert being sent to the authorities. He'd evaded them up until this point and didn't need to attract their attention at the penultimate moment.

All he saw was a standard latch that kept intruders out from the inside. He couldn't get to it and wouldn't risk breaking the glass, which meant he needed Sunny to unlock it for him.

He rapped on the glass lightly, trying to awaken her. He was unsuccessful with the first few attempts, but as he increased the force slightly, he saw her start to kick at the blanket, her slumber disturbed.

She slowly sat up, wiping the dreams from her eyes.

It was a beautiful sight, Evon thought. He hadn't seen his daughter with his own eyes in close to a year. Only his memory held visions of her, a memory he was glad wasn't impaired due to his fall. He tapped faster and more excitedly on the window to draw her attention. She looked at him and they locked eyes for a moment. She seemed confused, as would anyone waking from a deep sleep in the middle of the night only to see a dark silhouette in their window. Evon smiled and pleadingly gestured for her to come to the window.

Sunny rolled out of bed and rushed to the window. Evon nodded and pointed at the lock that was impeding their union. He told her to unlock it, but he wasn't sure she could hear the muffled directions through the glass and falling rain. She must've understood, though, because she grabbed the latch with her right hand and twisted it. The window was now unlocked and Sunny grabbed a handle inside to lift open the barrier.

"*Daddy*!" she exclaimed.

"*Shhh, shhh*," he sounded, putting a finger up to his lips. "Keep it quiet, baby girl. How are you? Are you happy to see me?"

Sunny nodded with a massive grin spread across her face and wrapped her arms around his neck, pulling him across the sill. Her touch felt good. This was his flesh and blood. His creation. He wasn't sure he'd ever get a chance to experience this moment ever again, but by the grace of God, here he was.

"Good," he said. "Where's mommy at?"

"You're all better, daddy! You're not sick anymore!"

"I know, I know, baby. We can talk about that later. But right now I need you to tell me where mommy's at."

"She's asleep in her room right now," Sunny said as she pointed to the door behind them.

"Ok, good."

"You're all wet, daddy! I'll go unlock the door so you can come inside!"

"Honey, no, it's ok. I'll be alright; it's just a little water. Look, you and daddy need to go spend some time together. Does that sound like fun?"

"*Yeah*!" Sunny screamed.

Evon rushed to put a hand over her mouth to keep her quiet.

"You can't yell, honey. Do you hear me? We don't want to wake mommy up, right? That wouldn't be very nice when she's trying to sleep, now would it?"

Sunny shook her head and Evon removed his hand from her mouth.

"Alright. Now, listen to me, grab a coat from your closet over there. I don't want you to get all wet like daddy."

Sunny let out a soft giggle.

"And put on some shoes. You can leave your pajamas on, though, ok?"

She left his embrace and happily set about doing what her father asked her to do.

He wasn't sure how much time had passed since he'd been at the window, but he knew he needed to hurry back out to Hank.

"Hurry up, baby. We need to go because I have a friend out here waiting on us," he said with increasing impatience.

While Sunny was sitting on the edge of the bed, putting her shoes on, Evon reached into his back pocket to get the folded pieces of paper he'd removed from the Bible. He shielded them with both hands so they didn't get wet.

Sunny was just finishing tying her shoes. He reached into the window and motioned her over.

"All done, baby girl?"

Sunny answered yes.

"Ok, here, take these papers and unfold them and lay them on your pillow," he instructed his daughter.

She took them in her hand, looking down at them, perplexed.

"What are they?" she asked.

"They are notes, to let mommy know where you are. Just do it and let's hurry up."

Sunny unfolded them and laid them flat down on her pillow.

"Ok, now come here and I'll help you get out the window."

She steadied herself and lifted one leg onto the narrow ledge and out the window, then the other. Evon locked her in a brief embrace once more and grabbed her by the hand.

"Let's get out of this rain!" he said with a smile.

With their hands locked together, they crept to the front of the house where Hank was still there waiting in his truck. He didn't see them approach the car and was startled when Evon pulled the door open. He ushered Sunny inside and got in after her.

"Took you long enough, didn't even see you come out," Hank said. "Who's this?"

"This is my daughter, Sunny. I'd tell you more, but I've already used up your time, having you wait for us. Let's just head back to the hotel."

"Wait a minute, your *daughter*? You're picking up your daughter in the middle of the night?"

"Yes, her mother and I have special arrangements."

"Kind of some weird arrangements if you ask me. You mean to tell me her mother couldn't have dropped her off to you?"

Sunny smiled at Hank, who returned it. Evon hadn't anticipated him being so inquisitive. He had to scramble to come up with plausible explanations so that things didn't become more difficult.

"She wasn't feeling too well. Drank a little too much for the holiday. We decided it wasn't safe for her to drive, which is why I asked you."

"Ah, ok. Makes sense, I guess. Well, I'm sorry, little lady," he said to Sunny. "We only have two seatbelts, so try to sit still while I drive."

"My daddy's here, so I'll be ok."

"That's right," Evon said as he placed a kiss on her forehead.

Hank pulled into the driveway, illuminating Chastity's car. Evon now saw that she'd gotten herself a fancy Range Rover, likely with the money he'd forfeited years ago.

Hank went into reverse, then drive, and carefully drove down the road with Evon's precious cargo in tow.

***

Hank dropped Evon and Sunny off in front of his new room before returning to the lobby to start closing down the inn for the night.

Evon unlocked the door to let Sunny inside. He imagined that, in the eyes of a child, the room would be utterly unimpressive compared to what she'd left behind, but she looked on in wonderment as the place her beloved father had been staying was revealed to her. She immediately hopped on the bed, testing its springiness.

"Daddy! Is this *your* bed?" she yelled.

"Yes, baby, it is. For now."

"And you have a TV in your room!"

"Yes, yes I do."

"You could watch TV and jump on the bed at the same time!" she said gleefully.

Evon watched as she jumped with her feet, landed with her behind, and repeated the process with childlike joy, even though she was a teenager. It was easy to lose sight of that fact, but what her condition had done to her development was apparent in instances such as the one he was witnessing.

In his past life, Evon would've taken on a more fatherly role, reprimanding her for jumping on a bed, with her muddy shoes on, no less, and for yelling as loud as she was. He was more than ok with it now because she was getting a last chance at enjoying life's simple pleasures.

This made him tear up slightly because he was witnessing his daughter mask her fears, her frustrations, and her sadness with behaviors that made it seem like she was truly and utterly enjoying life in that mind, that body of hers.

He knew different, though, and he was proud to be in this important position, as her father, but soon as her savior.

He looked around the room, at the materials that were on the floor that he'd gathered from Hank's garage. It was time to start putting them to use. He bent down to start picking them up.

Sunny took notice and stopped bouncing on the bed.

"What's that stuff for, daddy?" she asked.

"Don't worry about it right now. It's for daddy's business he has to take care of later."

This seemed to satisfy her curiosity, and she sat down on the bed, ceasing her jumping once and for all.

"Getting tired, baby girl?"

"Yeah…" she hesitated. "Are we gonna do anything fun?"

"We will, honey. Why don't you lay down or something for a little bit? Daddy has to make a run real quick."

"Where are you going?"

"Just right around the corner to another room. I won't take too long, so just hold on and stay in here, ok?"

Sunny hopped off the bed and ran over to her father to give him a hug. She crashed into him and knocked him off balance, not realizing the power her size brought. He returned her embrace and gently nudged her back to the bed. He looked at the phone sitting next to it.

"Do you know mommy's phone number?"

"There's a three in it!" she said. "But I can't remember the rest."

"Ok, good. Be a good girl and don't mess with the phone, ok? If it rings, just let it ring."

Evon kissed her on the forehead, picked up the materials he needed, and headed outside in the rain to room 14.

TWENTY

Deon was asleep and taking shelter underneath a blue tarp that had been set up to protect from the rain, when the honking awoke him. He was not only physically worn from the day, but was mentally and emotionally tired, too. Even though the sound of the horn awakened him, it was only from the worried, half-rest he was getting.

It wasn't a quiet night, with the sound of the rainfall meeting plastic and metal and the rustling of whatever leaves remained on the surrounding trees. There were also a few night owls up bristling about and ignoring the rain as their friends and family lay dormant in their makeshift homes.

Those that were still awake were the least startled when the silver SUV came speeding and honking into the encampment, bright headlights blasting rays of halogen light into the darkness.

The combination of that noise and the commotion amongst the people got Deon to finally shake off what was left of his slumber and he peeked out to see what was going on. The driver of the SUV relentlessly blared the horn as the car sat in park.

Then the driver-side door opened.

Out came Chastity into the rain.

She was wearing the same clothes as Deon had last seen her in hours before.

"*Deon*! *Deon*! Where the fuck *are* you?" she screamed, hurriedly walking towards the camp.

He struggled to get on his feet, his body still doggedly spent and not fully cooperating with his brain when he needed it to.

He went out from under the dry safety of his shelter into the rain. There was no hood on the jacket he was wearing and he didn't spend time looking for anything to cover his head with; his dry hair soaked up what little it could, but the rest of the water cascaded down his face. He wiped some of it out of his eyes before meeting Chastity a few yards away.

"Deon! Oh, God, Deon! Where the fuck *is* she?" Chastity screamed.

"Hold on, slow down. What are you talking about? What's going on?"

"*Sunny*! Sunny is *gone*, goddammit!"

The cobwebs brought on by the mental toll of everyday life and the struggle to recuperate that came with it, especially that of the last 24 hours, made it hard for him to comprehend what Chastity was saying to him as they stood in the rain.

"Gone? Wh– what do you mean *gone*?"

"Dammit, Deon, I got up to use the bathroom and heard the rain from outside coming from her door. It sounded louder than it should've so I opened the door and the fucking window was open and she wasn't in her bed!"

Deon's steadily beating heart started to pound in his chest.

"She wasn't in the bathroom or the closet or anywhere else in the house? Did you check everywhere? Was she outside?"

"Deon, I looked *everywhere.* She wasn't in the fucking house and she wasn't outside anywhere that I could see. But this was on her pillow."

Chastity pulled out some paper from her back pocket. There were several pages and they were already damp from being in her wet jeans and being exposed made them even more so. There was text on them that suggested they were typed and torn from the inside of a book.

"I can't even read those, it's too dark and they're getting soaked," Deon said.

"Come to the car, then," Chastity replied.

They jogged over to her Range Rover and got inside. It was a warm, dry reprieve from the elements outside. The rain made muffled pings off the roof of the car that mixed in with the subdued purr of the running engine.

Chastity turned on an overhead light and handed Deon the thin pieces of paper. He peeled them away from each other, as the rain had made them stick. They didn't appear to be full pages, just sections that were torn out. From first glance at some of the text, he could see that they appeared to be Bible verses with some of the text crossed out with a pen or a marker.

The first piece read: *Matthew 9:18* __________ *"My little daughter has just died," he said, "but you can bring her back to life again if you will only come and touch her."*

The next piece read: *Numbers 18:17* __________ *the firstborn* __________ *must be sacrificed to the Lord.* __________ *shall be burned as a fire offering; it is very pleasant to the Lord.*

Deon was confused by the first reading, but the second one made the gravity of the situation very clear to him. He was starting to get a vivid picture of what the perpetrator of Sunny's disappearance wanted to do, and it meant he and Chastity better find her *fast.*

There was one last passage that he read and it sent chills coursing through his body: *Deuteronomy 28:41 You will watch as your* __________ *daughters are taken away* __________ *Your heart will break with longing for them, but you will not be able to help them.*

Deon looked at Chastity and their gazes locked; he knew she felt it, too.

"This is serious shit," he said. "Whoever took her likes the Bible and wanted you to get a sense of what he's going to do through these verses."

"What? That doesn't make any sense."

"Did you even read any of this before you came over here?"

"I scanned over it. I didn't know what the hell it all meant."

"Well, the person who left this stuff definitely wanted you to read them."

"Deon, I don't give a fuck about some Bible verses! I want to know who the fuck it was that left them and who could possibly have my daughter!"

Think, Deon.

"I– I don't know. These," he said, shaking the pieces of paper, "aren't enough to figure that out. Did you notice anything else that was strange in her room? Was there mud or wetness or anything like that anywhere?"

"No. The window was pulled all the way up. Other than finding those, nothing else was tampered with or anything."

Think, Deon.

"Well, we know that whoever took her obviously *left* these," he said, "but was anything else *taken*?"

Chastity fell silent and thought for a moment.

"Her shoes. And one of her coats. She put those on and must've gone through the window."

"Meaning that whoever took her didn't come inside her room, and *told* her to put those on for her comfort… Is Sunny the type to listen to strangers who show up at her window in the middle of the night?"

"No, she's not. She knows to call for me if she feels unsafe or scared. She struggles mentally sometimes, but she knows that much."

"So, that means she knew this person… fuck…"

"What?" Chastity asked.

"Do you have any relatives that live in town?"

"Not in Oak Harbor, no."

"Actually, you do…"

They both fell silent. Only the sound of the rain hitting the car could be heard.

"Evon," Chastity said.

"Evon," Deon replied.

"Wh–, *how,* though? He doesn't know where the hell I live! I didn't leave my address or number or anything for him when I visited!"

"Well, he found you anyway."

"*Goddammit, Evon*, where the fuck did he go with my daughter?"

Chastity dropped her head in her hands and started to weep uncontrollably. Deon wanted to offer some comfort, but he didn't know what form that should come in. He couldn't relate to having a child taken away, being that he never experienced fatherhood, but he could empathize. In his situation, though, his loved ones were taken away for what he understood as a reason, a just cause, not by someone with a specter of nefariousness surrounding him.

"Could you tell what the hell any of that even meant?" Chastity asked, wiping away tears from her eyes.

"These verses? I'm not completely sure…"

Deon's voice trailed off. He could tell Chastity what was really on his mind and what were his worst fears, that he was actually quite sure Evon meant for these to be understood and taken literally, which didn't bode well for Sunny. The cryptic verses could be metaphorical, but this wasn't a time to make that determination. A child was gone in the middle of a rainy night, and nothing good happens when it's shrouded in darkness.

They would have to act as though the worst was coming to her and *before* that even came to fruition.

Your heart will break with longing for them, but you will not be able to help them…

Someone rapped hardly against the passenger window, startling Deon and Chastity. It was Flip, standing out in the downpour that was quickly becoming a deluge.

Deon rolled down the window.

"Ok, what the hell is going on out here?" Flip asked.

"Get in and we'll tell you," Deon replied.

After filling him in on why Chastity was here and what happened to Sunny, Deon showed Flip the torn-out Bible passages to get his interpretation of them. Flip read over them carefully, only making subtle grunts at what he thought of them. He handed them back to Deon.

"And you guys think Evon has her?" Flip asked.

"Who else could it be, Flip? What little girl do you know who puts on her shoes and coat and willingly climbs out of a window in the middle of the night without making so much as a peep to suggest she's in trouble? Chastity says there wasn't anything else wrong in her room. She *had* to have left with someone she knew."

"I don't know, man. Maybe you're right. But if that's the case, why the hell are we still sitting here? Let's go find them!"

"Do you guys have any idea where he might be?" Chastity asked.

"Yeah, we went by where he said he was staying the last time we saw him, the Dutch Inn, but he wasn't there. I say we go back there," Flip offered.

"That's a good idea, but what if we just miss him again or if he comes back here? Someone needs to stick around," said Deon.

After a moment of silence, Flip said, "Ok, I get the hint. I'll stay behind while you two go search. But how will I know if you guys need help or that you've found them?"

"You won't. But just stay here and keep an eye on things. If we all come back here soon then you'll know everything is ok. If Evon happens to show his face here, keep him here. I don't care what you have to do but make sure he does *not* leave. Got it?" Deon asked.

"Yeah, yeah, I got it. You guys get the hell outta here."

Flip got out of the car, huddling against the rain as he jogged back to some shelter a few yards away.

"Do you know where the Dutch Inn is at?" Deon asked Chastity.

"Everyone here knows where that's at," she replied. "Let's just hope he's there."

"That black bodyguard of yours, is he with you?"

"*Shit!*" she said, slapping her hands against the steering wheel.

"I'll take that as a 'no.' How about we hope that we don't need him."

***

The windshield wipers fought furiously to provide a clear view of what was in front of them as they approached the inn. Amidst the street lamps and the lights emanating from the surrounding buildings, the obscured view they got was the hint of billowing black smoke rising and illuminated from what seemed to be the vicinity of the hotel.

Chastity stopped a few yards away and put the car in park, leaving the engine running. They both hurriedly hopped out of the car, and Deon noticed the innkeeper he spoke to earlier frantically running in front of the building. The anxiety and fear that was ravaging his body in the moment was physically apparent in his face.

Deon ran up to him.

"What's happening?"

"A goddamn fire in the back! That's what's happening!" the man said. "You're the guy that showed up earlier…"

"Deon."

"I'm Hank. But look, I can't chat right now. Gotta find out where this fire is coming from!"

… shall be burned as a fire offering; it is very pleasant to the Lord…

"I'm coming with you!" Deon shouted. "Did you call the fire department?"

"*Shit*! Not yet. For fuck's sake, what the hell's the matter with me? I was just trying to figure out what on earth was going on! I'll go inside and do that now!"

Hank ran to the entrance, retrieving a set of keys from his pocket as he got closer to the door.

Chastity, who had been standing by her car during the exchange, ran up to Deon.

"Does he know what's going on?" she asked.

"There's a fire somewhere in the back, but he doesn't know exactly where it's coming from."

"Oh, God… This is where you think Evon took my baby?"

Deon nodded. "Look, I gotta go find where the fire is."

"I'm coming with you!"

Chastity ran back to her car and turned off the ignition, then put the keys in her pocket. When she made her way back to the spot where Deon was before, he had already taken off around the building to continue the search.

The rain and darkness were obscuring his vision, but with that impairment to one of his vital senses, the others seemed to be exponentially enhanced.

The sense that isn't one of the five taught to school children is the sense of urgency. It can't be strengthened through practice, nor can it be understood and utilized until those moments arise that call on its use. It isn't like sight, smell, taste, touch, and hearing that are always there at our beck and call; urgency arrives unannounced and already at its maximum level if the situation calls for it, and this was certainly a situation that Deon needed it for.

He looked up to see the smoke still fighting its way through the rain and discerned that it was coming from the back of the building.

Rounding the corner of the building, Deon and Chastity came up to the same room he and Flip had visited earlier when they came looking for Evon and Ruthie. He could clearly see that this was the room that was on fire.

He'd fought it up until this point, but he could no longer block the flooding back of the memory of a similar scene. Though this wasn't his home and his parents weren't the ones in peril, all Deon could think about was being held back by firefighters as he stood there watching his life reduced to ashes.

This time, he was older, wiser, and there were different lives at stake: Ruthie, Sunny, and even Evon. This time, there was nothing holding him back, nothing to suppress his urge for action in the face of immediate and life-altering danger. Though fear didn't have a paralyzing grasp on him, it was there with a hand on his shoulder, lightly reminding him that he could either use it to propel forward or he could turn away from the task in front of him, allowing fear to take him up in its icy and immobilizing embrace.

Deon chose the former and grabbed the room's doorknob. He immediately regretted that decision when he felt the extreme heat sear his skin. He didn't hear a sizzle, but imagined that if his hand held onto the knob any longer, his skin would surely have begun to cook on the metal. He shook his hand, waving it around in the air hoping the rain would cool it a bit. It offered some pain relief but not a solution on what to do next.

"What the hell are you doing?" Chastity chastised. "You can't just grab the doorknob and make your way inside when there's a fire!"

"Well, I know that now! How the hell else are we gonna get inside?"

Chastity turned and looked around, hoping to find something of significance to break a window but to no avail.

"*Shit!*" she said.

Earlier, when Deon and Flip came, he'd tried to get Hank to give him the key to this very room. Now, he figured Hank would oblige, being that his business was going up in flames.

"Look, we can't just sit here! They're inside there! Help me barge in!" he shouted to Chastity.

"*How?*"

Deon hoped that the heat had done enough damage to the structural integrity of the building, allowing for a relatively easy opportunity to rely on their own strength to get inside.

He rammed his shoulder into the door as hard as he could. Chastity followed his lead. It took them a number of tries, but they felt the door start to give, the locks on the inside wilting away from the intensity of the heat and the strength of their abundant will.

Upon the force of their last combined blow, they broke through the door, crashing through to the inside. They stumbled to the floor, quickly rising up for fear that they'd fallen headfirst into the blaze. There was indeed an enormous frenzy that was whipped up, but it hadn't made its way to the door to block any advancement. What the fire *did* do, behind the closed hotel door, was create a furnace inside the room, but the rush of cool air from outside did much to relieve what would've been an unbearable heat.

From his spot near the door, Deon deduced that it started in the corner opposite from what appeared to be a bathroom, but he wasn't sure because the door was closed.

The fire had leapt from the floor and was quickly engulfing a desk and the bed; the filling in the comforter was undoubtedly aiding the blaze. He thought briefly of trying to put out the fire, scanning for an extinguisher on the wall. He located where one had likely been attached.

It was gone.

A strong stench of something other than what the fire was burning was joining in with the smell of burnt wood and fabric. It was a foreign smell, one his nose hadn't experienced before. Considering what he expected to find in the room, panic started to course through him as he realized what that odor might mean.

Chastity was next to him, shielding her face from the heat and pulling the collar of her shirt up to prevent the inhalation of too much smoke. Deon did the same and scanned the room.

Muffling through her shirt, Chastity asked, "Where are they?"

"I don't know! This is the room Evon rented! That's what Hank told me earlier."

"Maybe they're hiding from the fire in there," Chastity said, pointing to the closed door. "That's the bathroom, right?"

It made sense to Deon that someone who was frightened because of an inferno in their room might hide in a closet or a bathroom because their exits were blocked, but in this instance it didn't add up because whoever was in this room had an opportunity to leave. They could've gotten out the same way he and Chastity had gotten in.

The fire was recent and it was clear it didn't have a chance to completely overtake the room yet. Either it started by accident due to an electrical mishap, which couldn't be the case because, from what he could tell, the spot where it started was clear of any power outlets, or someone purposely started the fire and left the area shortly before they arrived.

Deon shuddered to ponder the answer his heart and mind were intuitively pointing to.

He put a hand out toward Chastity, motioning her to stay put before he approached the closed door. He didn't want both of them to test the relative safety from where they stood; they could easily back out the door and were free from any real danger from the encroaching fire, save for having to inhale some smoke.

The odor he'd detected before that was separate from everything else that was burning got stronger, filling his nostrils with a sickly-sweet smell. He'd smelled a lot of things in his lifetime and knew the profile of certain things. This was a decaying pungency, *that* he was sure of, but this wasn't a food smell or even that of excrement left exposed too long.

The advancing fire didn't afford him much time to consider all the possibilities. He needed to act fast and continue the search for everyone if what was behind this closed door didn't yield any answers.

Deon looked back at Chastity, whose eyes were watering and pleading for him to take swift action. He lightly put his hand on the knob to make sure he didn't make the same mistake twice. It was warm to the touch, but not searing. Assured of his safety, he twisted the knob and pushed the door open.

The overwhelming smell that rushed him almost pushed him right back out of the bathroom. It was dark inside and he fumbled against the wall to flip on a light switch. He saw that a shower curtain was closed, concealing the tub. He quickly swiped at the curtain and saw the unmistakable remains of Ruthie's body.

She was piled into the tub, lying in an unnatural position. Her skin was no longer the peach-cream blend that Deon fondly remembered. It had instead turned a purplish-black with dark green splotches that hadn't made the turn to that darker color yet. She was wearing the same outfit he last saw her in, but it was tightly stretched around her body, as it had become bloated and much larger than it would've been.

There was dried blood on her neck and shirt. Her head was leaned back, eyes protruding from their sockets and mouth wide open with her tongue hanging out like that of a parched canine or as if there were unspoken words left unsaid.

Deon felt his stomach preparing to churn up some vomit to spew from his mouth and quickly placed a hand over it.

This was not a sight he was prepared for, mentally or physically, and he felt every emotion begin to swirl up inside of him. Shock, at seeing the decaying corpse of a friend he'd grown close to and having that image forever burned into his memory. Sadness, at arriving too late and being put in a position where there was nothing left to do but stare and try to recall gentler times. Anger, that someone had done this to Ruthie and dumped her body so unceremoniously, as if her life meant nothing.

Evon.

Deon's fists clenched and he turned away from Ruthie's corpse. He silently walked past Chastity, not acknowledging that she was still in the room with him, and entered the rain once more.

"What was in there?" she said worriedly as she followed him back outside.

"A dead body," Deon said flatly.

"*A body?* Whose? Oh, God, don't tell me…"

Chastity tried to rush back inside, but Deon firmly grabbed ahold of her wrist, wrenching her back.

"It's not Sunny and it's not Evon. You didn't know her, but it was my friend, Ruthie. She was killed and whoever did it was trying to burn the evidence."

"*What*? Who? Wasn't that the room Evon ren–"

Chastity's voice trailed off.

"Yes, and we need to find him, fast. He's still around here somewhere. He couldn't've set that fire too long ago. Probably just minutes before we got here. He's not driving, as far as I know, so he's got to be around."

They both stood a few yards away from the entrance of the burning room, drenched from the downpour. They expected to hear the wail of sirens anytime now, but there was only the sound of crackling wood and flames whipping through the air, fighting for new material to engulf.

Deon looked on helplessly because he knew that soon, Ruthie's corpse would become fodder for the flames unless an emergency crew arrived quickly. The fire hadn't made its way through the roof yet, but when it did, that room was as good as gone.

His mind raced as he tried to put together the frayed pieces of the puzzle.

How did it come to this?

Why?

Was she in there the whole time he and Flip were here knocking?

Where was Evon?

How did Sunny play into this?

Where the fuck was the fire crew?

"Deon, look," Chastity said, pointing in the air.

Her finger was pointing in the direction of the other side of the building.

More smoke was lifting into the air.

TWENTY-ONE

"Go to the lobby and tell Hank to hurry the hell up!" Deon directed Chastity.

He assumed Hank had already alerted an emergency crew and couldn't really get them to move any faster than they probably were, but this situation was becoming more dire than he imagined it would, and warranted Hank making another call to warn them of more fire.

Chastity hesitated for a moment, letting the rain continue to drench her and pleading with her eyes for Deon to let her continue to accompany him, but she finally acquiesced with a nod and ran toward the lobby.

Deon watched her round the corner before running off in the direction of the new appearance of smoke.

The images of Ruthie lying in that bathtub flashed through his mind. He *knew* that Evon had done that to her, and if he had Sunny, there was no telling what else he would do or what he was capable of.

That meant he needed to protect himself. He hadn't been in a physical fight in years and certainly not under the conditions he found himself in now, but he knew that this was evil he was dealing with. Fists would only do so much.

He reached the other room the fire was coming from and stood a few feet away. The window of the hotel room was brightly illuminated, and Deon knew that meant a fire inside was ferociously blazing. The door was shut and sure enough, smoke was filtering through the crack in the bottom. He looked around on the ground in the area where he stood. He needed to find *something* to arm himself with besides adrenaline.

That's when he spotted a concrete parking block directly in front of the door. It was crumbling with age and on the corner where the re-bar had fastened it to the ground, a large piece of concrete was barely hanging on. Deon kicked at it fiercely with the side of his foot until it completely came unattached. He bent down to pick it up; it was slick from the rain and years of being exposed to the elements.

As he approached the door, he knew better than to touch the knob again, but he had to get inside. When he and Chastity shouldered their way through to the other room, he understood he could credit an assist to the damage the fire had already done. This attempt would be no different except he couldn't rely on Chastity's additional strength.

He rammed into the door several times to no avail. His shoulder began to throb and he knew he couldn't continuously throw his body against the door for fear that he would injure himself. He stopped with his shoulder for a brief moment and continued to try to break his way through with the force of his foot.

This proved fruitless, as his wet sole kept slipping against the surface of the door, not providing enough friction to allow for a forceful breach. Deon decided to hammer at the door knob with the piece of concrete he'd kicked loose, allowing the rush of adrenaline to fuel him. He felt the door begin to budge, and that hope that he would eventually burst through drove him to push harder and faster with all his remaining strength.

The wooden door began to splinter and he heard metal clanking. Black smoke and heat started to escape through the crack he was opening, searing his eyes and face. The last forceful blow knocked the doorknob off and he lost the grip of the piece of concrete he was holding. The door hadn't opened yet, so he sent one more kick to it that finished the job.

The room had a cloying smell of gasoline, and there was no doubt that was the accelerant used to set the room nearly fully ablaze. The bed was upturned and pushed against a wall near the remains of an air conditioner. The walls and curtain were black, as the flames of the fire had danced across and left their dark telltale sign that man-made material was no match against the strength of a raging fire. In the open space where the bed had once occupied, a perimeter of fire had been set as if to block anyone from entering or leaving that area. In the middle of that perimeter, in the corner where the wall and bathroom partition met, sat a shirtless Evon. And he wasn't alone.

Sunny's prone body was lying next to him, with her head face up and in his lap. She wasn't moving, and Deon couldn't tell if she was breathing, either. She was wearing an oversized green bomber jacket and her pajama bottoms.

Evon sat motionless, skin glistening from the profuse sweat that the intense heat had coaxed out of his body. His legs stuck straight out, two metal canisters in front of him, the type that would typically be used to transport gas. He had a needle in one hand with the tip pointing at his arm. He appeared ready to inject himself with something, but was interrupted when Deon came through.

Deon bent down to pick up the concrete he'd dropped, and Evon dropped the needle. He grabbed Sunny and drew her lifeless body close to his.

"The Spirit of the Lord God is upon me, because the Lord has anointed me to bring good news to the suffering and afflicted. He has sent me to comfort the brokenhearted, to announce liberty to captives, and to open the eyes of the blind," Evon started. "He has sent me to tell those who mourn that the time of God's favor to them has come…"

He rocked back and forth with Sunny's body firmly in his grasp and kept talking, spewing forth words even when Deon tried to interrupt.

"Evon!" Deon said, "why did you kill Ruthie, you son of a bitch?"

His grasp on the concrete tightened, straining and hurting his fingers.

"…all shall realize that they are a people God has blessed. Let me tell you how happy God has made me! For he has clothed me with garments of salvation and draped about me the robe of righteousness…"

"*Answer me, dammit!*" Deon shouted at him.

"…I will not cease to pray for her or to cry out to God on her behalf until she shines forth in his righteousness and is glorious in his salvation…"

Deon took a step toward the huddled couple. Evon clutched Sunny tighter.

"…*the Lord, announcing your salvation; I, the Lord, the one who is mighty to save*!" he said, with a painful wailing in his voice.

The fire inside the room was roaring, but Deon could hear the faint sound of sirens approaching in the distance. Evon must've heard them, too, because he stopped talking and rocking briefly.

"What did you do to Sunny, Evon?" Deon shouted.

He didn't answer; he just continued to rock back and forth with her body. His eyes were closed and his head was down. He started to shake his head from side to side, the universal sign for refusal, for wordlessly saying *no.*

The fire in the room was starting to approach Evon and Sunny in the corner. The encirclement he'd made as a barrier was quickly tearing through the carpet on the floor, looking for something else to engulf.

Deon shook, his body being pumped with chemicals that told him to *move.* He couldn't waste too much time talking to Evon; he wasn't even listening. He feared the worse had already happened to Sunny, but he still needed to *act.*

"Evon, give Sunny to me, *now.* Chastity is here for her."

Evon ignored his command.

"Sunny? Sunny, can you hear me?" Deon asked, hoping for a response from her.

He received nothing.

Act, dammit, he thought to himself, but he wasn't sure what kind of danger he'd put himself in. He didn't know if Evon was hiding some form of weapon or if he'd do something to Sunny, if she was even alive.

The sirens became louder, but so, too, did the roar of the flames. They were starting to reach the ceiling, and it wouldn't be long before debris started to collapse on everyone in the room. But Deon refused to leave until he had Sunny.

He could rush Evon with concrete in hand, but that wouldn't be smart. There would surely be a tussle and everyone in the room would be consumed by flames.

Deon felt anger swell up in him, both because of his inaction and the fact that the man sitting yards away from him had taken one life and potentially another: that of his own flesh and blood. Deon did not want him to get away with such evil.

"*Look at me, motherfucker*!" he screamed at Evon.

Whether it was the word choice or the force in Deon's voice, Evon reacted and looked up at him through the blaze. Deon could see the reflection of the fire dancing in his glossy eyes as they locked on each other, but they were otherwise dark, soulless.

Deon reared back and threw the piece of concrete as hard as he could at Evon's face. Evon quickly took his hands off Sunny to shield his face and kicked his leg to the side, knocking over one of the cans of gasoline and spilling its contents.

The gasoline inside spilled and made contact with the ensuing fire.

Everything from that point moved in slow motion. Deon watched as the flames on the ground sparked and quickly raced up the nozzle of the gas can. Only one thing could happen once the fire met a full reserve of fuel trapped inside the can.

That's when the explosion happened.

The concussing sound of the exploding gas can was brief, but loud, and made Deon's ears ring. The suddenness made him turn away to shield himself, so he didn't see that the metal can had shredded, sending debris flying.

He felt some of it hit him, but Evon had caught the worst of it.

Once the ringing had subsided, Deon heard agonizing screams coming from Evon.

He turned and saw him writhing in pain on the ground. His hands were clawing at his face, trying to clear away whatever made its way to his eyes. His pants had caught on fire, but Deon was sure that he didn't feel it, for the pain in his face was probably worse.

He looked down at Evon's side to see Sunny lying face down. The jacket she was wearing had caught fire. Deon still couldn't tell if she was breathing or not, but he quickly rushed toward her, shielding his face with an arm, knowing that no less than his shoes might catch fire as he jumped through the growing flames, but he wasn't going to stand still and watch her body be engulfed.

He reached down and frantically pulled the coat off her, flinging it aside as an offering to the fire in exchange for her body. Then he grabbed her by her arms, trying to lift her limp, but heavy body up to hoist over his shoulder. He felt resistance as he lifted and looked down to see that Evon had reached out and took hold of her ankle with one hand. Despite what he'd just suffered, he was incredibly strong with just that one arm, pulling her back down toward him.

Deon yanked upwards, taking one side in the tug of war over Sunny's body, but Evon wouldn't relent. His screams had turned into muffled moans as he turned his attention to making sure his daughter did not leave his side.

Deon briefly let go of Sunny and turned his attention to Evon. Deon grabbed a fistful of Evon's hair and yanked him backwards. Evon loosened his hold on Sunny's ankles and swung his arms wildly in an attempt to make contact with Deon, but he failed.

Deon cocked his arm back and struck Evon in the face, hoping to stun him enough to buy himself some time, but it was only a glancing blow, as Evon's flailing arms caused him to miss his mark. Undeterred, Deon struck him again, this time landing a shot on Evon's jaw and sending him crashing to the ground.

He stopped moving but for a brief second before he started to stir once more.

Deon looked around and spotted the piece of concrete he'd hurled at Evon just moments before. He picked it up and came crashing down on the back of Evon's skull.

Once, twice, eliciting a sickening thud each time.

Blood started to ooze out of his head and trickled down the side of his neck as he lay inert. Once he saw that Evon wouldn't offer any more of a struggle, he resumed trying to get Sunny's body out of the quickly deteriorating room.

Her dead weight protested against his attempt to lift her. He considered dragging her but erased that thought knowing he'd be dragging her through the encroaching flames.

With one last heave, he managed to hoist her over his shoulder. Her arms slumped over, touching his back, and he marched as quickly as he could through the burning perimeter Evon made and toward the relief outdoors.

When he got outside, he was able to hear that the sirens had arrived at the hotel. Emergency personnel ran toward him. Chastity and Hank weren't far behind. Deon carefully laid Sunny's body down on her back in the parking lot. He took a moment to let the cool air soothe him and relieve him of the heat his body endured while he was inside the hotel room. The emergency crew rushed to Sunny's side, lightly pushing Chastity away as she screamed and tried to make her way to her unresponsive daughter.

"Is there anyone else inside?" one of the responders yelled to Deon.

"Yes," he said, pointing at the room he'd just left. "There's one more man in there."

***

Evon slowly rose on his hands and knees. His head felt funny, cloudy even, like there was water swishing around inside his skull.

Just cobwebs.

He shook his head a bit and tried to shake them out. When he tried to open both his eyes to assess his surroundings, only his right one cooperated. He reached up with one hand and touched his left eye. He rubbed it with his fingers, trying to coax it to open for him, but it wouldn't budge. He could only manage to get it to send waves of dull throbbing through his head.

That wasn't the only discomfort he felt; there was a powerful heat rising from his legs. He looked down and noticed his pants were ablaze and only then did he realize he was surrounded by orange and yellow flames.

Evon was confused. He didn't remember what went on to get him to this point. His shirt was off and the hotel room door was open.

What on earth is going on?

The bed was missing.

Where is the bed?

He strained to look out to see what was happening, but the images his one good eye could muster were quite blurry. He heard muffled voices outside.

Who's out there? Why are they here?

He began to crawl toward the door to get a closer look but halted when he placed his hand right on top of a rising flame. He thought he should feel some kind of pain, yet there was nothing but a brief, itchy feeling before he noticed the fire moving up his arm. He tried to crawl forward once more, tried to will his body toward the sound of the voices, but he collapsed. His arms refused to work with him.

Fine, my legs will do.

His legs wouldn't move.

Evon opened his mouth, preparing to call out to the voices he heard outside.

No sound escaped his lips.

His throat felt dry, mouth parched, devoid of all moisture.

There was a peculiar taste on his tongue, though he didn't know what.

The heat he felt from his legs had moved its way up his back.

Why can't I move? Maybe I just need to rest for a moment.

He strained to look outside again and saw his daughter lying down.

Sunny? Why is Sunny here?

There were people kneeling around her. It was dark outside, that much he could tell. His vision cleared slightly, enough to see that there was rain silently falling from the sky. The people outside started to move around. They looked right at him and started to point. Then they ran away.

Where are you guys going now?

There was Chastity. And Deon. And Hank. They were all here.

But why?

Evon couldn't feel the heat anymore. It finally left him alone.

Good, now I can get outside.

He gave his body the command to nudge forward, but it disobeyed.

Just a few more minutes of rest, that's all I need.

He laid his head down and closed his eye. The heat was completely gone. He knew there was fire all around, but there was no heat.

This is strange. Fire? With no heat?

So strange.

His breathing became shallow. Then he didn't hear the voices from outside anymore. It became silent all around him.

So… strange…

Images passed in a flurry throughout his mind. Sunny. Chatity. The trees by the bridge. Ruthie. Craig. Jillian. The squirrel on the highway. *Sunny…*

A feeling came over him. He hadn't felt anything like it before.

It was a… new experience.

TWENTY-TWO

"Once I heard those sirens and then saw the trucks and ambulance racing down the street, I knew some shit was going down," Flip said. "I was just stuck, couldn't do shit because you made me stay and miss out on all the action."

"Good thing, too. I don't think you would've wanted to deal with temporary hearing loss and some burns and shrapnel."

Deon raised his arms and turned them to show Flip the damage he'd missed out on.

"You didn't need to see all of that going on there. Probably would've shit your pants," Deon said.

"Hey, fuck off," Flip replied.

"*Hey*! Watch the language in front of my daughter, you two!" Chastity said.

After the events of the early morning hours before, they were all huddled into a room in Whidbey General, surrounding Sunny as she lay in a hospital bed.

The paramedics at first suggested that they transfer her to Seattle after tending to her at the scene, but Chastity decided against it. She wanted quick medical treatment and her motherly instincts had probably saved Sunny's life.

The doctors found that Evon had injected Sunny with a dose of ketamine. It was enough to knock her completely out for a short while, not enough to do any kind of lasting, permanent damage, but had they not hooked her up to a respirator to help her breathe, the situation could've been much worse. She had inhaled a lot of smoke and soot and her body's natural reaction to cough had been suppressed because of the injection.

Deon wasn't one hundred percent sure what kind of designs Evon had for them as they sat in that burning blaze, but he imagined that the needle Evon had was full of the stuff, too, and he was booking a one-way trip for him and his daughter. Only Deon interrupting their path on the runway prevented them from reaching a point of no return. Or at least he prevented that for Sunny.

He couldn't say the same thing for Evon.

"So, you saw him burning? And didn't try to rush in and help the guy?" Flip asked.

"Yeah… He was trying to crawl to the door, but then he just stopped. I couldn't get back in there even if I wanted to. The damn room was gone at that point. And besides, I came for Sunny and Ruthie, not him," Deon said.

"Damn…" Flip said, shaking his head.

Deon thought that reply was for the fact that Evon had perished the way he did, but also for the reminder that Ruthie's life had been snuffed out as well.

"I know I've told you several times on the ride over here, Deon, but you just gotta know that I'm so thankful for what you've done and I'm really sorry for the loss of your friend," Chastity said. "I don't think any of us thought that Evon would do the things he did. He must've been really screwed up. I mean, who the hell *does* that? Kidnaps his daughter? Sits in a room surrounded by fire, spouting off Bible verses or whatever? That's creepy as hell. Definitely not the guy I married years ago."

Deon was in agreement about the strangeness of the situation but waved her apology and gratitude away with a swipe of his hand. He had been placed in a position to do something and imagined anybody else would've done the same thing.

This was real life he was experiencing and he had a chance to affect the lives of others. To *act*. There were many times in his life where he didn't do that or was prevented from acting; this made up for all those times. Especially the time he tried with all his might to reach the burning house that took his parents away. This was a redemption of sorts. His only regret was that he couldn't do it sooner and prevent the loss of two other lives.

Ruthie deserved better than what she got. He couldn't say the same for Evon, but maybe with a different set of circumstances they could've helped the guy some way.

That decision was up to someone else now.

"How long did the doctor say she'd be here?" Deon asked, inquiring about Sunny's condition.

"Probably just another day. They just wanna make sure the lingering effects of that crap aren't drastic and to make sure she can breathe ok," Chastity answered.

"Ok. Well if it's ok with you, I think Flip and I will take off and leave you two alone."

"Oh, don't be silly," Chastity said. "Park your tail somewhere and stay here. You *know* she wants you to stay. Ain't that right, baby girl?" She asked Sunny.

Sunny was lying in her hospital bed, the white linens pulled up to just beneath her armpits. She was completely quiet, staring out the window, listening to adults talk around her, which was par for the course for Sunny. If she was at all affected by the combined effects of ketamine and smoke, it wasn't by much. She was exhibiting normal behavior by her standards as far as Deon was concerned.

Chastity was standing by her bed and started to gently rub her daughter's leg.

"Isn't that right?" she asked again.

Sunny turned her head to Deon, who was standing on the other side of the bed. They looked at each other for a moment and he offered her a smile. She weakly returned a faint one back. That was all the confirmation he needed.

He didn't want, didn't *need* the rewards or the adulation. He knew that Sunny was thanking him in her own little way and that was more than enough for him.

He just wished that she was never in a position to have to offer any kind of thanks. However, he knew in his heart of hearts that everything happened for a reason. He wasn't sure what that reasoning was and wasn't even sure he was supposed to ever know, but he knew it was a purposeful part in the grand scheme of things.

"See there?" Chastity said, "She likes you, Mr. Giddyup, so you and Flip here are staying put for a little bit. Might as well make yourselves cozy."

Deon wouldn't argue anymore. When she looked up at him just seconds before, with those hazy eyes created by what she had endured the past several hours, the decision was made. She saw him, *really* saw him. Not just his physical form, not just a guy standing next to her hospital bed, but what he really was.

Try as he might, he couldn't be invisible anymore.

"We'll stay just a little bit longer," Deon said. "I don't think the hospital wants us overstaying our welcome, unless we had a different reason to be here."

"Which your crazy ass almost gave them," Flip said.

"I'm sure you would've done the same thing, Flip."

"Eh, maybe. For her. Can't say the same for you."

In reality, Deon knew that translated as "I'd go to the ends of the earth for you."

***

That day time continued to flow at its normal speed. Life, although harshly interrupted, was picking itself up and dusting itself off after a momentary stumble on the road to wherever the destination ended. Was it just death? Eternal life? Deon pondered over that briefly but only because he had to. Being involved in what he was—seeing death laid bare in front of him, and being in a hospital where so many lives were either saved or passed on—had called for it.

These were thoughts he didn't want to be stuck thinking about any longer than he had to. His time would come, where he himself might be laid up in this exact same hospital. That was when he would think about the great mystery of life again. For now, he just wanted to get out and experience it.

Doctors and nurses made their way in and out of Sunny's room over the course of the morning. Everyone that occupied the room—himself, Flip, Chastity, and Sunny—had their circadian rhythms interrupted and they were sleepy at a time when they should've been at their most alert. There was a reason for this, of course, but Deon still had a little bit of energy in him.

He watched as everyone found their own little nooks inside the hospital room and drifted off to sleep. First, it was Sunny, who'd been through the most out of anyone and more than deserved a chance to rest her weary body. Then, Flip, who was in the fetal position in an oversized, cushioned chair, dozed off. That left Chastity and Deon as the only ones left awake.

He couldn't blame Chastity for wanting to stay up. The last time she'd closed her eyes to fall asleep, her daughter disappeared. Though irrational, Deon knew full well that she'd be awake by the side of her beloved daughter until the Sandman himself forced her into a slumber.

"You're next," Chastity said.

"Huh?"

"Sunny, Flip. They've checked out for a while. I'm too worked up to fall asleep, but you, you're probably next."

"Nah, I'm just as worked up as you are, probably."

"You mean jumping through fire to save a big ol' teenaged girl and fighting off a crazed demon hasn't worn you out?"

"Nope. All in a day's work," Deon joked.

"So, what? You're just going to sit there in silence?"

"Actually, I'm thinking about taking a walk for a little bit. You know, to gather my thoughts and to get some fresh air into my lungs. I can only take so much of this hospital smell."

"Ha, I can't blame you there."

"Yeah… Well, I'm off. I'll be back before too long, if they wake up and start asking questions."

Deon rose out of his chair and Chastity waved him goodbye as he walked out of the room. He took one more look at Sunny. She was lying still, breathing deeply, and getting the rest she so dearly needed.

As he walked down the halls to the exit of the hospital, he couldn't help but to be nosy and steal a few glances into other people's rooms.

Aside from Sunny, there wasn't a young person to be found. Every room or partition that he peered into was occupied by someone older, some much more so than others.

He saw a few gray-haired women lying lonely, discarded by their families, waiting for their numbers to be called. One was propped up in the big hospital bed watching the TV that protruded from the wall. She had a big, gray remote in her hand, listlessly pressing buttons to flip the channels. She sensed that Deon was staring at her and turned her head to face him. They stared at each other for a fleeting moment, but in that short time, Deon saw in her eyes that she had enough of the mundanity of everyday life on this earth and had done what was necessary to earn herself a ticket to a more pleasant one.

He smiled at her but received nothing back in return.

The hospital wasn't as big and fancy as he imagined the one in Seattle to have been. It still had an old charm that harkened back to decades prior. Color schemes, instruments, even the furniture all served as relics to the past. Not to be outdone, even some of the doctors and nurses looked to be at an advanced age and probably had been employees here since the early days.

They all busily went about their tasks, not taking notice of Deon, who was still somewhat disheveled from earlier in the day. That suited him just fine because he wasn't in the mindset to want to entertain any conversations.

He reached the exit of the building and pressed on the metal push-bar of the door to get outside. The morning sun was peeking out of the remaining clouds that had just blanketed Oak Harbor with rain hours before. The lingering aroma of rain and dampened earth filled the light breeze; he deeply inhaled, slowly, to fill his lungs completely with the comparatively pleasant smell.

Shallow puddles lined the curbs and filled in any cracks or holes in the pavement. He made sure to step over and around them as he began his stroll; he wanted to avoid getting any *more* wet after the past couple of hours.

It was surprisingly warm out, too. Not warm in the sense that it felt like spring, but in the sense that he wasn't in need of a coat. It made for good, morning walking weather, which he set out to do.

Even though officially Thanksgiving was over, it didn't feel like it. Judging by the scant human activity on the streets, which was odd considering it was Black Friday, he guessed that people were still inside in a pumpkin pie and tryptophan-induced hibernation.

Hibernation was exactly what he'd been doing year after year, holiday food notwithstanding.

Oak Harbor wasn't that big of a city and considering its size, Deon thought it was shameful that he hadn't fully explored it after all the time he spent there. He relegated himself to staying in the Dregs, only venturing out from its confines when it was necessary. He had no reason to really be out and about anyway, especially since he used his lack of income as an excuse to not take delight in the pleasures of the small town. Now, that would be an excuse no more. He owed it to himself to get out and enjoy life despite his social status.

After the last 24 hours, it became clear to him that at any moment, by the hands of any person, life could be cut short, without a moment to prepare and tell your loved ones. And then what? What was next? Just like everyone else he knew, Deon had been made aware that good deeds here in this realm led to abundant rewards beyond man's wildest imagination in the next. The only bad thing was that he feared uncertainty and the only way to be certain that these tales of riches were indeed true, was to trade in this life for another. He wasn't about to do that, though, not now, not anytime soon, at least not voluntarily. So, he had to live. Truly *live.* He'd used up about a third of his life doing nothing, but that ended today.

Deon's life had been indirectly affected by the death of his friend, Ruthie. Just as he owed it to himself to get out of the doldrums, he owed it to people like Ruthie, who had their chance to live snatched away from them, to enjoy the life he was fortunate to still have. He owed it to people like his parents to turn that fire they'd succumbed to into the fire that fueled the furnace in his heart, to let it drive his desire to make something more of it than what he'd done thus far.

What it took to realize that was being in the presence of another innocent life and playing a part in preserving it so that she could have a chance to live herself.

He didn't want the adulation, didn't want to be put on a pedestal and considered some type of hero, although he knew Chastity would probably make an attempt to have him recognized, but when Sunny woke up and was healthy, he wanted something from her. He wanted her to make a promise to him that, no matter what, she'd never let her zest for living get dull, to keep it sharp despite the obstacles that tried to blunt it. That's all he wanted. If he could keep even one person from wasting most of their life in a melancholic stupor like he did, then he considered that a success. However, he had a feeling in his gut that Sunny wouldn't need to make him any promises. Despite her condition, that girl was riding on a full tank through life and what had almost happened to her would only make her love life *more.*

As he continued walking, he made sure to take notice of all his surroundings. This was his home that he needed to explore. Even though autumn had taken hold of the once lush, green oaks, he knew how beautiful they'd be once the spring returned, and he couldn't wait to walk among them. For now, he cut across the street from the hospital and walked through the adjacent park that was ringed with the native oak trees.

They were barren, yes, but that didn't stop the local critters from enjoying them as they were. Squirrels scurried about the trunks and branches and birds perched themselves high above, sounding warnings that they were being joined by a bi-ped this morning. Deon wasn't the least bit a nature freak, but he couldn't help but to take joy in seeing the animals live. They, too, had obstacles in the form of harmful and ever-advancing human encroachment, but that didn't stop them from living full lives. He thought about saying hello to them, but thought that would be silly, so he silently acknowledged them and kept walking.

Deon had a destination in mind, but was taking the scenic route to get there. When he reached that spot, he'd circle back and go back to the hospital to say, not 'goodbye,' but 'see you later' to Sunny and Chastity.

Being that Oak Harbor was a small town, most everything that was needed was in fairly close proximity to each other, so it was no surprise that when he emerged from the park, he ended up down the street from the scene of *THE* Dutch Inn.

The place was absolutely crawling with activity and Deon walked in that direction, even though it was a little bit out of the way of where he was heading.

There was a group of vehicles made up of police cars, firetrucks, and news vans that occupied the street, access to which had been closed off. Yellow police tape was set up to form a perimeter that extended even beyond the footprint of the hotel. There was clearly an investigation ensuing, and Deon knew what the police would eventually find, if they hadn't already. He and Chastity hadn't been questioned right after the events of the past few hours, having been allowed to leave the scene because of Sunny's condition. The police did show up at Sunny's hospital room later and briefly interview everyone, but whatever else they discovered now was up to their hard work and whatever else Hank could provide.

The building didn't at all resemble what it did just a day before. The combined effects of the fire and the watery efforts to save it had done considerable damage. The fact that there was anything left standing was remarkable. He thought he detected some lingering smoldering, but as he got closer he realized his tired eyes were playing tricks on him.

There were people standing all around, some taking pictures, some presumably assessing the damage, some talking amongst themselves. He saw reporters meandering and figured if what had happened wasn't morning news by now, it would be shortly because these kinds of things didn't happen here, and the fact that it was a well-known institution would surely make it a headline.

Deon spotted hefty Hank talking to some policemen. Although he couldn't hear what was being said, he saw that Hank had his arms crossed with eyes pointing to the ground and he was shaking his head. Either he was still in disbelief at the nightmare he was living, or he wasn't liking whatever it was the policeman was telling him. Whatever the case, Deon felt sorry for him. He didn't deserve to be swept up in Evon's madness, but he was sure that Hank was resilient and would do whatever it took to be back up and running soon.

After the policeman finished talking, he walked away and climbed into a nearby car. As he pulled away, he passed by Deon and continued down the street. Hank lifted his head to watch the car leave and spotted Deon looking in his direction.

He squinted his eyes at Deon, trying to see if it was who he thought it was, and after confirming that it was him, he slowly uncrossed his arms and walked away.

Deon imagined that he was angry at him because he was in some way attached to the events that cost him his business. Perception is reality, though, and Hank would forever associate the people who came away unscathed with the destruction of his property and the interruption in his stream of revenue.

There was nothing else to see. Deon walked back in the direction of Dreg City.

The moment he was dreading had come, and it was time to let everyone there know what had happened before they heard it elsewhere and misinformation was spread.

Their matriarch was gone.

No.

She was *taken*.

Ruthie was a beloved figure for years and one of the few reasons people even tolerated living there in the first place. She made everyone feel loved and didn't pass judgement, no matter what they'd done that led them there or what they continued to struggle with.

She'd truly earned the mantle of "matriarch," but after the unfortunate events, someone else had to be declared the leader of the camp.

That's where Deon came in.

It was only right that he took the initiative and continued what Ruthie started. He wasn't a natural born leader, but by being around her all those years, some of her endearing qualities had rubbed off on him.

He wondered how they would take the news, though. Would they mutiny? Would they disperse to other areas of the town? Would mass chaos ensue now that the person they trusted to help them through life was gone? Deon liked to think he got a taste of what it took to be the person they needed when he made sure their Thanksgiving wasn't ruined, and hopefully that earned him some credit, but only time would tell how they took to him running the show. No one else in the camp that he knew could step in and fill her shoes, anyway, so he was doing this by necessity just as much as he was because he actually *wanted* to.

He'd had many regrets and one of them was that while he was living there, he didn't feel like he really knew the people he was living among. He had Flip, Ruthie, and at one time, even Evon, but aside from them, he only knew a few others he lived beside and they were by name only. That was one thing Ruthie was deft at. She knew everyone by name and knew their stories. There was a time months ago when he and Ruthie were conversing about some of the nicknames of the residents; he could barely recall any. She chided him for this, saying there might be a time when he really needed to know everyone in the camp. He'd brushed it off back then, but he knew he couldn't be a leader of the people if he didn't even know the names of the people he was leading. That took a top spot on his list of priorities.

Next on his list was to make sure what happened between Ruthie and Evon *never* happened again. He understood that it would be impossible to try anything close to doing a background check; in their environment, it was inevitable that some unsavory characters would slip past their defenses. However, that didn't mean that he wouldn't scrutinize new members of the community even more so than was done in the past.

It was all part of building new relationships to him, adding to the foundation, bridging the gap. Maybe that's what his lucid dream the previous night was trying to tell him. He remembered it clearly.

Just a few hours before his life changed forever, he was lying on the ground, fighting to get *some* semblance of sleep when Chastity came roaring through.

He was half asleep, but he remembered that he was dreaming about a bridge. He didn't know what the bridge was called, or where it was even located, but it was suspended high above the ground. He was walking right down the middle of it. There was no one else around. No cars, no animals, *nothing*. He remembered walking over to the edge of it, to look down and see how high up he was.

He was so calm; there was no fear. There were no sounds either. No rustling of any trees, not even a whisper in the wind. As a matter of fact, he remembered there was no wind; the air was completely still. When he peered over the edge, he couldn't see anything. The ground, if there even was one, was completely obscured by thick, white clouds. He moved away from the ledge and returned to the road, but this time, instead of walking straight down the middle as he'd done before, he moved to the left lane. Then he sat down.

That was it.

He didn't have a chance to complete the dream because that's when Chastity interrupted it. Deon didn't even have a chance to *think* about his dream because of the events that followed, but the long walk allowed him to revisit his reverie.

He was no expert in dream analysis, but he knew that dreams weren't just random collections of visions that ran amok through the brain. The images that came, came for a reason, whether it could be made sense of or not.

The bridge meant *something*. The fact that Deon walked it alone meant something. Him not being able to see the ground beneath meant something, as did the way he moved from the middle of the road before looking over the edge, to picking a particular lane after.

Try as he might, Deon couldn't unlock the meaning to that something, and it was frustrating him to grasp at nothing. Maybe some things were better left not understood.

Before he knew it, he'd arrived back home in the Dregs, back among his hodge-podge family. The atmosphere was already buzzing, which meant they'd heard some news, although he didn't know what. If he had to guess, he figured the news about the hotel was being talked about, but he didn't think it had been revealed yet who was found inside.

People started coming up to him, asking him if he knew what was going on. He told everyone that he did and that he had something to add to that news. Deon asked for help rounding up everyone and he stressed that what he had to tell everyone was going to be hard to hear, but that it was important that they hear it, for it marked a profound change in all their lives.

It took a few minutes, but they were eventually able to get everyone together. They huddled in front of Deon, who'd taken position against a wall.

The light breeze he felt when he left the hospital picked up and briefly gusted, rustling some leaves and debris.

"I'm sure you've all heard some news about what's been going on around here lately. It's probably a good idea for me to answer any lingering questions," Deon said.

He took his time and told everyone all the details of what happened and the role he played in the early morning events.

Some people let out wails, some preferred to silently cry and not draw attention to themselves. There were others who were angrier than they were sad and could be heard cursing to the high heavens. Despite all that, everyone there tried to offer comfort to one another the best way they knew how.

What they were hearing was difficult, life-altering news—Deon understood that more than anyone—but he tried his best to allay their fears of what Ruthie's exit from this world meant for their collective futures. He assured them that he would do everything in his power to make sure their home was still a home despite the noticeable loss of one very important member.

He didn't explicitly say that he was now the patriarch, he didn't feel that was necessary, and the term was more suited for someone older, more seasoned, but he imagined it was understood nonetheless.

Deon didn't want to come off as someone in power, he wanted to be viewed just as he was before, but he also wanted to convey that he was more than capable of taking on the new responsibility of steering the ship.

After he was done talking and answering any lingering questions, he watched as the crowd that gathered around him started to disperse and everyone was left to digest the developments that were fed to them.

A gale picked up and made him shiver slightly. He told a few people that he was going to walk back to the hospital but would return shortly.

As he crunched through some of the leaves that were whipped up in the wind, he looked down and noticed a piece a paper amongst them. It stopped him in his tracks because of the condition of the paper: it was slightly burnt, blackened around the edges. He pressed his foot down on top of it to keep it from floating away and looked around to see if anyone was watching him.

Deon removed his foot and quickly knelt down to inspect the paper. He realized he'd damaged it further, as some of the burnt edges broke away. He picked it up and discovered it was a page from a Bible. All but a few verses had been burnt away, reduced to ashes that were undoubtedly flying through the wind.

He read the only remaining verse that had all its words intact, and although he wasn't a religious person in the slightest, what he read on the half-burnt page was a message delivered just in time, meant only for him.

TWENTY-THREE

The days had become too boring for him at this point. They were filled with menial tasks at his job in Moses, Washington.

With his physical state, too weak to do any heavy lifting, but too strong to just sit around and be completely useless, his boss used him for the in-between stuff. The stuff that no one else liked doing. That had suited him just fine for the past year, but no more.

So, at the end of his shift on Tuesday, he told his boss he wouldn't be coming back. The boss looked stunned and asked him what he was thinking not giving him two-weeks' notice, but he was given no explanation. Just a goodbye and thanks for the paychecks. The boss told him not to bother coming in to get his last one because it would be mailed to him. Something about making sure disgruntled employees didn't come back and jeopardize the safety of everyone else. He wasn't disgruntled, though. He just thought it was a good time to depart permanently.

After leaving, he walked back to his lonely home that overlooked Eastern Washington's portion of the Snake River. He was glad to be living out there alone now. He didn't have to worry about being bothered and there were no surprise guests, save for the animals that roamed his property at night. The solitary life afforded him privacy, serenity, and after watching the news and reading the paper over the past year, a renewed purpose.

He sat in his cushioned, brown recliner looking out the window and rested his dogged feet, but figured he shouldn't get too comfortable or else he wasn't getting back up.

The day was still young, which meant he had plenty of time to make the thirty-minute trek over to Clarkston. It would be much faster if he'd had a car, bike, or friends to rely on, but lacking those, his feet would be put to work. Not that he minded it, though. People had way too much reliance on lazy modes of transportation and given the obesity rates in this country, they could use much more walking. Besides not wanting to be added to the growing number of overweight people, he wanted time to enjoy the outdoors and hear the rushing water of the river that lined his path to Clarkston.

It was warm out, even unseasonably so for these parts in the Pacific Northwest, even though he was on the far eastern part of the state. The sun gleamed off the subtle ripples on the river's surface and each sparkle seemed like a wink at him. Ponderosa pine and shrubbery lined the banks and provided sanctuary for the various bird species that inhabited these parts. Sometimes he would take delight in becoming familiar with the natural environment, but today they were of no consequence.

When he finally made it to town, everything was as usual. The same number of citizens busying about, the same number of cars occupying the roads in an orderly fashion. In fact, there was no reason for Clarkston to be any different than it usually was, only *he* felt different and he half-expected his change in aura to affect the environment around him. It wasn't to be, however, because he was still essentially a nobody to everyone else in town and even though he felt a tingle of excitement thinking that people around him would pick up on the change that occurred in him, he didn't mind remaining anonymous. That would be beneficial later anyway because he wanted to remain inconspicuous, nothing but a wisp in the wind.

He thought about stopping to get a bite to eat while he was in town and he hadn't eaten since he left for work in the morning, but he was thirstier than he was hungry and stopped by a convenience store for a one-liter of Diet Coke instead.

He stood outside the store, twisting off the cap of the bottle to take a long guzzle. Then he paused to laugh at himself. If he kept up this practice, he'd undoubtedly be counted amongst the obese that he thought about on his walk to town. He took a few lengthier sips of the sugary drink and sat the bottle down on the sidewalk outside the store. He was sufficiently satisfied and wouldn't finish the rest.

There was business he needed to tend to while he was here and he needed to get it over with before daylight ran out; he didn't want to walk home in the dark. That meant he had to hightail it over to Saint Cecilia Catholic Church.

On his way there, he passed the school and flower shop erected in Saint Cecilia's honor. He also passed the churches of other denominations and didn't consider entering them. Only one church would do on this day because he had a confession to make. He wasn't even a patron of Saint Cecilia, but he figured the priest inside wouldn't turn him away.

Saint Cecilia's was an exquisite structure. The architecture harkened back to the days when people spent days, weeks agonizing over the most minute details. He imagined it took years to finish the erection of the church whereas in this day and age it would likely be finished before the year was over.

As he climbed the concrete steps, he noticed the year 1915 etched in stone near the entrance. This place, or at least the original foundation, had stood for more than 100 years, meaning it had felt the feet and weight of both mortal and venial sins from thousands of lost souls. If walls could talk, they would have a century of stories to tell for sure.

It was quiet inside, as he expected, because Tuesday was the day of least activity. It was dark as well, but the stained-glass windows let in enough light for him to see the wood paneling and the ornately carved pews that were situated on either side of the aisle. On the floor was a long, red carpet that led to an altar that was about two feet off the ground. He slowly walked up the aisle to stare at an enormous metal cross that was affixed to the wall.

He heard a rustling and held his breath so he could hear better. He slowly turned his head around to see if anyone had followed him in, but he was the only one inside to confess on this day. The rustling he'd heard must've been the priest getting ready to absolve him of his sins.

There was a long, red curtain draped over an opening to the left of him and in the direction where he heard some rustling, so he figured that was where he must go to deliver his confession.

He pulled back the curtain and his assumption had been confirmed. The area was no bigger than a closet, with a small bench situated in the front of a partition with a latticed screen planted firmly in the middle.

As he was told was customary, he performed the sign of the cross and heard a slat of wood being pulled back from the screen.

It was dim inside, but he could make out the figure of an old, white man with glasses hidden behind the screen.

"Bless me Father, for I have sinned. My last confession… well, I've never really done this before. So, this is my virgin voyage."

"That's quite alright, son," the priest said. "What do you want to confess today?"

The man pressed his face up to the screen and whispered, "Father, I haven't *done* anything yet, but I think I might soon."

"What do you mean?" said the priest.

"Well, I've been thinking about killing people. In fact, I *know* I will soon. But you're not allowed to tell anybody that, right?"

Silence fell between them for a moment before the priest replied, "That's correct. What you say to me in here is something I cannot share with anyone else."

"No matter what?"

"Yes, no matter what."

"Good… good…"

"Are you a member of this church, son? Do I know you?"

"No… no. But you *do* know my name, or at least I'm sure you've heard it before."

"And what is your name, son?"

The man took a deep breath and exhaled slowly out of his nose before saying, "My name, Father, is Evon Brisk."

Acknowledgements

There are *so* many people to thank that I'm sure I'll forget, so I won't attempt to name you all. However, you know who you are, the people who read the early versions of this book when I was just getting started. All your feedback and comments definitely helped me craft the rest of the story and I hope I didn't disappoint! Specifically, Mrs. Yeager, your first comments gave me the fuel I needed to keep going! And Mr. Quinn, I hope I gave you everything you were looking for. Ms. Magee, thank you for your endless needling! Dr. Morris, many thanks to you and your daughter! Ms. Neill, thank you so very much for everything you did during the whole process of me writing this book. *Save Them All* couldn't have reached its polished state without your initial work. Andrea, thank you for all your advice and suggestions on how to make this story better. Everything you said will help any future stories I create! Beth, your keen eye caught things that no one had considered, and I can't thank you enough for all your hard work. Lastly, the biggest thank you is saved for the city of Oak Harbor. Thanks for letting me turn your wonderful town upside down! I hope Evon didn't do *too* much damage!